BLACK SPIRAL DANCERS™

ERIC GRIFFIN

author:	eric griffin
cover artist:	steve prescott
series editors:	eric griffin
	john h. steele
	stewart wieck
editor:	philippe r. boulle
copyeditor:	jeanée ledoux
graphic designer:	allen mills
art director:	richard thomas

ISBN 1-58846-822-4
First Edition: December 2002
Printed in Canada.

White Wolf Publishing
1554 Litton Drive
Stone Mountain, GA 30083
www.white-wolf.com/fiction

World of Darkness Fiction by White Wolf

The Tribe Novel Series
Tribe Novel: Shadow Lords & Get of Fenris by Gherbod Fleming & Eric Griffin
Tribe Novel: Silent Striders & Black Furies by Carl Bowen & Gherbod Fleming
Tribe Novel: Red Talons & Fianna by Philippe Boulle & Eric Griffin
Tribe Novel: Bone Gnawers & Stargazers by Bill Bridges with Justin Achilli
Tribe Novel: Children of Gaia & Uktena by Richard Lee Byers & Stefan Petrucha
Tribe Novel: Silver Fangs & Glass Walkers by Carl Bowen & Tim Dedopulos
Tribe Novel: Black Spiral Dancers & Wendigo by Eric Griffin & Bill Bridges

The Predator & Prey Series
Predator & Prey: Vampire by Carl Bowen
Predator & Prey: Judge by Gherbod Fleming
Predator & Prey: Werewolf by Gherbod Fleming
Predator & Prey: Jury by Gherbod Fleming
Predator & Prey: Mage by Carl Bowen
Predator & Prey: Executioner by Gherbod Fleming

Other Titles by Eric Griffin
Clan Novel: Tzimisce (Vampire Clan Novel #2)
Clan Novel: Tremere (Vampire Clan Novel #12)
Vampire: Widow's Walk (Clan Tremere Trilogy, part 1)
Vampire: Widow's Weeds (Clan Tremere Trilogy, part 2)
Vampire: Widow's Might (Clan Tremere Trilogy, part 3)

For all these titles and more, visit **www.white-wolf.com/fiction**

For Damon,
Who knows when to root for the monsters.

The First Circle
The Dance of Insight

The two Garou that sat hunched forward on the cold cave floor were about as different as day and night. The first was proud, regal of bearing. He was a legendary warrior, a cunning strategist, a man prophesied to rally the Garou Nation to the Final Battle.

The other was a no-account of humble beginnings. A drifter who couldn't manage to hold down a freelance job. A self-confessed and unrepentant layabout.

"Again," Stuart ordered. Judging from his tone, he might have forgotten for a moment which of them was which. He sounded more than a little like a frustrated schoolmaster. "The spiral. There's got to be something we're missing."

Arkady angrily wiped the cave floor of its complex diagrams and elaborate plottings. Slowly, he started over again at square one. With a single motion, without ever lifting the blackened tip of the bone stylus from the uneven surface, he drew a perfect, continuous spiral. Nine times the figure looped back in upon itself before vanishing in a final singularity. A crude, coal-black smudge.

"There must be a way," Arkady repeated as if trying to convince himself of the fact. "A way of walking the spiral without being corrupted. Of striding into the heart of the labyrinth and emerging victorious on the far side. It is prophesied. It must be possible." He struck the cave floor soundly with the flat of his fist.

"Unless, of course, the prophets were just engaging in a little wishful thinking," Stuart said. "Or later scholars were just trying to find a way to explain away the fact that Lord So-and-so had just flipped out and gone over to the other side."

"That's not funny," Arkady said. "I've lost too many kinsmen to that promise for me to start questioning it now."

"Seems to me like an ideal time to start questioning it," Stuart said. "And I can't read a damned thing you're writing anymore. The whole floor here is smeared black and I think my eyes are starting to cross. How about we just call it a night?"

"You said you would help. You said that there might just be a way."

"There might be. But we've been over this a dozen times and I'm damned if I can find it. Maybe in the morning things will be a bit clearer. The late morning," he added hastily.

"Sleep then. I will keep watch," Arkady snapped. He rose to his feet and began pacing out the interior of the cave. His steps instinctively carried him in an ever-narrowing gyre.

Stuart lay stretched out full-length on the floor, his chin propped up on the back of his hands. "It's no good. Even if you can win through to the spiral—a doubtful proposition at best—there's still nothing you can do when you get there except repeat the same mistakes made by all those who have gone before you. Once you set foot on that Black Spiral you are lost. Period. There's no turning back, no turning aside, no escape. It's got you and it's just going to work away at you until you crack."

The winding path of Arkady's pacing brought him back around to Stuart again. This time he brushed past him on the inside and continued his circuit.

"Is that monologue helping you to clarify your thoughts, or was it intended for my benefit?" Arkady asked.

Stuart sighed and pushed himself to his feet. "Forget it. Forget I even said anything." He stared after Arkady's retreating figure, saw the scuffle blackened footprints trailing out behind him like a loose thread.

Absently, he followed the path of the tracks backward, saw the twin sets of prints where they ran closely past him on either side.

But if those prints were the path of the Black Spiral, what was this narrow stretch of floor where Stuart was now standing? With a growing sense of excitement, he took out his pocket notebook. Quickly rifling through to a blank page, he rendered a copy of the infamous nine-gyred spiral. Then he squinted at it closely until his eyes refused to focus on the diagram any longer and everything blurred about the edges before snapping back into sudden clarity.

"There!" he cried aloud.

Arkady stopped dead in his tracks and turned, a look of concern on his face. "Where?" he said, taking a step toward Stuart.

"No! You have to stay on the path," Stuart reprimanded him. "Make your way back to me, but do it the right way. Stay on the Black Spiral."

Arkady sighed, but humored his excitable companion. Soon he stood by Stuart's side once more.

"Now you walk the pattern again," Stuart said. "Just like the last time. Only this time, I walk with you."

"This is your plan?" Arkady asked incredulously. "You would walk with me into the lair of the Wyrm?"

"Uh, no. My momma didn't raise no fools and there's no way in hell that you're dragging me down to Malfeas with you. This is for demonstration purposes only. Walk."

Arkady shrugged, feigning disinterest and again began to retrace the black footprints. Stuart kept pace right beside him, shoulder to shoulder. They finished one complete circuit of the room.

"I really don't see what this has to do with…" Arkady began. But Stuart hushed him and urged him on through a second circumambulation. And then a third.

"And the point of this little exercise is?" Arkady asked, at last losing patience.

"The point is," Stuart replied with a triumphant grin, "that I am still at your side—through three complete circuits of the pattern—and I have yet to set one foot upon the Black Spiral."

Arkady stopped dead in his tracks. "But how can that be?" he protested softly.

"Look here," Stuart said, tapping his pencil rapidly against the open notebook page. "It's something I just realized about the nature of spirals. All spirals. Here's the Black Spiral I drew. But there's another spiral here, nestled within it. In this case, it's a White Spiral, white for the paper peeking through. It's a negative spiral, sandwiched in between the lines of the black one. And if you were to walk on *that* spiral, like I was just doing, it should be possible—at least theoretically possible—to reach the center without ever taking a single step on the Black Spiral. Without subjecting yourself to its corrupting touch."

Arkady just stared at him. Then a smile split his face. And then he threw back his head and laughed, slapping Stuart heartily on the back. "You are a wonder, Stuart Stalks-the-Truth. Almost I wish you would repent of your earlier decision and agree to accompany me. Are you sure that you are not in the least bit tempted to put your fine theory to the test?"

"Don't you worry about me," Stuart said. "If you manage to pull this off, I'll know about it. Hell, I imagine we'll all know about it. But I've a different path to walk. A road I've avoided for far too long now."

And it was only in that moment that Stuart realized where the White Spiral—if such an improbable thing even existed—must surely lead. It was a path leading unvaryingly home.

The Second Circle
The Dance of Rage

With a great heave, Arkady rolled aside the Three Day Stone that sealed the entrance to the ancient tomb. Moonlight gleamed off the peerless snow-white fur that covered him from crown to paw—the mark of a proud and ancient lineage. He wore his warrior skin—the towering half-man, half-wolf Crinos form. Thews as thick as tree boles bunched and knotted with the effort of dislodging the hoary old boulder. Even bent beneath the task, Arkady in his war form stood half-again as tall as a grown man.

The slab itself was of no less epic proportions. In some distant, less troubled age—before the last of the White Howlers to submit to the Wyrm had vanished into this very tomb, never to emerge again—two squads of cubs might have played atop the stone and used it for their ball pitch.

Its entire surface was carved in an intricate pattern of Celtic knot work. Arkady found himself trying to ferret out the secret concealed in that untraceable tangle of loops, arcs and crossbacks. Perhaps, if he only stared long enough, with eyes half squinted, the pattern might resolve itself into an image of the labyrinth that lay beyond—the Black Spiral itself. He quickly abandoned the effort. If that were the case, he thought, then this stone was more than a legendary obstacle, it was a warning as well. No one could ever hope to navigate such an incomprehensible labyrinth. Arkady couldn't even take it all in.

Arkady broke off to catch his breath, then put his other shoulder to the stone and began anew. Perhaps the pattern had another purpose. Maybe it traced out the true path into the very heart of the spiral. A meandering golden thread, showing the way, if only one were clever enough and patient enough to commit its twists and turns to memory. If that were the case, the stone *should* have come with a warning. A false hope was worse than no hope at all. Crueler.

With a scrape and a groan, the stone shifted. A breath of fetid air billowed out to meet him as the stone rolled aside. Arkady had to leap aside to keep the boulder from crushing his foot. When it at last came to rest again, he peered cautiously around its edge.

All was dark and silent inside. Not even the echo of his monumental struggle echoed back to him from the depths of the tomb.

There was something in his nature that instinctively distrusted a silence. If there was a stillness, his immediate thought was to fill it up with action, exertion. The best possible outcome of any period of forced contemplation was a catharsis of physical exertion. Arkady took the silence of the tomb as a challenge and reacted accordingly.

His howl dislodged tiny cascades of debris from the tunnel's ceiling all along its length. He paused only a moment, to hear the sound of his own voice borne back to him and then stormed through the dark aperture, ready for anything—screaming legions of fomori, hordes of gibbering Banes, packs of rabid Black Spiral Dancers.

What he was not prepared for was the tiny form that shrank back from the arc of light streaming through the opening at the sight of the Silver Fang lord in his full battle rage. The nine-foot tower of bristling fur and knotted sinew checked, nearly stumbled and ground to a halt.

The girl could not have been more than seven years of age. She was pale and trembling. Her matted tangle of shoulder length hair might once have been blond or brown; now it was the exact color and texture of a flaking scab. One of her eyes was blackened and swollen, and her shins, where they peeked from beneath the torn, knee length T-shirt, were covered in angry purple bruises.

There was dried blood at the lower hem of the shirt.

Blood pounded in Arkady's ears as he brushed her aside with one hand and squinted farther into the darkness, trying in vain to pick out some sign of his foes. Something to hit, to rend, to shred. The cloying stench of the Wyrm's corruption hung heavy in the still air of the tomb, but he needed no further corroboration of the atrocities that had been enacted here. He took a step forward, interposing himself between the girl and whatever lay beyond. She squirmed backward into the very corner of the cavern, as if she might wriggle into some cranny in the rock and escape him.

"Where?" Arkady demanded. Even in his own ears, his voice was more threatening than comforting. It was an effort to force some semblance of human speech past the taut lupine vocal chords, tuned to fierce howl rather than calming whisper. "The ones who… who did this to you. Where are they?"

The girl's face was a mask of terror. Her back was already to the wall, but her feet kept scrabbling at the floor, pushing her backward still.

"Well?" he demanded.

The words tumbled from her like a dam breaking. "Don't hurt me. Please. I didn't do anything. I'm sorry. I'll be good. I waited, just like you said—"

"Like *I* said?" Arkady's voice came out in a bark, startling her, cutting off the flow of words midstream. He had raised one hand between them in instinctive denial. He saw her eyes fix upon the lethal silver claws and quickly dropped his hand again, confused and embarrassed.

He was only terrifying the girl further. With a nervous glance over his shoulder for enemies that he knew very well might be lurking nearby, he took a deep breath and shuddered back into his more vulnerable human form.

At the sight of the transformation, the girl shrieked anew and dug frantically at the rock wall.

Arkady could smell new blood streaming from her torn fingertips.

He reached out and took her by the shoulders, but she recoiled from his touch. "Now wait a minute. Just calm down," he said. "It's all right. Look at me. I'm not here to hurt you. Just look at me."

Gradually, her frantic efforts subsided into a low broken sobbing. He turned her by the shoulders to face him.

Without raising her face to meet his eyes, she reached down and lifted up the front of the T-shirt from the knees, exposing the bruised pink flesh where her legs came together.

"What—? No!" Arkady nearly shouted at her. His hands, sure as swords in battle, fumbled to smooth the hem of the shirt back down to cover her.

"I don't understand…" she muttered miserably. "What did I do wrong?" She was afraid again now. "I'll do just what you say. I always do. You told me… I mean, *they* told me to wait here, and I waited…"

"How many of them are there?" he began and broke off, wincing at the crassness of his own words. The girl was hurt and frightened. His questions weren't helping matters. The hulking warrior was finding himself more than slightly over-matched at the sight of the small girl in distress. He tried again.

"What's your name, child?"

There was a flash of defiance in her eyes as they came up to meet his. As if she knew this was just some new way to get at her, to hurt her. She wrestled with it for a while, but apparently couldn't see the angle. In the end, her gaze dropped again. "Sarah," she mumbled.

"Sarah? Well, Sarah, we're getting you out of here. Right now. Nobody's going to hurt you anymore. Come on."

She shrank back from his touch, trembling and shaking her head vigorously from side to side. "I have to wait here!" she moaned. "Right here. The Lady said so. She will be angry if she returns and finds I am not here."

"What lady?"

"The Dark Lady. She's the one that made them all go away. The ones that paw at you and poke you. The burned dogs. You know. The ones like…" she broke off and pressed back farther into the cranny of the rock.

"Like me." His tone flat, emotionless. He was not angry or resentful. Instead, he found himself wondering at what this child must have suffered here, at the hands of her "burned dogs."

"I didn't mean… please don't hurt me!"

"No one's going to hurt you, Sarah. I've told you that already. You have my word."

She glared at him.

"You don't believe me," Arkady said. He shook his head in amazement. This child was so fragile he could snap her in two with nothing more than his raised voice, but here she was doing what even a grizzled Garou warrior might well shy away from—questioning his word to his face. There was something stubborn in this child, a core of iron hidden beneath a fragile glass casing. But perhaps, Arkady realized, it was only this peculiar combination of qualities that had allowed the girl to survive here, upon the very threshold of the Wyrm's lair.

"I am Lord Arkady of House Crescent Moon." The name and title rang out as he had hurled them so many times before, like words of challenge. "The most ancient and esteemed of all the noble Silver Fang houses. You have my pledge that no one will harm you in my presence—no one. Do you understand, child?"

Sarah's voice was barely audible. "She'll send you away," she muttered. "The Dark Lady, she'll send you away. Just like the others."

Arkady drew himself up regally and bit back an angry retort. "I'm not like the others," he explained with straining patience. "I'm going to help you."

"You're not like the others," she parroted, without emotion, without conviction.

"I'm going to get you out of here. And then I'm going to find these burned dogs and this Dark Lady of yours and give them a reason to wish they'd dug a deeper hole to hide in."

Again, a squawk of pure animal panic escaped her and she shook her head stubbornly. "I'm not…

I'm not going," she said with sudden determination. "I won't go. You can't make me."

Arkady arched an eyebrow. "I can't?" he retorted, before he could stop himself.

"You said you weren't like the others," she accused. She fought to hold back a fit of sobbing, but he could see it shuddering up through her.

He stood and waited for the worst of the shaking to subside. "Sarah, I'm sorry." He reached out to comfort her, but that too was exactly the wrong thing to do. He cursed and backed off. He began to pace. This was not going at all well.

"All right, you don't have to leave. I won't make you leave. You just stay right there and stay quiet. All right? I'll go see where these others have gotten to. They could still be nearby. Once the coast is clear—"

"They're gone now," Sarah said flatly. "You'd hear them if they were still around. Their laughing and dragging their spades behind them. Up the steps from the coal cellar."

"Well if they're gone, why don't you just... No, never mind, it's all right. Look, you see that light just over there?" In the darkness, the moonlight was blindingly bright. She rolled her eyes at him.

He ignored the gesture. "That's the way out. If you change your mind, you can just go out that way. Out there, in the light, you'll be safe. You can run away, far away from here. Where they'll never hurt you again."

Black Spiral Dancers

"The Lady said to wait." Sarah shook her head stubbornly. "It wouldn't do to disappoint her. She would be angry with me. She's far worse than the burned dogs. They only hurt you in the one place."

She made to show him again and he stopped her.

He heaved a sigh of resignation. "All right. I can see that there's nothing short of throwing you over my shoulder that's going to get you out of here. So you just sit right there and wait for the Lady and—"

Sarah snorted derisively. "You don't know nothing. I'm not waiting for the Lady."

"You said you were…"

She shook her head in denial. "I said the Lady *told* me to wait. But it's not her I'm waiting for."

"Okay," he said in a terse voice, clearly loosing patience. "Who are you supposed to be waiting for then?"

"The Last Gaian King," Sarah said. "Whatever that is. The Lady told me I was to wait right here and not to budge an inch until the Last Gaian King came."

The Third Circle
The Dance of Endurance

"The last what?" Arkady could not believe his ears. At the mention of the Last Gaian King, his thoughts went immediately to Albrecht and that damned Silver Crown. Albrecht was a longtime rival who had usurped his inheritance and thrust himself in Arkady's way time and time again. The throne of Jacob Morningkill should rightly have fallen to Arkady. He had worked so hard and sacrificed so much. And Albrecht had just walked in and taken it all away.

The legendary Silver Crown was a sign of Falcon's special favor. It was said that whoever wore it was the rightful king of all the Silver Fangs and thus, by extension, all werewolves.

Arkady found his eyes scanning the shadows, as if he expected Albrecht to stride out of the darkness, that same self-satisfied smirk on his face. The gleaming crown on his head.

There was a sudden taste of acid in his mouth and all Arkady's senses screamed, "Trap!" If Albrecht were here ahead of him! Could the upstart steal even this from him? This exile, this desperate assault upon the front gates of Malfeas itself, it was all Arkady had left. All that remained to him. He had lost the crown. He had lost his place in the Silver Fang hierarchy. And he had dishonored his peerless bloodline. Albrecht had driven him from the sight of his people. And now he would take even Arkady's last sacrifice, this final hope of redeeming his line. It wasn't right.

"The last Gaian King," Sarah repeated wretchedly. "The Lady said I had to wait here for him. And I waited, just like she said. I'll be good, I promise. I'll lead him to her. He is meant for her. Or they're meant for each other. It's all foretold…" She shrugged and broke off. "I won't go. If the Lady finds out that I was away, even for a minute, she'll punish me."

"Where is he?" Arkady barked. His fingers bit into the girl's shoulders. Angry white blemishes spread from each of his fingertips where he gripped her skin. "You have seen him already. He's been here and you are not telling me…"

"No! I swear it," she sobbed. "I'm a good girl. I do just what the Lady says. Don't hurt…"

"For the last time, I'm not going to hurt you!" he shouted.

"You're hurting me," she said, her voice a whimper. She tried, without success, to pull free of his grasp.

Deliberately, he unclenched his grip, finger by finger. Released, she puddled to the floor. "I'm sorry. I didn't mean to…"

"Doesn't matter," she muttered, drawing her knees up under her T-shirt and wrapping her arms around them. "You didn't hurt me. You can never hurt me. I'll just go away. To my secret place. It's a place where you can't follow, none of you! You're just like the others. Oh, I knew. I knew! You look different than them, but the Lady, she looks different too. It's not the looks, it's the words. Words that hurt and burn, like coals. Burned black as coal…"

"Stop it!" he shouted directly into her face. He drew back his hand and, for a moment, even he was not sure that he wouldn't strike her.

"Just like the others," she muttered stubbornly, as if already feeling the hot sting of fingers slapping across her face. Her tongue darted out, perhaps to catch a phantom trickle of blood from her lip. "All you do is hit. And burn with your fingers. And I've got the marks to prove it…"

She screamed as he grabbed her. Scooped her up in one arm, as if she were no more substantial than a rag doll, and threw her over one shoulder. "We're getting you out of here. Right now."

Sarah kicked and shrieked and bit and clawed. She was a tempest of teeth and elbows and fingernails. But Arkady took no notice of her struggles. She was a seven-year-old girlchild; he was one of the foremost warriors of the Garou. He was ashamed to think how sorely she had wounded him already. He headed back up the tunnel at a lope.

After a while the scratching and kicking stopped, as suddenly as it had commenced. Perhaps the child realized that force would not avail against the burly warrior. That the only effectual weapons that remained to her were her words. Coal-hot words.

"It doesn't matter," she said, her voice calm, quiet. "It's too late now anyway. They're already here."

Something in her tone, in the ice-cold certainty of it, drew him up short. His pace faltered and he caught the first subtle hint of motion in his peripheral vision. Then he saw the eyes. The gleaming pairs of lupine eyes, reflective, impassive. He counted at least a dozen forms emerging from the shadows. Stunted, crouched, manlike forms covered with the knotted sinew and bristling coal-black fur of the wolf.

Sarah's voice was calm, a level whisper, but Arkady could see the flicker of terror in her eyes. She was sinking away from him already, plunging down deep, into the comforting depths of her "secret place." Her body had gone limp, all the defiance and outrage had gone out of it suddenly. She was lost to him. It was as if he were carrying a drowned corpse.

Cautiously, without making any sudden moves that might be construed as the prelude to an attack, he lowered her body to the floor. She lay just inside the mouth of the tunnel. If she stretched out her arm, it might have reached the arc of moonlight falling through the opening.

Straightening, he turned to face them. The burned dogs, that's what she'd called them. He knew them by another name, however, an older name. The name the White Howlers, that werewolf tribe that had long ago fallen to corruption, had taken for themselves: the Black Spiral Dancers. He threw back his head and howled his challenge directly into the face of the massing foe.

They were burned, all right. Black as pitch, their features twisted and disfigured as if they had been sculpted by the caress of fire. Their fur had been seared away, leaving patches of coarse bristles, sharp as steel wire. But Arkady knew that the corrupting flame that had so marked them—that had bent their very bodies to its purpose—had not fallen upon them from without. It had ravaged them from within.

These monstrosities were the Garou that had known the caress of the Black Spiral. They had sought out its touch, courted it. Its kiss meant power for those with the strength and courage to walk the spiral, follow its tortuous logic through its nine gyres to its very center. But these were of a different breed. The suitors who had courted that power and been rejected. Those who had come crawling back from the brink of the spiral.

My predecessors, he thought and snorted contemptuously. *If I'm lucky enough to win through to the spiral. And, of course, return again.*

As he took up a defensive stance between them and the girl, the burned dogs came creeping, bubbling up from the darkened passageways and pits beyond. There were dozens of them, perhaps half a hundred. Some came shambling and upright, some bounding forward on all fours. Others dropped from the rough-hewn ceiling with the piercing cry of bats. And then there were the unfortunates, the wretches too broken in mind, body or spirit to do anything more than drag themselves forward, crawling along the floor in mingling trails of their own foul secretions.

He met the eyes of the foremost of this wave of twisted foes. Arkady watched for the reaction there as he shifted into his warrior form. Watched for the reflection of his greatness mirrored in this glass darkly. But he was denied even that small pleasure.

The eyes of the lead dog were milky white and unseeing. There was something disturbing about those eyes. They bothered Arkady and he found himself staring into them as the others closed upon him. They were too shifting, the whites of those eyes. *Too liquid*, he thought. They puddled in their sockets as if whatever flame had brushed the wretch had half-melted them.

Arkady shook himself to throw off the hold those eyes had upon him. His pelt suddenly blazed white in the darkness. As if that were some prearranged signal that they had been waiting for, the entire mob of Black Spiral Dancers fell upon him at once.

Arkady no longer had time to take stock of the enemy; he ripped upward with his claws. The blow caught the foremost of them low, in the abdomen. The force of the uppercut was such that it lifted the Dancer off his feet, even as the flesh parted and peeled away to either side of Arkady's fist, like water breaking across the bow of a ship.

For a moment, Arkady thought he saw something flare in those blind, milk-white eyes. A flicker of recognition, perhaps. A realization of a greater darkness rushing in upon him. It lasted only a fraction of a second and then Arkady felt the jarring impact of his claws catching upon the first bones of the ribcage and he pivoted, ripping his hand back out, before it could become lodged there.

The body of the burned dog continued in its motion, as if unaware that there was no longer any will directing it—bounding forward (its own vector) and upward (the one Arkady had imposed upon it).

For a moment it seemed to Arkady as if the corpse might take flight—suddenly sprout leathery bat wings in one last desperate bid to reach the opening beyond. To escape from the pit of Malfeas that had spawned it.

Then, almost self-consciously, like a cartoon character suddenly realizing he had already overrun the cliff's edge, the body reached the apex of its trajectory, hung there a half-second more and then fell lifeless to the ground. It landed within two feet of where Sarah lay. She did not even stir at the impact.

Arkady did not wait to see it hit. He was already moving away—fists, feet, deadly jaws going through the graceful motions of an elaborate and deadly dance. Then the music of the battle, a symphony of rage, carried him into the midst of his foes.

He rode the excitement of it, the pure adrenal rush, slamming his body forward. Two of them were down before they could even close the circle of their line around him, cutting him off from all hope of retreat. Three. Their front line gave ground before his freight-train rush, but held ranks. Soon, he knew, they would recover from the initial shock and then their pack instincts would take control.

Even as the thought formed, he saw the circle drawing tighter around him. The boldest of his adversaries darted forward from the ring, claws slashing, only to dance away again as Arkady turned to face him. Immediately, another assailant was at his back, powerful jaws snapping. Arkady's backhanded swipe sent the Dancer skittering back to the circle, but already a third assailant was on him.

They harried him from all sides, wearing him down. It was all Arkady could do to keep them at bay, much less actually mark any of them with fang or claw, until the fifth one to try him. He did not manage to dance away from Arkady in time and paid for it. Still, the circle shifted and drove Arkady farther along the darkened passage, and the body of the fallen adversary vanished.

He was surrounded now by a tempest of claw and fang that tore at him like an icy wind. For a moment, Arkady pictured himself standing high atop a windswept crag, peering up at a vast brooding storm that stretched like a shroud from horizon to horizon. He leapt, cut, thrust and slashed, but all his efforts were ineffectual, futile, ridiculous. One might just as well wade out into the surf to do battle with the tides.

And this tempest could well afford to be patient. The Dancers were merely testing his defenses. They were waiting for him to tire before the onslaught, to stumble or merely to overreact to one of their lightning fast probing attacks. Then the full force of the maelstrom would fall upon him, a dozen slavering dark thunderheads descending upon him en masse, dragging him down, pinning him beneath the sheer mass of their black wire-bristled pelts.

Arkady knew that if he went down, there was little chance of his getting back up again. They would slowly press the life from him and then open up his chest to let the last of his breath escape him in one final unimpeded rush.

Arkady saw all this, and still he leapt directly into the face of the dark churning storm of Black Spiral Dancers.

His sense of time blurred with the blossoming of his full-blown battle rage. He quickly lost count of the number of bodies that darted at him, the number of blows slipped, dodged or parried. When one of his assailants proved just a fraction of a second too slow or his lunge just a touch too sloppy, Arkady's claws marked him.

Arkady was splashing through the bowels of the fifth or sixth such unfortunate when he heard, rather than felt, the crunch of bone. Viselike jaws snapped closed over his left shoulder. The lightning flash of pain was only a fraction of a second behind.

He stumbled and a howl of anguish tore from his throat. In a single motion, his klaive flashed from its sheath and the swift upward stroke caught his attacker just behind the ear. It laid his brainpan wide open and lodged there.

If the blow had not been so instantly lethal, the attacker would certainly have released his locked jaws in pain and surprise. The swiftness of the deathblow, however, preempted even this response. If anything, the jaws of the dead Black Spiral Dancer clamped down harder and clung there.

Arkady struggled to free himself. With a great heave, he wrenched the klaive free, and the body of the Dancer crumpled to the stone floor. But already it was too late.

The total amount of time that both of his arms were pinned could not have been more than half a minute. But that was half a minute too long. White-hot pain flared as claws pierced his back, not rending, but puncturing straight in. A moment later, the full weight of the pouncing Black Spiral Dancer hit him, crashed over him with the force of a freight train. Arkady's back bent and his legs went out from under him as he crashed, face-first, to the stone floor.

Three times he tried to rise and three times they drove him back to the ground, with vicious cuts to his legs and an ever-increasing mass of snarling bodies heaped on top of him, grinding him down. He clawed desperately for the surface and then went down for the third and final time.

The Fourth Circle
The Dance of Cunning

The Rottebritte skirted the thickest press of the melee, urging the warriors of his hive to even greater feats of reckless bravery. He accomplished this largely by singling out an unblooded cub, one who was putting on airs by hanging back at the edges of the fray—a privilege jealously guarded by those who had earned it. Grabbing fistfuls of fur between the cub's shoulders and at the small of his back, the Rottebritte would fortify the recruit with a string of curses that would make a breeding-pit slave blush crimson and then hurl him toward the gleaming silver killing machine that roared and thrashed at the heart of the throng.

The Rottebritte spared himself one half-grudging glance at the intruder. The Gaian whirled and groaned like a rusty old combine tractor, laying waste to everything foolish or unfortunate enough to come within reach of its deadly threshing blades. He glowed white hot and sang like a kettle about to boil over. Only the constant supply of viscous lubricant—his own blood and sweat, and that of his victims—kept the puffing and rattling machine from overheating and tearing itself to pieces.

The Dancer snorted contemptuously and turned away. The Rottebritte knew the scuffle here at the threshold was a foregone conclusion. The Gaian was a formidable opponent; already a half dozen of the Rottebritte's own men were down, dead or wishing they were. But there were another three dozen clamoring (with the proper encouragement, of course) to take their place.

He heard the screams of the dying, recognized each of them by his voice, his distinctive howl. He had trained them all—drilled them, lived with them, *raised* them—from the time they had first crawled from the birthing pits...

No, that wasn't precisely true, he thought. Not from the *first* time they had crawled forth, but from the third. If a cub couldn't fight his way free of the pits three times, he was no warrior-born.

It was disgraceful how few whelps nowadays survived their first minutes of floundering around amidst the vile secretions of the breeding pools. Many were clawed to ribbons beneath the press of their fellows, clamoring over each other's backs in their desperate struggle to escape. Others fell victim to the sinister caresses and guilty pleasures of the pit slaves, soon finding themselves inexorably bound within the strict ghetto hierarchy of the pits, never to emerge as long as they lived. And the weaklings and litter runts just drowned, of course, or fell victim to the dark wriggling things that sloughed through the slime that coated the floor and walls of the pits. Even a full-grown warrior would have sunk to the waist in that murk—the remains of generations of accumulated afterbirths, stillborns and also-rans.

The howls of the dying broke in upon the Rottebritte's bitter reflections and he barked back encouragement. His howl poured the strength of the Hive into them—its age, its traditions, its destiny, its ability to endure. The music of it was filled with promise of living to fight another day and they drank it down eagerly, a last meal for a condemned man.

And the promise was not mere platitude. The Rottebritte knew that some of the casualties, even the mortally wounded, could and would go on to serve the Hive for quite some time. If nothing else, the broken husks of their still-living bodies would be turned back under the fertile soil of the breeding pits—buried alive to ferment in their own juices against the night of hatching, or to warm the pink wriggling things that had been cut from the pit slaves' bellies with knives of bone. Perhaps one of those who lay dying here would, one day soon, serve as the fleshy cradle for the Rottebritte's own son. The thought warmed him, a swelling feeling of pride.

He smiled broadly, unable to keep it all in, and clapped the nearest warrior heartily on the back in an overflow of camaraderie. The blow sent the unfortunate lurching off balance into the heart of the fray. The Rottebritte heard his howl of pain, and something that might have been an ear soared past.

But he wasn't about to let a little thing like that spoil his good mood. Tonight he would have a great victory and he would father a son! He warmed to the thought. It had been too long since he had visited the pits in anything other than an official capacity—drafting reinforcements. But tonight, the Lady would be pleased with him and no one could deny him this small self-indulgence. He had earned it. Yes, he would definitely pay a call upon the breeding pits once this business here was settled.

Leaving the crowd of combatants behind him, he crossed to the small figure lying huddled at the cave mouth. He prodded her unmoving form with one foot. "Get up!" he barked at her.

"Don't hurt me, I—" Sarah began.

"I said get up!" He grabbed her by her bedraggled mane of hair and hauled her to her feet. She yowled and for a moment that scream filled the chamber, cutting clearly through even the clash of blades, the howls of defiance, the wails of the dying. It brim-filled the chamber and echoed down the dark passageways.

"That's enough of that caterwauling, litter runt," the Rottebritte snarled, turning her around and giving her a shove forward, deeper into the tunnel. It was a shove that would have served to propel a grown warrior through a press of bodies to the heart of a fight. As the air went out of her with a whoosh and she left the floor, the Rottebritte realized what he had done and made a grab for her, but she was already beyond his reach. She tumbled in the air and her head hit the tunnel floor with the almost musical sound of hollow bone on stone. She rolled a half-turn and then another before she came to rest just outside the circle of hive warriors.

The nearest saw her flight, grimaced at the impact and then prodded her experimentally with one foot. When she let out a raspy whimper, he shrugged. He looked up to the Rottebritte to say something but, catching the look in his superior's eyes, thought better of it and slipped into the crowd to avoid the commander's unwanted attentions.

The Rottebritte crossed the intervening space in three crisp steps. Stooping, he grabbed her by the wrist and, unmindful of the harm that might be done in moving her, hauled her again to her feet. "You will not escape responsibility for this so easily, Sallah. The Lady would like to have a talk with you." He growled the threat through clenched teeth, directly down into the girl's face. An acrid string of spittle struck her cheek and clung there.

On his lips, her name sounded like a curse. It seemed to cut through the fog of pain and cotton and terror in her head. Some distant part of her, a spark of instinctive defiance, growled back. "Liar!" she shouted. It was her big voice again, the voice that had cut cleanly through the din of battle. "I have to wait here. The Lady herself told me. I have to wait for…"

"Idiot cub," he spat and cuffed her soundly on the side of the head, where the blood still showed (as well as the slightest indiscreet hint of bone white) from where she had hit the floor. Her body went limp, dangling from the wrist where he still held her firm.

With his free hand, he got the attention of the nearest warrior.

"What the hell? Oh." The warrior wheeled, rubbing the back of his sore head, but he hastily choked down his indignation as he found himself facing the Rottebritte.

"You. And you." He got the attention of another volunteer in a similar manner. "Both of you. Listen to me and don't screw this up. Take this cub directly to the Lady. You don't stop for anything or anyone along the way. You understand?" He waited for their nods and pressed on before they could interrupt with any stupid questions. His pleasant anticipation of the evening's activities was already souring. The Lady hadn't said anything about the girl-cub having to arrive in good condition, but the Rottebritte was all too familiar with her fickle ways. The crack of her anger was more fearsome than the lash she carried, and there was just no telling what might set her off.

Another good reason not to go himself. He smiled a predatory smile at his two recruits. "If anyone tries to fuck with you on the way, you tell him you are on an urgent errand directly from me to the Lady herself. You don't stop to discuss it, you do not accept any challenges from anybody—and I don't care what they call you—over the right to play with, feed on or mate with the she-cub. All right?"

They looked unconvinced. Perhaps they were already picturing the treatment they'd be in for if someone did challenge them as they made their way through the nether reaches of the hive. Begging off fights and admitting that they were mere errand-boys would rankle.

"Yeah, but what if—"

The Rottebritte was only waiting to see which would be the first to object. "If anybody gives you a hard time, puss brain, you show them this." He forestalled further objection by punching his claws into the recruit's chest and raking downward at an angle. Three claws found their mark and scored a trio of deep parallel tracks in his flesh.

"Puss brain" howled and stumbled backward, falling instinctively into a fighting crouch. He was breathing heavily and clutching at the wound with one hand, his free hand braced on the floor before him for balance. The Rottebritte saw the muscles of his back bunch to spring.

"Don't be an idiot," the Rottebritte growled back. "And get back over here so that I can finish putting my mark on you. That's going to have to pass for your credentials. You know what credentials are, right?" he added as an afterthought.

Gathering the shreds of his wounded dignity about him, the recruit straightened. "My name is—" he began in a threatening tone.

"I don't give a shit what your name is. Get over here." The Rottebritte tossed the girl into the arms of his other volunteer, the more cautious one, and again sunk his claws into puss brain's chest, this time tracing two lines, running straight down, from sternum to groin. In a good light, the hasty effort might have resembled the letter T, its triple crossbar listing drunkenly to one side.

Puss brain clenched his jaw and didn't cry out this time, although the last was certainly the more formidable cut.

"Now, as I was saying," the Rottebritte continued. "You take her straight to the Lady. If anyone tries to stop you, you're on an urgent errand to the Lady and you've got the credentials to prove it. You will find the Lady…"

"Yeah, we know where we'll find her, all right," the Dancer holding the girl in his arms said with a smirk. *A shame*, the Rottebritte thought. *And I had pegged him for the cautious one.*

"After you have delivered the cub," he pressed on, his voice raising ever so slightly in disapproval, "you will await the Lady's pleasure."

At that they paled visibly and he allowed himself a satisfied smile.

"But, sir!" they protested, almost in unison.

"And when she is… done with you," he paused meaningfully to let the full impact of that phrase sink in, "you will haul yourselves, or what's left of you, down to the pits to report to me directly. If *I* hear of any detours along the way—either way—I'll have your manhood carved out and sell you for the ugliest pair of pit slaves in the hive. Understood?"

"Yes, Rottebritte," they barked.

"Then get the hell out of my sight."

They hurried to comply and the Rottebritte turned back to the melee still raging just across the threshold. *Nothing left but the mopping up now,* he thought. *Still, can't hurt to be cautious.*

He gave them another five minutes and then waded into the thick of the fray, pulling his warriors up bodily, one by one. Wrestling them back up off the untidy mass of blood and broken bone and achingly white pelt that lay crumpled on the floor.

The Fifth Circle
The Dance of Combat

Arkady came to, only to immediately regret it. He found that his body had instinctively reassumed its accustomed human proportions when he blacked out—a reaction he always found an unpleasant reminder of the vulnerability of childhood. Of the maelstrom of confusion, anger and terror that dominated the time before his First Change. It was like breaking down and going into the fetal position under unbearable stress.

Unfortunately, as his body had taken on his true form once again, other things were also revealed for what they really were—such as the true extent of his injuries. Wounds that had been little more than stinging distractions to him in his lumbering Crinos war form were now revealed to be deep bleeders. And each of the truly horrific wounds he had suffered, he now realized, was life threatening in its own right.

Just beneath the throb and spurt of pain in his forehead, he could hear the low groan of shattered bone grinding over bone, trying to reknit itself. It was the bellowing creak and moan of the arctic ice floe expanding and contracting. It filled his perceptions, glaring and pain-bright, from horizon to horizon.

To aid his already unnaturally accelerated healing, Arkady tried to shift to his more substantial Glabro form. This hulking Neanderthal shape was easy half-again as massive as his accustomed human proportions. It could handle an awful lot of punishment. In it, he was stoop shouldered, knuckle dragging and ungainly, but Arkady knew he wouldn't be making any sudden moves anyway—graceful or otherwise—any time soon. Right now, what he needed was his strength, resiliency and, if he were lucky, a little time.

He was rewarded for his efforts by a sudden blinding pain from something cutting into his wrists. They were bound, he realized, a second before the creaking and straining cords snapped with the echoing retort of a pistol shot.

There was a flurry of motion and invective around him and then he crashed to the floor and found he had more pressing things to worry about. Like the pain and the rising blackness of oblivion. He fought it back down, or thought he had, until he was interrupted by a sudden sharp pain in the ribs. A kick.

An unfamiliar voice cut through the fog of pain and cotton in his head.

"That's enough!"

There was a brief scuffle and then another voice, aggrieved and complaining. "But the bastard's awake now. Look at him!"

"So you're going to kick him until he passes out again?"

"Yes!" The reply was belligerent but soon gave way to mere frustration.

"Fine. You drag him for a while then. Shit, he must weigh 300 pounds like that, but it's your back."

A grunt. "You awake?" Another prod with a foot, gentler this time, but the rib was already broken. *Before* the first kick. "I said, you awake?"

Arkady tried nodding (nearly passing out again) and then speaking, but with little more success. It came out somewhere between a moan and a shuddering sob.

This elicited a scattering of derisive laughter from his captors. There were probably at least a half dozen of them, he thought, from the sound of it. He couldn't see a damned thing. Couldn't focus on anything beyond the matted tangle of hair and blood plastered across his eyes. The brow ridge over his left eye was definitely shattered and the eye swollen shut.

Someone cursed and Arkady braced himself for another kick, but it never fell. Instead a mocking, high-pitched voice, looming right over him, called, "Wake up, sweetie. It's time for school."

More coarse laughter and then something warm and wet splashed against Arkady's face. He recoiled instinctively, but the stream followed him and did not abate. The liquid seeped into the open wound that was once his forehead and burned like fire.

"Quit fooling around. Just drag him, will you? Here, take his other arm."

He was grabbed by both wrists and dragged forward across the rough stone floor.

"I don't see why we can't keep him here. Have some fun with him for a while."

"Idiot. You heard what the Rottebritte said. This one is bound for the pit. The Rottebritte claimed his blade and the Lady has claimed… well, the rest of his sorry carcass. Can't imagine why she'd want it, though. It isn't much to look at."

"Oh, I can imagine it all right. I can imagine," said a new voice. His words were met with a coarse barking laughter. "So unless you'd like to go down there yourself and take it up with her, I'd suggest you pull. The sooner we're rid of him, the better."

This did not seem to satisfy the brute who had been giving Arkady's ribs the working over. "All the same, I'm just gonna cut me a little souvenir off him. I'm the one that beat him. You saw that! Hell, if you poke around in that mess of flesh where his back used to be, you can still see my finger-prints all up and down the bones of his spine. Say you can't," he challenged.

"Oh, you laid him out good, all right."

His voice was beaming. "And I deserve a little something for that. The Rottebritte took his sword. The Lady gets his mangy remains. I just want a little something to remember him by."

"Oh, just shut up and get it over with already. It's your funeral. When the Lady gets to wondering where all his choice bits have disappeared to..."

"That's not the part of him I'm interested in. I just want to get me one of these silver fangs of his. I keep hearing so much about how these Silver Fangs are better then everyone else. I figure they've got to be talking about the teeth."

Arkady's face exploded in white-hot pain as the foot smashed into it.

He lost consciousness again and when he came to, he was bleeding freely from the mouth. From the feel of it, the extraction had taken more than one try. He was still being dragged by the arms but could not tell how long he had been out.

"Sleeping beauty's up again," said a familiar mocking voice.

"Would have been easier on him if he'd just stayed out. You wanna kick him again?"

"No. I cut my damned heel the last time, getting those teeth. And you know what? They're not even silver! What a gyp. Come to think of it, it looks more like a red talon to me."

"Well, if you'd wipe the blood off of it..."

"You can't trust them damned Gaians for nothing. They can't even name something without bragging or lying or both. Why, I once got a peek at a damn Black Furry—down below, I mean—and it wasn't even..."

"That's Black *Fury*, you idiot. Not Furry."

"No, it was furry, all right. What I was trying to tell you was that it wasn't black!"

The conversation continued on as such, a series of off-color jokes at the expense of the Black Spiral Dancers' Gaian cousins. Arkady didn't spare it much attention, as he was focused on directing his body's efforts to reknit its broken bones and tattered flesh. It seemed an eternity before their slow, bumping, dragging progress came to a halt.

Arkady squinted up through the bloody mat of hair plastered across his eyes. The floor sloped down sharply away from him towards the chamber's center. There was a jagged cleft in the rock floor there, some kind of vent hole. Waves of hot air that smelled faintly of smoke and kerosene and chemicals wafted up from it, causing everything within his field of vision to ripple.

He lay, face down, in the layer of filth that covered the floor. He tried to raise his head free of the muck and failed, falling back again. He nearly blacked out from the stab of pain in his back that accompanied this effort.

"Here, look, he's going to crawl the last little ways and save us having to drag him the whole way."

"He sure took his time about it. I don't know what these Gaians have against a little honest work…"

"Well I, for one, am tired of dragging his sorry carcass around. Just roll him down to the pit and have done with it."

There was grumbling and then a foot was inserted under Arkady's shoulder. It rolled him over onto his back. He bit back a howl of agony. One part of his mind was aware that his body wouldn't lie flat; he had obviously broken more than a few ribs.

He was rolled over again. And again.

"Enough!" he spat through a mouthful of blood and broken teeth.

"Well, I'll be damned…" The burned dog who had been kicking him stepped back a pace. One of his packmates came forward, claws extended, to slap the Silver Fang back into oblivion, but was prevented by his packmate. "No, don't. This I want to see."

As they watched, Arkady again forced his head up from the muck, fighting down the agony that raced the length of his spine. Slowly, torturously, he rose to his elbows.

"Son of a bitch! He's actually gonna do it."

Someone laughed. "Who says you can't teach a whipped dog new tricks? Hey, Silver Fang, when you see the Lady, make sure to tell her who taught you to crawl on your belly. Every good wormling needs to learn to crawl on his belly."

Arkady waited for their mocking laughter to die down so that the broken whisper of his own voice could be heard.

"Who?"

"Who what? You mean, who kicked your ass and taught you to crawl? That would be the Rain-of-Terror Pack. Remember that; it'll be on the quiz."

"It's easy to remember, cause we rained down terror on your sorry ass, see?"

"I thought we was the 'Rape of Terror' pack."

"Idiot. Don't you remember when…"

Arkady never got a chance to hear what the burned dog was supposed to remember. All conversation had come to an abrupt halt as Arkady pushed himself up to his hands and knees. He clamped his eyes and jaw shut in the effort to keep the raging pain at bay.

"I'll be damned. I think he's actually trying to get up."

"Don't bet on it."

The temptation of a clear shot at Arkady's exposed ribcage proved too much to resist. The kick caught him squarely, with a crack that could be heard from across the room, and sent him tumbling again. He came to rest on his side, closer to the edge of the pit, facing them. The filth that coated the floor was deeper here, but he hardly noticed it. He had little attention for anything but the all-consuming pain in his ribs.

When the pain finally receded to a low throb, he became gradually aware of the conversation again.

"Got nothing to say to that, huh? I didn't think so." The Dancer spat and the spittle hit the floor an inch from Arkady's cheek. "I'm tired of kicking this guy. It's no fun anymore. Just shove him over the edge there and let's go."

"I got nowhere to be." Another kick landed, in the pit of his stomach, and Arkady curled around it. "I could keep kicking this bastard all night… Hey!"

A jagged row of broken teeth clamped down upon the aggressor's ankle, eliciting a cry of pain. As Arkady had doubled up under the force of the blow, he had shrugged into his wolf skin. His jaws gnashed, quick as thinking and, finding their mark on the offending leg, held on for all they were worth.

With a howl of agony, the Spiral Dancer shifted into his warrior form. His pinned ankle doubled in girth but was still held firm. Hot blood and spittle ran down over his foot as he tried to shake the wolf free.

Even in his lupine form, Arkady could not seem to get his feet firmly under him. He was wrenched violently from side to side. It was like trying to keep hold of the arm of a wounded bear.

"Get it off of me!" the Dancer yelled, but his packmates were enjoying the show so much, they were slow to come to his aid. Alone, he delivered crushing blows upon Arkady's head and shoulders in an effort to dislodge him. The Silver Fang held firm, though, and bulked up into the huge primeval dire-wolf Hispo form.

With each transformation, he felt stronger, surer of himself, as his body reknit bone and sinew, healing a bit more of the grievous wounds he had sustained. The powerful jaws of his Hispo form would, once he gathered his strength some, snap his foe's bones like kindling.

At this point, even those not involved in the fight could see that things were getting clearly out of hand. From the corner of his good eye, Arkady could see them closing in on him, circling around. In a desperate gambit, he released his grip on the Dancer's ankle and twisted around, throwing all of his now-considerable bulk against the back of his opponent's knees.

He had thought to buy himself a small measure of time and space to face his new assailants. But the attack proved even more effective than he had hoped. Already wounded and off balance, the Dancer did not take the blow to the back of the knees gracefully. He buckled and went down.

For a moment he flailed, scrabbling to catch himself at the brink of the pit, but he found no purchase in the foul muck. Arkady could see the flash of terror in his eyes as he slipped over the edge and vanished from sight. The howl of the felled Dancer rang in his ears for some minutes even after Arkady had turned to face the rest of the pack.

They circled him warily, knowing all too well that a wounded and cornered animal could prove the fiercest of foes. Arkady's hackles rose and he snarled a warning.

"Will you look at that? He's *still* trying to fight!"

"Shut up. Just keep closing in. Nice and slow."

They methodically herded Arkady toward the crevasse. They did a good job of it, slow measured progress. Every once in a while, one of them got too close and paid for it. Even on all fours, Arkady was having trouble keeping on his feet. It was only the pulse of the battle—the spurt of rage and adrenaline—that kept him upright. If he were more certain of the treacherous footing here at the brink, he would have shrugged into his towering Crinos warrior skin. But he could not chance a misstep now, and four legs—even four shaky ones—were far safer than two.

Then suddenly, they were all on him at once. Arkady did not catch the unspoken signal, but that hardly mattered now. At this point, all he could do was to try to give as good as he got. Falcon willing, he might yet drag a few of them down with him, or at least give them a little something to remember him by.

In defiance, he sprang directly into the teeth of the nearest Dancer. The sudden counterattack startled the assailant and he tried to deflect the brunt of the attack, rather than getting well clear of its path. That would have been the most sensible reaction to seeing a few hundred pounds of bunched muscle and gleaming claw pouncing straight into the path of his charge.

The two adversaries crashed together with bone-jarring force and the Dancer fell over backward. He hit the floor and all the wind went out of him, even before Arkady's back claws raked open a double row of long gashes in the unfortunate's lower belly.

Arkady immediately bounded up and over his foe, kicking off from the tangle of spilling intestines. But the footing betrayed him and he stumbled, nearly slamming flat to the stone floor. He scrambled upright again, but the slight delay proved his undoing. An iron bar came crashing down upon his already mangled back. He yelped as he heard vertebrae pop and crack. He wheeled, bringing on a renewed agony, his deadly jaws snapping at his attacker.

The bar rose and fell again and this time it did drive him to the floor. The third time it came down upon his skull and everything started to go black. He shook his head to clear it, opening his muzzle and howling his defiance at the attacker. He gathered his remaining strength for one last spring.

The Black Spiral Dancer before him saw the motion, of course, the bunching of the muscles of haunch and shoulder. He braced to receive Arkady's final desperate pounce, cocking the crowbar back in both hands like a baseball bat.

Arkady leapt. His opponent swung, but he had misjudged Arkady's leap. His blow was too late and a good three feet to the right of where Arkady's form hurtled through the air. The force of his own swing spun the Dancer around.

Only then did the object of Arkady's leap become apparent. It was not aimed at his crowbar-wielding antagonist, or any of the Rain of Terror pack. With a final bark of defiance, Arkady plunged, claws first, over the edge of the precipice.

• • •

Long into darkness, Arkady fell. He hurtled downward, a falling star. A rebellious angel cast down from the heavens into the nether dark. He had taken his fate in his own hands, chosen a self-imposed exile over defeat at the hands of his foes. But what had he won? He spiraled downward, his dignity intact, but uncertain how long he would have to relish this small victory, this flare of defiance.

The wind howled in his ears as he plummeted, taunting him for fleeing, for leaving his enemies in control of the field of battle. Try as he might, he could not shout it down or block out its mocking refrain.

Nine times the sun and moon traded places in their chase. Each in turn soaring high above him and then, laughing, plunging down past him. He would not rise to their challenge. He stuck doggedly to the straight and narrow, as if afraid he might lose his way if he for a moment strayed from his path. As if he had a choice in the matter. He had made his decision in the cavern above, when he stepped out into this domain of wind and vertigo. And now he was committed. Disappointed, the celestial orbs soon tired of him and resumed their game, tracing mirror-image gyres across the heavens above and the void below.

Only the ever-present winds remained by his side. "You should be dead," they whispered. "Why don't you just let go? Leave things to us. There is no sense in fighting further. You are in our domain now, safe. Why do you keep fighting? What is there to fight here, my brave young warrior?"

He made no reply. There was no reply to give them. He was alone with the winds.

It seemed an eternity later when the voices tried him a second time. "Look at it this way," they began—for the wind is nothing if not reasonable, except when provoked. "Either this fall is going to end, rather abruptly and messily, or it isn't. And it's all much the same to you, I'm afraid. Better to just rest now, to let go. To let us take things from here."

Again he denied them. They were right, of course. Already all the fight had drained out of him. He was empty, adrift, at their mercy. The winds could buoy him up, or they could just as easily withdraw their favor and abandon him to Gaia's pull, the desperate and lifelong clutch of the jealous lover.

He wanted to offer them a deal, to bargain for his life, his freedom. But he could not think of a single thing he could offer them. The only thing he knew they wanted of him was his volition, his unconditional surrender. And that he could not give them.

So he fell headlong, down through the layers of whispers and temptations, dreading the moment he would come to the end of his fall, dreading the moment he would find that his fall had no end.

A third time the wind tested him. "If you will only pledge to serve us, my brothers and I," it coaxed, "we will save you. It is within our power. Do you doubt it? Good. Come, there is something we wish to show you."

Arkady felt himself suddenly jerked upward, as if he had reached the end of some invisible tether. He screamed as his body was forced to take up the familiar burden of his own weight once again. He half expected that the winds were just toying with him, that he would not be able to make out anything here amidst the maelstrom. But as he squinted into the teeth of the wind, his eyes watering and straining to focus, he could make out something struggling there in the distance.

A bird of prey circled in its characteristic narrowing gyre, its feathers so white they seemed to shine with their own light. But something was wrong. As Arkady watched, the majestic bird veered suddenly, fought for altitude. It was a losing battle; the winds had hold of it already. They toyed with it at first, tossing it this way and that, one to the other. And all the while, the buffeting winds increased in intensity, egging each other on until they had swelled to hurricane force. He saw a tail feather ripped away and then another.

It was a cruel game and there could be no question of either its object or its eventual outcome.

"Enough!" Arkady bellowed, but the winds tore away his objections, shredded and scattered them, as soon as he voiced them.

"Tell us what you see, wolfling."

"I see only the casual cruelty of a tyrant and a coward. What insult has this creature offered you? What threat could it possibly represent to ones such as yourselves? If you have arranged this bird's torture in the hopes of impressing me, you have failed miserably."

"Do you not recognize the pitiful creature?" the winds crooned. "From your bragging and posturing, I should have thought you two were better acquainted. Look closely at its plumage. It is distinctive, yes? Nothing in its haughty bearing is familiar to you? The predatory curl of its beak or talons, perhaps?"

And then, as if a veil had been lifted from between him and the struggling creature, he saw it clearly for the first time. It was a falcon, there was no mistaking it. As difficult as it was to judge things like size, distance and time here—in this realm far from any conventional points of reference—Arkady got the sudden impression of overwhelming vastness. The falcon was so huge that it would have been hard pressed to settle on any perch so humble as a mere mountaintop. An involuntary cry escaped Arkady's lips.

"Good. You do recognize your patron after all. We wanted you to understand—to see with your own eyes—that even Falcon cannot help you here, child. What is a mere Falcon compared to the majesty, the fury, the reach of the winds? We reach out a hand, and Falcon soars. We withdraw our favor…"

Falcon plummeted like a rock. Arkady lurched in that direction, but he was too late. Already the noble bird had vanished, batting its wings in vain where there was no resistance and screeching defiance as it fell.

"Your devotion," the wind suggested, "is misplaced. Reconsider it. Serve us and we will bear you up, carry you over the threshold of the night sky and to safety. Refuse us and we will not reach out our hand to you again, even if it means that you are dashed to pieces against the very floor of Malfeas itself. Let the consequences be upon your own head."

It didn't take him much deliberation to come to a decision. But then again, deliberation wasn't his long suit.

"Go to hell," he said.

"An interesting choice of words," the wind said, shrugging him off. His body immediately resumed its headlong fall. "Hell—coming right up."

Arkady suddenly felt the weight of rock all around him, above him. Rushing past him on all sides. The impression of vast open spaces was gone. In its place, Arkady was left with a sense of claustrophobia and an oppressive hot wind billowing up at him. It smelled of smoke, kerosene, chemicals and less savory things. He could see a light flickering there, far below him, an unhealthy glow that grew stronger and steadier with each passing moment.

But there was something else down there as well. At first Arkady thought it merely a part of the flickering fires below. But soon he could see that it was something distinct, a patch of white, not rising up to meet him from below, but also plummeting down into darkness. Something inside Arkady leapt toward it in recognition.

He howled out to it, hoping to bridge the gap between them with the tenuous lifeline of his voice. He seemed to be closing the distance between him and the struggling white form, which should not have been possible if they were both in freefall. But there it was, just below him, its wings beating frantically, struggling for altitude. A white falcon.

Arkady wanted to call to the falcon (or was it actually Falcon himself?) to reassure it, to let it know that he had not betrayed it. But his words were torn instantly away from him and upward.

Then, as he watched, the falcon folded its wings to its sides, curling in upon itself, and began to tumble downward end over end.

"No!" Arkady howled. His lunge toward the bird was so wild, he himself began to tumble and he lost sight of it as he struggled to right himself.

"Wait! I didn't abandon you. The winds, they tried to make me, but I didn't. I…"

The voice he heard then did not carry up to him borne on the rushing wings. Rather it seemed to come from somewhere inside him. It was deep, rumbling, resonating along his very bones and filling him up with its vastness.

"AND I," said the voice, "NEVER ABANDONED YOU."

The voice was too much to be contained in such a fragile vessel. It tore up through him, seeking egress. It broke from his throat with a howl of defiance that shook debris loose from the rock face on either side of him. It streamed from his eyes with a blazing light that drove back the encroaching shadows. It blossomed out of each of his gaping wounds, searing and cauterizing as it went.

And slowly, with excruciating patience, the voice unfolded from his mangled back in crackling wings of purest white flame.

The Sixth Circle
The Dance of Corruption

Arkady awoke, coughing and sputtering, floating facedown in a burning lake. It was only then that he discovered Falcon's final gift, the fact that he could not recall the details of those last terrible minutes of his fall.

The shock of impacting the surface of the lake and of plunging deep beneath its fetid waters had brought him back to himself. He was fortunate enough not to have surfaced directly beneath one of the slicks of mingled oil and sludge that floated on the lake's surface, blazing and sending up roiling black thunderheads.

Disoriented, choking on lungfuls of tainted water and noxious fumes, he struck out for what he hoped was the nearest shore. It seemed to take an eternity. Every muscle in his arms and legs ached by the time he dragged himself from the turgid waters. But it was the ache of honest exertion. Arkady felt better than he had since he had first rolled aside the Three Day Stone and entered the Gaia-forsaken Black Spiral Dancer hive.

A sheen of blood and oil clung to him, a glistening second skin. Or perhaps, in his case, a third. He slipped into his wolf skin and the thick dark rivulets soaked his fur, dripping and puddling at his feet.

He staggered no more than three steps from the water's edge before collapsing. He retched violently onto the stone tiled floor. Absently, he noted that someone had obviously gone to great effort to scour the granite until it was featureless, perfectly smooth and nearly white. They would not thank him for coming.

His mouth split into a wide grin as he wiped it against the back of one paw. He intended to give the inhabitants of this place far worse insult before he was through here.

Still on all fours, he shook himself all over, throwing a spray of dark liquids in all directions. He was startled to catch a sudden answering movement of someone or something stepping back out of the range of the splatter. He came instantly into a fighting crouch.

A woman stood before him, not five paces away, even after her hasty retreat. She was tall and regal, crowned with a mane of thick midnight hair that hung down to the small of her back. Her eyes were proud, and they held him there, defying him to look anywhere else.

Arkady rose unsteadily to his feet and tried on his human form experimentally, pleased to find that it held and for the moment kept him upright. Standing before her as an equal, he allowed his eyes to travel up and down her form, slowly taking her all in. She was clad in a long garment of white wolf's fur—an outrage that instinctively sent the hair at the nape of Arkady's neck bristling. The garment might have been a coat, at least on someone who was wearing anything else beneath it. Perhaps a robe, then. It gaped open at the front, revealing slight teardrop breasts. And below them, six wine-dark nipples trailing down her taut belly in two straight lines.

She followed the line of his gaze and snorted contemptuously. "I am Illya, a handmaiden of the Lady Zhyzhak. You are Arkady of House Crescent Moon."

It was clear from her inflection that this was not a question. What was less clear was what she wanted of him. "Handmaiden," he repeated, shaking his head, his eyes never rising from the gentle curves of her chest and underbelly. Even in the uncertain light of the oil fires and thick black smoke behind him, he could make out the warm flush of her skin and the downy peach-fine fur that covered it. Covering all, concealing nothing. A false modesty.

"My mistress bids me to welcome you to the Temple Obscura," she said.

He could trace the delicate latticework of the fine white scars that crisscrossed her flesh. Apparently this Zhyzhak had not only an eye for beauty, but a heel for it as well. With a visible effort Arkady came back to himself. "Is it she who has done this to you?" he demanded.

She looked confused for a moment before she realized just what he was referring to. Self-consciously, she began to pull the furs closed. Then she caught herself, unknotted her fingers from the fur and trailed them, slowly and deliberately down the line of nipples. She treated him to a patronizing look. "With her own hands," she said defiantly.

"Then," he replied, "you are a handmaiden no longer, Illya. I free you. You are no longer bound to this creature. You may go. And you need have no fear that she will come after you; I will attend to that personally."

At this declaration, she threw back her head and laughed out loud—a series of musical lupine barks. When she recovered herself she said, "The Lady did not tell me that you were such a wit, Lord Arkady. If the truth were known, she had painted you as a bit slow and more than a little self-important. But I see this was only another of her little cruelties at my expense. You will have to be very entertaining indeed if you would aspire to usurp my place in the Lady's service. I am one of her special favorites." All hint of amusement had suddenly gone out of her tone.

"You misunderstand," Arkady said gruffly, "but it makes little difference. Bring me to your Lady and I will settle this matter with her directly. I have said you are free, therefore you are free. There is nothing more to be said."

She regarded him for a long while. "Why should I want to be… never mind. I have a message for you from the Lady. And also a gift. I was instructed to meet you here and deliver them. Are you going to allow me to do so? Surely even you will grant that I cannot be 'free' while I have not yet fulfilled this task that I have undertaken."

"You might have mentioned it earlier," Arkady grumped.

She ignored him. "Here is your message: The Lady Zhyzhak informs you that she knows why you are here and that she will await you upon the spiral. You will meet upon its fifth gyre, which is the circle of combat."

"We will?" Arkady could not quite conceal his smile.

"What are you laughing at?" she challenged.

"I was just thinking that, judging from her message, your mistress doesn't have any idea why I'm here. But I'll certainly keep an eye out for her. Was there anything else?"

"Yes, this." Illya untangled a small sack that was tied within her furs. Without a glance at it, she tossed it to the ground at Arkady's feet. It hit without any appreciable noise and neither bounced nor skidded. "Now I am free?" Her grin was taunting.

"I have said as much," Arkady replied, stooping to retrieve the sack.

When he straightened he was alone. His keen ears could pick out the pad of bare feet receding across the stone tiled floor. He did not follow.

Arkady fumbled at the string that held the sack closed. Delicate manipulations had never been his forte. Brute force projected upon a stage of epic scale—that was more his style. He was a force of nature and of destiny.

He struggled with the knot for a full minute before extending a claw and, with a single irritated flick of his finger, slicing neatly through the entire mouth of the pouch. He upended it over his upturned palm.

For a moment nothing happened. He could feel that there was something inside, but whatever it was clung tenaciously to the inside of the sack. In mounting frustration, he shook it. The contents tore free of their moorings and fell into his hand with a wet plop. It was not one object, but two. A pair of sticky orbs, still trailing viscous strands of tendon, nerve and congealed blood.

He rolled them around in his palm absently, musing over the meaning of this macabre keepsake. It wasn't until the orbs were aligned—both pupils facing upward, returning his stare—that he realizing what his hands were doing. With an effort, he forced them to stop and closed his fingers into a fist, closing the eyes in death.

What did it mean, this enigmatic present? The Lady Zhyzhak awaited him on the Black Spiral. Did she think he was too blind to find his way to the heart of this benighted realm? Was that it? Was she mocking him?

She had not sent her champion to treat with him, but only her handmaid—a mere wisp of a girl, a bit of pillow fluff she had lying about her bed chamber. Did the Lady intend this envoy as an insult? Or was her message more subtle? Perhaps she was offering the girl to him, to try to buy him off, to turn him aside from his terrible purpose.

But if that were so, why did the Lady say that she would await him farther on, in the midst of the Black Spiral itself? That certainly did not sound as if she meant to divert him.

Arkady shook his head. There was too much he did not know. This Lady Zhyzhak said she would await him. Very well, then; let her wait. It was not Arkady's intent to set foot on that spiral at all.

If he were right, and all his hopes now were contingent on this one surmise, he would not need to walk the Black Spiral. It had all looked so simple when he and the Fianna, Stuart Stalks-the-Truth, had stumbled upon this desperate plan. Arkady would walk the white mirror spiral nested between the gyres of the black and arrive at the same destination—the very center of the labyrinth. And he could do so without ever once suffering the corrupting touch of the Black Spiral.

That was where all the others before him had failed. Arkady would not fail. He could not afford to. He was the last of his proud and noble lineage—the purest of the blood born in a score of generations. The fallen Silver Fangs that had gone before him had to be redeemed. So that their sacrifices would not be in vain. They had all waited so long already.

The Lady will await you on the spiral.

"Well, let her wait." Silently, he slipped his grisly present back into the sack, twisted the mouth closed and hurled the bundle far out into the burning lake.

Purposefully setting his path away from that which Illya had taken, Arkady struck out into the darkness at random. Illya had named this netherworld the Temple Obscura, a name usually invoked only to frighten disobedient cubs. In the tales of the firewives, the temple always figured prominently as the most infamous of the approaches to the realm of Malfeas and the dreaded Black Spiral Labyrinth.

But surely she was having some sort of joke at his expense. Arkady had not paid any more heed to these cautionary tales than to anything else his elders had said to try to bring him to heel. But in his memories, the Temple Obscura loomed as a sort of Gothic cathedral, filled with clouds of overpowering sulfur and brimstone. If he now actually stood before the altar where the Black Spiral Dancers came to pay homage to the Wyrm and test themselves by dancing the Black Spiral down into the depths of madness and corruption, then the reality bore little resemblance to the romantic notions of his childhood.

First of all, he could not remember for the life of him any mention of a long fall, and that plunge was not one Arkady was likely to soon forget. Second, there was the lake of fire to consider—a glaring omission even given that the firewives would never have had occasion to visit the site firsthand. It was the sort of detail they should have checked on.

In the old tales, even something as basic as the physical dimensions of the temple was the subject of wild conjectures and hyperbole. Its nave alone was said be lined with lamps of sickly green balefire so numerous that the unbroken procession stretched farther than the eye could see. From Arkady's vantage point, however, such lights were nowhere in evidence, which was something of a sore point at present. He would have welcomed even one such light just now, as he squinted to pick out any details of his surroundings with only the flickering and uncertain glow of the smoky oil fires behind him.

He distinctly remembered the (conspicuously missing) lamps ceaselessly churning lava and effluvium—and that would have been something worth seeing in and of itself, even setting aside the purported magnitude of this spectacle. The oldest tales put the number of these erupting luminaries at nearly twenty thousand! The story of Iron Peter went so far as to fix their count at precisely 19,683.

But even Arkady had to admit that such an exact figure was surely the result of a simple poetic conceit, rather than anyone bothering to count the interminable array of lights. He also noted that 19,683 was, not coincidentally, three (the number of the Wyrm) raised to a power of nine (the number of the Black Spiral Labyrinth). And, in the perfect hindsight of an adult perspective on cherished things from childhood, the tale of Iron Peter really amounted to little more than a ghost story with a questionable moral tacked on.

No, everything about this place was wrong. Even the most disreputable of accounts agreed that the Temple Obscura was a place covered with intricate patterns and designs—story glyphs captured by the Black Spiral Dancers during their raids upon the Garou's Silver Record Lodges. But Arkady had not seen so much as a single hastily scrawled pictogram.

If the truth were known, it looked as if someone (or -ones) had gone to great pains to scrub the floor to a featureless shine. So much so that Arkady had to conclude that over the ages, several layers of the granite must have been worn away with the effort. It was as if someone had embarked on a systematic effort to eradicate all hint of history or personality from the vast chamber.

Arkady had been traveling for some time before it occurred to him that he really ought to have a better plan of attack in mind. The problem was that his options were miserably limited. There were really only three significant directions here in the underdarkness. One, backward toward the lake of fire—the only visible landmark in the unbroken gloom of the hall. Two, he could repent of his earlier stubbornness and strike out in the direction Illya had gone. That option, he had to admit, was growing on him. Besides the obvious attractions that could be marked off in Illya's personal favor, this path would also give him a much-needed semblance of progress.

Arkady had a natural disinclination toward retreating that bordered on the pathological. He flatly refused to retrace his steps when there was still any other option open to him—even a hopeless one like plunging headlong into a midst of a few dozen armed enemies. Also, there was a good chance that Illya would be returning to her mistress directly to report their encounter, and that might at least lead him *somewhere* in the direction of Black Spiral Labyrinth. He could not say so much for his current course.

But this option still stuck in his craw. Perhaps it was the thought of being manipulated by the two women, of being led by the nose. But the only other option was, three: to continue to wander around blindly in the dark.

He considered. If he put the burning lake to his back and kept walking in a straight line, directly away from it, sooner or later he was bound to strike a wall. No matter how vast this hall might prove.

And if there were any other point of ingress or egress, besides the rather precipitous way he had come, he was certain to find it if only he followed the wall long enough.

And so, perhaps only out of sheer stubbornness, that is what he did. It seemed he had been running for hours, if not days, when he at last stumbled upon something besides himself in the unbroken darkness. It was impossible to say for sure that he had stuck to a straight line as he had intended. The light of the oily flames was still behind him, although now it had receded to little more than the pinprick of a single star puncturing the vast canopy of the night sky. Of course, the light still *seemed* to be directly behind him, he thought angrily. Even if he had meandered drunkenly from his original course. There was simply no other point of reference here.

Once it became obvious that he had already covered a distance far greater than could possibly be contained in a single building, he had shrugged into his lupine form. He could not only travel more quickly this way, he could also maintain the ground-eating lope almost indefinitely without tiring.

So it was that, when at last there was a subtle shift in the darkness ahead, he did not discover it by bumbling face first into it, as surely he would have in his human form. Even at a run, his keen lupine senses picked up on the change, like mounting solidity in the dimness ahead. A thunderhead forming on the horizon, billowing, piling higher upon itself.

Arkady checked his speed, slowing to a cautious walk. He circled wide to one side. Meeting the same resistance, he doubled back to circle around the other way. The looming thunderhead was again there before him. It ran in an unbroken line, straight as a plumb line, as far as he could make out. Here then, Arkady thought, was a wall. Or at least what passed for one in this place.

It was not a conventional wall; there was nothing solid about it. It was not carved from blocks of polished granite like the floor. Arkady inched closer, sniffed at it and snorted. It was difficult to say just what it was made out of. Arkady shifted back to his Homid form to see if perhaps eyes trained from birth to grasp and interact with manmade artifacts could make any more sense of the barrier.

It was a commonly held misapprehension that the human senses were somehow inferior to those of other animals. Arkady, however, understood that just as there were many things invisible to the human senses that were obvious to those of a wolf, the opposite was true as well. There were some experiences that could be taken in only through the filter of human perceptions.

As Arkady shifted, the wall seemed to shift as well, mirroring his every motion as if it were stalking him. Its new form fell upon it with the suddenness of a steel trap snapping shut. Arkady staggered back away from it, reeling to catch his balance.

The wall no longer appeared as the impenetrable bank of a mounting thunderhead—a hazy line marking the outer boundary beyond which a benign Gaia let her darker aspect peek through. To his wolf senses, the wall had seemed the farthest outpost of the Mother's sheltering care. Outside the face of her incomprehensible, unreasoning fury raged—the realm of howling isolation, madness and loss.

It was not only dangerous to move into the barrier, it was nearly unthinkable that any wolf would choose to do so. Only the sick, the gravely wounded or the broken in spirit would willingly leave the community of the pack for the keening loneliness of the outer darkness.

To his human senses, however, the wall wore a different aspect. It was not a presence at all, but rather an absence. It was as if something that should have been there suddenly was not. The feeling was not a pleasant one—a queasy mixture of disorientation and apprehension. It set to work grating directly upon the nerves.

Arkady shook his head angrily to clear it. The idea was ridiculous, of course. How could he perceive an absence? How could he see something that was not there? And yet somehow, that was exactly what he was experiencing.

The wall toyed with his expectations, frustrating them. It reminded him of coming home late at night, fumbling for keys, only to realize that his front door had been kicked in. Arkady stood there gaping at the blank expanse of wall, dreading what he might find within.

The thing that most disturbed him was the feeling of incompleteness about it all. The wall felt to him like a work in progress, unfinished but moving toward some final form that could only be dimly guessed at from the evidence at hand. It went to work on his frazzled nerves like a story or song repeated over and over again, each time with the single glaring omission of its last line.

The wall was not, he realized, something caught in the midst coming into being, but rather, something in the process of going out of it. It was a truth being systematically expunged. A song being unsung. A story being erased, word by word, from the end to its first beginnings. Once upon a...

Arkady's mind leapt to the pictures and stories he had seen in the Silver Record Lodges of his people. Myths and memories so potent, so vital, that they could not be rendered in any medium more ephemeral than living rock. Stories carved upon the hearts of mountains.

But here, at some more primal level, deeper even than the roots of mountains, the stories were being unwoven. Taken apart at their most basic building blocks and scattered. Split like atoms with results just as calamitous and irreversible.

This was the Elephant's Graveyard, he realized with sudden clarity. The place where the oldest of stories—the hoary old tales that made up the history, the cosmology, the religion of the Garou—came to die. To lie down and be forgotten.

It was only then that Arkady knew the dark purpose to which this Temple Obscura had been built and consecrated. It was a refutation of all the Garou held dear—the counterpart and utter negation of their cherished Silver Record. This was the hole where the stories bled out of the world.

The Seventh Circle
The Dance of Loyalty

He could not say how long he stood, staring mesmerized at the play of shadows before his eyes as the last living memories of valiant conquests and cowardly betrayals—tales that had defined his people and given meaning to their struggles, their sacrifices—passed from the world.

He was their last mute witness, an audience of one. It was as if the entire course of history was no more than a shadow play staged for his private benefit. He could not break away from it. It held him pinned and wriggling. He barely dared to breath or even blink lest he miss something in that fraction of an instant that could never again be recaptured.

He could feel hot tears on his face. He may have cried aloud. But despite his pleas, there was no pause in the damning procession of image and song. It was not his own life, but the lives of count-less others, that flickered one last time before his eyes. And then they were gone. Utterly lost.

He threw back his head and howled and from somewhere in the vast darkness behind him, his cry was answered. Not a howl of defiance, as his had been, at a proud and noble tradition that was rapidly slipping through his grasp. The sound that came back to him from the darkness was a mock-ing echo. A small broken sob. In the voice of a young girl, lost and without hope of finding her way back to the light.

Arkady knew that voice at once and the shock of it managed to break in upon him, to twist his head away from the wall of the Temple Obscura.

"Sarah," he bellowed. "Sarah, where are you?"

The small voice fell to a whimper and then was silent. Arkady shifted into lupine form again. The storm front was there before him again and he edged sideways away from its fury. It could break at any moment and it would not do for him to be caught in the downpour.

His keen ears had little trouble picking up the sound of muffled sobbing and he broke away already at a run. Arkady called out to her again, but this time his voice came out as little more than a series of quick barking yips, the crisp efficient signals of a pack spreading out to find a lost cub. Some distant, human part of his mind winced at the sound, imagining it would only frighten the girl further.

She was still a long way off, but it was difficult to tell if he was racing on all fours toward the girl's position or merely toward some point where the echoes of her cries rebounded from one of the walls. Arkady could only hope that he was getting closer rather than farther away from her.

Arkady found himself bounding first one way and then another. At times, the distant prick of light that he imagined was the lake of fire (and not just some ghost image playing across his retina) was at his right; at other times it seemed straight ahead, or even off to the left. With a sinking feeling in his stomach he realized that he had no reason at all to assume that there was only one light source here in the Temple Obscura. The lights he glimpsed might actually be from different sources—torches or cooking fires or reflections of distant daylight streaming in from some crack above. Perhaps the temple was so vast that it encompassed not one, but several burning lakes. He thought again of the legends of the temple being lined with twenty thousand balefire lamps and cursed aloud.

The problem, he thought, with taking a story for your guide was not that stories were hardly ever true. It was in what they left out.

Arkady squeezed his eyes shut and concentrated on the sound. Only the sound.

Perhaps the details of the old tales didn't really matter, he thought. Perhaps the words themselves were like his sense of sight here in the underdark. Blunted and rendered unreliable. Maybe what was really important was the sound. The rhythm of the words. The steady rise and fall of them, like the familiar pattern of four feet pounding across a granite floor.

Maybe it didn't matter at all what was said here, he thought, but rather the spirit in which it was voiced. He threw back his head and howled again, defiant. She was here somewhere. And even a darkness this vast and complete could not stand between them.

The only result of his renewed call, however, was a faint frightened shriek.

"No!" came the small distant voice. "Go away. Leave me alone. Don't hurt me. Don't hurt me again."

It was like a litany. The girl mumbled the words over and over again, until they lost all meaning. Until only the inflection, the rhythm of their rise and fall mattered.

Arkady pace matched it, redoubling his efforts in a burst of speed that set his heart thundering against his ribs. And then suddenly, she was there before him. A small huddled thing on the floor. Knees drawn up to chest, elbows wrapped around knees, face in hands. She was rocking slowly back and forth, and the singsong rhythm of her rocking was exactly the same as that of her litany of denials and that of the pattern of his four pounding paws.

He checked his speed suddenly, nails scrabbling for purchase on the polished stone tiles. He was going to crash right over her, like a wave. Like a breaking thunderhead. To obliterate her utterly.

With a violent heave he threw his bulk to one side and leapt, sailing past her, a powerful forepaw passing within a handbreadth of her face. He skidded to a stop, wheeling fast, afraid he might lose her again to the darkness. But she was there, exactly as he had left her, rocking and crooning softly to herself.

Arkady padded forward cautiously, as if afraid the sound of his voice would be enough to set her to flight. To scatter her. As if she might dissolve back into mist and darkness without a trace.

"Sarah," he whispered, padding closer. The sound was little more than a growl. He froze, stock still, one paw still hanging in midair. Afraid to put it down. Slowly, he shifted back into his human form. He hoped it might be a little less frightening.

Finding himself now on hands and knees, he crawled one step closer and then sat facing her not three paces away. At these close quarters, the fear that she might just vanish on him, leaving him alone again, receded.

"Sarah," he repeated, more confident this time. He tried to make his voice comforting, knowing that even his human voice, tuned to seasons of battlefield command, might be enough to set a small frightened girl to flight.

She did not look up at him, would not lift her head from her hands. "You should have told me," she accused and then suddenly reversed tack. "Even if you did tell me, I wouldn't have believed you. You're a liar!"

This took him off guard. "I… I'm sorry. I…" He was still trying, with mixed results, to puzzle through the labyrinthine thread of her hurt and accusation. "I didn't leave you on purpose. I was trying to defend you, but there were too many of them. They knocked me out. Dragged me off…"

She was having none of it. She raised her head to face him and his words died unspoken. He made a noise that was halfway between a curse and a gasp.

"You said you wouldn't hurt me—that no one would ever hurt me. Ever again. And then you just left me there. I hate you." Her words stung, but Arkady could not focus on those words. He was staring at her in horror and outrage at what they had done to the girl.

"Oh, Sarah," he said and then faltered. "I'm so sorry."

Dirt, blood and tears streaked her cheeks. She had tried to wipe the stains away, many times from the look of it, but there were always more where those had come from. She stared straight at him, the cock of her head defiant. Arkady did not return her stare. Could not.

Where Sarah's eyes had been, there was now only the skin of her eyelids, stretched parchment thin over sunken and empty sockets. Someone had taken the time and trouble to stitch those eyelids closed with thick black catgut. The handiwork was methodical and exact—nine neat stitches sealing each socket. The puckered pink flesh bunched around each of the pinpricks might heal cleanly, but there would never be any mistaking what had been done to her.

Arkady could contain himself no longer. "Who did this to you?" he growled.

"Why should you care?" she shot back. "You don't care. You're just like them."

"I said, who did it?" he barked. The whip crack of his voice snapped her head back.

"You did!" she shrieked at him. She could not have seen him draw back his hand, but perhaps she felt its passing. She set her jaw, struck it forward defiantly. Moments passed, but the blow did not fall.

"I'm going to get whoever did this to you, Sarah. Whether you want to tell me about it or not. I'll get them," Arkady said, struggling for control. "But I will not sit here and let you say that I did this to you. Do you understand me? Someone has hurt you and he's going to pay. Now, can you walk? We've got to get you to somewhere safe, wherever that might be."

"No!" she grabbed for him, trying to make him understand, to shake it into him. "No. You have to promise me. You won't send me away. You won't…"

"Then answer my question. Who has done this?"

For a moment it seemed she might argue further. Then all the resistance drained from her body. She slouched, her head falling back to her hands. "The Lady," she said. "It was the Dark Lady. There, are you happy? Now are you going to make *her* pay? *You?*"

"Yes."

Mingled hope and disgust flickered across her features. "Liar," she muttered, but without her earlier venom or conviction.

After a long while he asked gently, "Do you want to tell me what happened?"

At first it seemed she would refuse him or yell at him again, but in the end, the words came tumbling out of her in a sobbing rush.

"She said all she asked me to do was to wait. That's all. And I managed to screw even that up. Why didn't you tell me?" There was a note of pleading to her voice.

"Why didn't I tell you what? I don't understand."

"I did everything she asked. I waited. I waited so long. But no one ever came. Only those like you. The white coats. The ones that went down into the coal cellar and become just like the burned dogs. All those years, but no one ever came."

Arkady could hardly credit it. Was the girl saying that others of his kind—other Silver Fangs—had come this way recently? That seemed unlikely. Against his will, his thoughts immediately went to Albrecht. Had his rival managed to arrive here ahead of him? To once again steal away a glory that was rightfully his?

No, that was ridiculous. Albrecht was thousands of miles away. No doubt, back in the North Country Protectorate, squatting like a toad atop the throne of Jacob Morningkill. A throne that did not belong to him.

Who then?

Then something else the girl said struck him. "All those years?" he repeated, shaking his head, and winced to catch himself at it, realizing the gesture was wasted upon her. But the girl could not have been much more than seven years old at the outside.

"How old are you, Sarah?"

She drew back her shoulders and wiped at her tears with the back of one grimy arm. "Seventeen," she said, her look daring him to contradict her.

He laughed aloud despite himself. "And you call me a *liar*? I am not so far from seventeen that I have forgotten what it looked like. You are seven, maybe."

She shook her head stubbornly and made a noise in her throat that said clearly that he didn't know anything. "Seventeen," she insisted and then hedged a bit. "At least as near as I can figure it."

"What year were you born?" he asked, thinking to trip her up.

"I don't count it from when I was *born*," she said. "Nobody remembers back to when they were born! I count it from when I first came here. And that makes it seventeen."

"All right," he threw up his hands. "I give. Can you tell me how you got here at least? Which way you came from?"

Without even pausing to deliberate, Sarah pointed off to her left.

"That way's as good as any other, I guess. Come on, now." He reached out and took her hand. She tried to jerk back from him, but he held firm.

"Now that I've found you again, I'm not letting go so easily," he said.

"I can do it myself." She did so. "Come on, then, if you're coming."

• • •

She led him deeper into the darkness of the Temple Obscura. Arkady was eager to reach their destination, but he forced himself to match his pace to hers and they progressed at a tentative shuffle. It was maddening.

In his lupine form, he could have raced ahead, scouting in all directions. Bounding outward and then back to her side a hundred times over. But he did not leave her side.

"Are you sure this is the way?" he asked after an eternity of shambling through unbroken darkness.

She nodded, then realizing that he probably didn't catch the slight gesture in the darkness, she cleared her throat and rasped, "Yes. It's straight ahead of us now, but still a long way off. Can't you hear it?"

He cocked his head to one side, a distinctly lupine gesture. "No," he admitted after a while. "Nothing."

"Not hear with your ears. I mean, hear with your spirit. And you'll never hear anything if you keep racing back and forth like that. Keep still."

Arkady started to retort that he was keeping still. That he said he wouldn't leave her and that he hadn't. Then realized that what she said was true. Every muscle in his body was straining ahead. In spirit, he was bounding ahead of her until he reached the end of the tether of his duty, and then racing back to her. The ebb and flow of it was ceaseless, like a tide. He exhaled noisily and tried to force his keyed-up nerves to relax.

"Reach out like you were going to step sideways. Only don't go anywhere. Don't you dare go anywhere. You'd never find me again here. Just reach out and touch the membrane between the worlds. Hear the thrum traveling along it. The sound of things coming and going."

It did not occur to Arkady to question her, to demand how she came to know of these things—particularly of the Garou's unique gift of stepping sideways into the spirit realm. Instead he closed his eyes and did as she bid him—and found himself plummeting straight down into the looming thunderhead he confronted earlier, the ominous outer boundary of the Temple Obscura.

His surroundings shifted suddenly and dramatically. Instead of the unbroken darkness of the Temple, Arkady now fought his way forward against the push and pull of churning waters. His clothing was soaked through and his legs were numb from the thighs down, plunged beneath icy waters.

His ears filled with the roar of the rushing water. The sound alone staggered him, nearly sweeping him from his feet. Somehow he remained upright and took another staggering step forward. The floor sloped down treacherously away from him. He reached out for Sarah, to keep her from being swept away from him in the maelstrom, but she was not there. He cast around desperately for her and thought he saw, some distance ahead, a shock of white hair vanishing beneath the inky waters.

He dove in that direction, powerful arms churning up walls of water to either side of him. He called her name, over and over again. But the waters had hold of him now and were sweeping him far from the point where she had disappeared. Carrying him away from her. He kicked out mightily against the current, but his efforts were utterly ineffectual. The waters swept him about in a great gyre, carrying him farther away and, at the same time, drawing him farther inward, to the very center of the spiral.

"Sarah!" he bellowed, and was rewarded with only a lungful of water for his troubles. He cast about for any sign of her as the current swept him around again past the place where he had lost her. With a powerful effort, he thrust his feet out for the bottom, made contact and skidded away again, swept onward, inward.

He realized then that it would be of no use stopping there even if he could manage to gain his footing. Sarah would not be there. She would be farther in, farther down.

Gathering his strength for one last effort, Arkady set himself toward the very center of the whirlpool and kicked off directly for its heart. If he were to ever find her again, it would be there…

The thought cut off abruptly as something brushed against his shoulder—a tree limb swept away by the flood perhaps, another bloated victim. And he found he was snagged upon it. He pushed off, only to find that the sheer weight of it was pushing him down beneath the surface of the churning waters. He had to get free of it before it drowned him. He twisted in its grasp, he shoved, he pulled. He tried to bring his feet around to bear upon it, struggling all the while to gain the heart of the maelstrom, the tip of the funnel where all the waters were brought crashing together. And presumably, where they drained out of it through some unguessed subterranean sinkhole. The point that Sarah must, even now, be rushing toward.

And then suddenly, he was free of the snag and landed with the whoosh of all his breath being knocked from him, upon the polished granite tiles of the floor of the Temple Obscura. Sarah stood over him, in the darkness, one tiny hand locked in a death grip around his shoulder.

The deadly maelstrom had vanished as suddenly as it had appeared; his clothing was not even damp.

"I told you not to go anywhere," she accused and then, satisfied that he would not rush off again, turned him loose.

He cursed and retched, trying to cough up lungfuls of water that were simply no longer there. "You all right? Where the hell was that place?"

"This place," she said. "They're both the same place. What was it you called it? The Elephant's Graveyard. The place where…"

"The place where the stories bleed out of the world." Then he caught himself. "And I never told you about that! How the hell did you know?…"

And then he saw it and all thoughts of Sarah, and what she did or did not know, were utterly expunged from his mind.

Up until that point, he couldn't have said exactly what he expected to find here. A spiral pattern burned or etched into the floor. A mosaic of granite tiles forming the outline of the infamous nine-gyred labyrinth. Whatever image he had innocently held in the back of his mind was blasted away in that moment.

He cursed. He was dimly aware of Sarah at his shoulder; he felt the shudder that wracked her even though, sightless, she was spared the full impact of the nightmare that arose writhing before them.

Black Spiral Dancers

"I told you," she said, her voice a whisper pitched to near hysteria. "Told you not to go anywhere."

The spiral was not some decorative pattern sketched out on the tiled floor of the Temple Obscura, it was a landscape unto itself. It was so vast that the mind could not take it all in. Arkady felt a wave of vertigo crash over him. He clenched his eyes shut against the mounting nausea.

In places the spiral reared up, its path describing the vaulted arch of a cathedral ceiling looming over them like a deadly viper about to strike. In other places, it plunged down through what should have been the floor, vanishing into some even deeper nether region.

In vain, he tried to trace its course, to see where—and if—the path emerged again from the depths. But the vertigo hit him with redoubled force and he broke off. Trying to grasp the scope of the spiral all at once hit him like being suddenly dangled by his ankles from a helicopter. The world he had known turned suddenly upside down and swelled to become both vaster and more terrifying than he had ever imagined it could be.

He heard Sarah whimper and drop to the floor beside him, curling into a tight fetal ball, and he knew that just screwing his eyes shut would be no defense against this onslaught. The contents of his stomach lurched and he choked them back down.

"It's all right," he croaked. He had hoped for reassuring, but even he could hear the edge of panic in his voice. "It's going to be all right. There's got to be some way to approach this thing. Just don't look at it..." He had been grasping at straws. He snapped his jaws down on the words as soon as he had uttered them, but they had already escaped him. "I'm sorry. I didn't mean..."

Sarah gave no sign of noticing, much less of having taken offense. She was rocking slowly back and forth, muttering something to herself in a childish singsong. He could not make out the words, but the rhythm of the chant jangled on his nerves, feeding the feeling of rising panic.

"Sarah!" He took her by both shoulders and shook her, but stopped upon catching sight of his white-knuckled fingers digging into her skin. Already he could see thick fur burrowing out from the pores of his hands, like the thrashing of albino worms suddenly exposed to the sunlight.

Muscles bunched and knotted. Vertebrae cracked and realigned themselves with the musical sound of shuffling ivory tiles. He stepped back, letting Sarah slump to the floor as he bellowed challenge.

He knew this was only a further frustration. There was no one here to rend, nothing to crush.

As Arkady faced the spiral, a picture flashed through his mind, hanging superimposed over the scene before him. It was a rough pencil doodle torn from a spiral-bound notebook, Stuart Stalks-the-Truth's depiction of the infamous nine-gyred figure, rendered in harsh black graphite against white paper faintly lined with blue.

Arkady was struck suddenly with how preposterous it was in the face of the mind-rending reality of the true spiral here before him.

Sarah's head jerked up at the broken sound that escaped him. Even to his own ears, it sounded like a noise that someone might make as he slipped into hysteria. Arkady had been unaware that he had laughed aloud before her reaction called his attention to it. He stopped. Her concern might not have been as unfounded as he might have hoped.

He had to be rational. All right, he thought, I'll be rational. "All we have to do now," he said, pleased at how steady his voice sounded, "is to find some way to get up onto that thing."

He sighed as if shouldering a pack for a long journey. He was strong and he was ready, prepared for hours—even days—of hiking round and around that thing. Trying to worry loose a single frayed thread from the maddening tangle, the faintest hint of a path leading inward.

Sarah got unsteadily to her feet. She was still struggling to block it all out. Arkady forced his eyes to focus on the small patch of ground directly before him where his next step would fall. Sarah was not so lucky.

All of her senses strained to compensate for her loss of sight. All of them fought for some point of reference to help ground her. To prove to her that all these things were real.

He saw her struggling, saw the panic rising around her like the floodwaters from his vision. She floundered and was suddenly swept under. "Arkady!" she choked out. And then he was there, holding her. All the strength had gone out of her legs and he held her there, caught halfway to the floor.

He felt the ground sloping treacherously down away from them, toward the heart of the spiral. He felt the weight of the churning waters crashing against his legs.

"No," he barked. "Don't go anywhere. You're going to stay right here with me. Hold on to me. I said…"

"It's no good," she choked and spat. "Can't swim. Can't stay afloat."

"That's bullshit!" he howled at her. "Concentrate on something, anything. That rhyme or song or whatever it was. How did it go?"

"It's gone," she muttered miserably. But he noticed she was no longer gasping and choking as if immersed in water to her neck. "Swept under. All the stories, the songs, the poems. Just draining away. Out of the hole in the bottom of the world."

Arkady could feel her slipping away from him as well. Going under for the third time. He reached out for her in the only way he knew he might yet reach her.

"They called him Chalybs," Arkady recited. "It was a strong name, a name of power. In the Old Tongue, the sacred words whispered among the hills before the coming of the Roman garrisons, it meant 'steel.' The People of the Wall called him this because, even from an early age, the blades of grown men would break against him."

He spun the tale out to her like a lifeline, hoping desperately that it was enough to reach her.

"His mother was to blame. She had lost one son already; she was not about to let them take another from her. The Folk called her Samladh, the White Lion, for she was fierce in spirit and in aspect. Her face shone like a vengeful moon as she defended her home and her young. The Folk revered her and invoked her protection against the Eagle-totemed legions."

It was the sound of that name that brought her back. The name Arkady had heard from her own lips. Not Sarah, but 'sau-lah,' the White Lioness. The scorned patron of the White Howlers. They were the Lost Tribe, the original victims of the Black Spiral Labyrinth, who descended into the darkness beyond the Three Day Stone. When they emerged from their coal cellar, they had been changed by the corrupting touch of the spiral—twisted and burned black. The cubs she had once watched over had become her tormentors, her burned dogs.

At the sound of that name, Samladh, her head pivoted toward the sound of his voice and he knew there was still a chance.

"The Lady Lion of the Moors was a formidable enchantress. Her magics were threefold. First, she was a master of the harp and the well-turned verse. Second, none of the dark secrets of the forge were hidden from her. Third, she was clever in the art of shaving faces. If she willed it that no blade should ever pierce the boy, well, they could hardly refuse her."

She lunged for the lifeline of his words, latched on to the rhythm of them. Their steady rise and fall. She clung fast.

"Chalybs spent his early years among the skirts of the wise women of the Isle of Glass. He played with the pigs and together they rooted for mushrooms within the hushed wonder of the wood's edge. He climbed the stunted black apple trees that grew there—those stark and foreboding guardians at the threshold between the worlds of the quick and the dead. He ate the tart blood-red apples and chewed their seeds.

"From this vantage point, both worlds were spread out below him, laid bare for his scrutiny. But Chalybs had eyes only for the world of the living. It was his habit to peer far out over the still waters of the lake to where he could pick out the swaying fields of wheat, the clatter and bounce of oxcarts, the wisp of smoke stealing from a peasant croft. His daydreams were filled with the distant glint of sunlight on iron—the blade of the plowshare sluicing through rich brown loam, the lullaby of the swinging of the scythe."

"Mother, may I go across the waters this year? To help bring in the harvest?" It was Sarah's voice that had taken up the narration. Asserting her ancestral right. Spinning out the ancient story that belonged properly to her.

"And Samladh laughed and brushed the hair back from his eager steel-blue eyes. 'The farmers of the lake country have hands enough for their task, my reckless darling. My daring young plowman.'

"Chalybs pouted. 'When I am a man, I will go across the waters, and you will not be able to stop me. Neither your bands of iron nor your clever verses will hold me. I will have a farm of my own and I will send you flour so fine that you will not even be able to hold it in your hands. And pigs so fat that the skiff will have to cross the lake perched upon their backs—rather than the other way around.'

"Samladh held him close, whispering tales of mysterious lands across the waters—of market squares filled with stolid peasant women crying their wares. Of the magic of strong wooden fences and boundary stones. Of rosaries of garlic and onions strung from the rafters."

Hand over hand, she began to inch her way toward him, fighting against the current.

"That's it. You're almost there," Arkady said. He took her by the forearm and squeezed hard. She was solid, tangible. Real. With one last great heave she fell heavily against him and clung there trembling and panting hard.

He held her there in silence for a long while. At last he said, "Don't try to take it all in, or to figure it out. Find something small to focus on—a sound. Your breathing would work; keep it measured and steady, in and out, slow. Or the pad of your bare feet on the stone, counting off the number of tiles, feeling for the cracks with your toes. Or you could try repeating a snatch of a poem or story or song over and over again. Something, anything. Reciting the multiplication tables even!"

She nodded and pushed away from him, stood upright on her own. "It's okay," she said. "I'm all right now. Thank you."

He turned her loose and let out another long sigh. "Actually," he said, "I was thinking that it might be best if you just waited here. I don't know how long it will take to find the way into that thing, but I can cover the ground a lot faster on all fours."

She shook her head puzzled. "What? I don't… Oh, I see." She was quiet then, struggling with something. Maybe just trying to steady herself, to listen to the sound of her own breathing. But her voice, when it came again, wasn't any steadier. It was fully that of a frightened seven-year-old.

"Don't leave me here."

He swore.

"I mean it," she said. "If you leave me, I'll…"

"I won't leave you," he interrupted.

"I'm serious. You promised me that you wouldn't hurt me, that no one would hurt…"

"I said, I won't leave you," he repeated. "Come on, we've got a long hike ahead of us." He set her back on her feet, and together they set off around the spiral.

The spiral itself, however, had other plans for them. Arkady caught the motion out of the corner of his eye and shouted a warning. Already he was shifting, preparing to meet this new threat. But there was no way he could have prepared for the doom that was descending upon them.

As he watched, the entire blasphemous pattern of the Black Spiral *shifted*.

Arkady felt the hysteria rising once again. Something that big—big on a cosmological scale—should not move. Or if it does, it should be a motion so grand, so ponderous as to be imperceptible to petty organic creatures such as him. A motion like the graceful swing of the planets or the procession of the equinoxes. Motions so sublime they had to be deduced rather than witnessed.

This motion was neither graceful nor stately. The spiral moved with the grating sound of scale scraping across scale. Of course, here the nerve-flaying roar was amplified to the scope of the grinding together of tectonic plates. The birth wail of mountains, clawing their way skyward.

Both he and Sarah froze at the cry only to find the spiral itself turning to face them. One long sinuous arc slipped from the tangle and reared high above them, poised to strike. They could only gape in horror as it began its whipping descent. They were too stunned to even leap aside, as if that would have done them any good. The looming tower of onyx ribbon was taller than a skyscraper. There was nowhere they could have run. Nothing to do but brace themselves for an impact that would obliterate them utterly, grinding even their bones to dust.

The entire floor of the Temple Obscura lurched like a ship caught in a maelstrom. A downpour of granite shards crashed over them, the force of the impact splintering the ponderous stone floor tiles like glass. Arkady found himself careening through the air. He made a desperate grab for Sarah, but missed her as they both hurtled directly away from the point of impact.

He landed hard, his head hit and he tasted the coppery tang of blood in his mouth. The only sign he had not blacked out was that he still held his Crinos war form. In a moment, he launched himself back along the line of the blast, a five-hundred-pound projectile of fur and sinew.

He spared only the briefest glance for the spiral itself, checking for any sign of its rearing back for another strike. Then he was running, eyes devouring the broken ground ahead. Calling Sarah's name.

No sign of either.

He frantically scanned the floor ahead of him, which was now rippled into rolling hills and troughs—afterimages of the sheer force of the impact. Watching the regular rise and swell of it, Arkady was reminded of the churning waters of his vision.

He did not bother counting the number of times he stumbled, the knife-sharp edges of the broken granite tiles biting deeply into his shins. Many of the tiles had been sheared in half by the wave of the buckling floor and jutted upward like a palisade of spears braced for the charge. Others teetered drunkenly atop the hastily erected embankments.

Arkady ignored their fortifications and plunged forward.

He nearly tripped over her before he saw her. A tiny broken moan escaped her as he shoveled aside the broken masonry that half-buried her.

She was singing softly to herself, the same childish singsong. *Good,* he thought. *Still fighting.*

"Up," he grunted, cradling her in his arms. In his war form, she was little more than a rag doll, limp in his grasp. "Nothing broken."

She punched him hard, in the chest. A full roundhouse swing with everything she had behind it. It barely startled him. He smiled, proud of her effort.

"Put. Me. Down," she growled, punctuating each word with another blow. She was trying to connect with his face but didn't have the reach for it. His chuckling only spurred her to a more furious flurry of blows. "Put me down!"

She would start kicking soon. He set her down as gently as he could under the circumstances. She gave him one last parting shot, a kick to the armpit that landed solid, before he had righted her and set her on her feet.

"Don't you ever touch me again. Ever!" She glared up at him defiantly and he didn't even wince at the sight of the thick black catgut stitches. He beamed down at her.

"Good. Better. That last kick, right on the money," he said.

The rumbling of the spiral had fallen still. The frayed end of the spiral that had crashed down directly in front of them lay still, not even twitching.

"That's it," Sarah said quietly. "Our way up onto the Black Spiral. Assuming it stays put."

It stayed put. The spiral could afford to be patient. It had time—all of time, in fact.

But Arkady was looking for something else. There had to be something here. Something. Stuart Stalks-the-Truth said that the solution Arkady sought was something inherent in all spirals, in the very nature of spirals. It was an experiment in fore- and background. In the case of the Black Spiral, there had to be a mirror spiral—a white spiral nested within the black. It was not just possible, it was logically necessary.

Arkady was well aware that logic was not the reigning force here in the Temple Obscura. Still, Stuart's white spiral was all Arkady had to cling to at this point. Without that faint hope, he would have no choice save to mount the Black Spiral itself. To expose himself to its corrupting touch. To place himself at its mercy as so many of his forebears had done. As Sarah's own children had done. He would not go down that road.

He peered intently into the darkness, trying to wrest its secrets from it. And there *was* something there. If it wasn't just some trick of the uncertain light. The spiral itself, darker than midnight, threw a sharp line of shadow across the tiled floor. Arkady set his feet toward that razor-thin ribbon of shadow.

The advance edge of the Black Spiral groaned and lurched, trying to free itself and throwing up a wake of shattered granite. But already Arkady had caught sight of it, the faintest glimmer of light eking out its existence in the spiral's shadow. He bounded forward, before the pattern could shift again, plunging into the greater darkness between the midnight coils.

What he saw there brought him up short. There *was* a path here, a route inward! He saw it plainly for the first time in all its glory. Stuart might have laughed aloud to see his tall tale become a reality. Arkady was not disposed to laugh.

He howled his frustration and his cry echoed throughout the vastness of the Temple Obscura until even its echo was swallowed utterly by the darkness. Coming quickly behind, Sarah bumped into him.

"What is it? What's wrong?" she demanded.

Arkady's voice was quiet now, resigned. "Nothing. It is here, just as I had hoped it would be. The mirror spiral."

"Then what's wrong?"

Words failed him, so Arkady could only gesture toward the path before him—an answer Sarah could not follow. The path before him was not a white spiral as he and Stuart had envisioned. It was a path of purest gleaming silver. It winked at him mockingly from its dark nest.

Arkady knew that the very touch of the precious moon metal was antithetical to all of his kind. Each step he took upon this Silver Spiral would burn him as surely as walking on fire. He pictured himself dancing from foot to foot in agony, forced into a mocking reenactment of the Dance of the Black Spiral. The faint hope that had brought him here, to the very gates of Malfeas, had betrayed him.

There was a triumphant roar behind him, as the loose end of the Black Spiral reared high for the coup de grace. The mercy stroke that would pound flesh and bone into fine powder. That would put an end to his ill-conceived venture once and for all.

Arkady felt the entire weight of the spiral, poised above him, begin its decent. There was only one way to escape it. He didn't have time to deliberate. He could stand his ground and have his existence snuffed out—his story finally expunged—or he could leap to the one place the Black Spiral could never touch him. Its own shadow.

Grabbing Sarah's arm, Arkady leapt toward the Silver Spiral.

The Black Spiral twisted and lashed out at him, but already he was beyond its reach. It vented its frustration by slamming into the floor and punching through it, its leading edge vanishing into the nether depths. Arkady held fast to Sarah as the floor behind them buckled, its tiles cascading up into the air.

He landed on all fours, howling agony searing into his hands, feet, knees. He bounded back upright in an instant. He could barely abide the merest brush of the Silver Spiral's touch.

Sarah had picked herself up and was standing beside him, a look of concern clear on her face. The touch of silver did not scald her.

Arkady, however, couldn't stand still. To do so was to give the pain the opportunity to mount. He had to move forward. But where was forward? Arkady shook his head to clear it; he was aware a fundamental disconnect had taken place from the moment he touched the Silver Spiral. The Spiral was discontinuous in both space and time. Arkady was now isolated, cut off from the flow of events, the world of causes and effects that had sheltered him since birth. He howled his confusion, pain and frustration, but no sound emerged. At least, not here.

Perhaps somewhere, in another place or at another time, the world-shaking howl emerged out of nowhere and disappeared again, back into nothingness. And people he would never know looked up and shivered at the sound of its passing. At the fall of a fellow creature into terror and madness.

He lurched into motion. Desperately, he glanced ahead to where his steps were carrying him. The silver path plunged into a dark canyon between steep cliffs of black scales. But he could not make out where the path was leading him. If, in fact, it was leading anywhere at all.

If this is what it was to walk the Silver Spiral, Arkady couldn't fathom what it must be to walk the Black Spiral itself. It was unthinkable.

He wheeled at the touch of a hand on his arm, ready to tear apart whatever minion of this accursed place he might find. But it was Sarah.

"You promised," she accused. "That you would not leave me."

"I have left them all," he said. "Only I hadn't realized it until now. My family, my sept, my tribe—the entire Garou nation. I am nothing to them now. It is as if I never existed."

"You will not," she said pointedly, "leave me behind so easily. I let them all go down into darkness alone—to walk the Black Spiral and challenge the forces of Malfeas itself. I will not do so again."

"I am not one of your children, Samladh. I am of Falcon's tribe."

She shrugged. "I have seen the falcon wheeling overhead. Its path is a gyre—the same spiral walked by my children. As above, so below. Do not seek to lecture me on my own children."

"I'm sorry. I didn't mean…"

"They were proud, my children. So proud. And I was proud of them in turn. A mother's pride. A lion's pride. Now I will go and see for myself the places where they walked. To see where they have fallen by the way. You would deny me this?"

"No."

"Then let's walk. Look at your feet. Already the fur of them is burned black as pitch. Like the burned dogs. If we stand around much longer, you will not have stumps enough to walk on."

He returned her gaze levelly, staring a long while at her sightless eyes, wondering how they could see his feet and the damage they had suffered. It was a hurt that even his superhuman recuperative powers could not hope to heal, because the wounds were dealt him by the touch of silver.

As he turned from her and struck off again, he wondered if Sarah's eyes would ever heal. He knew now that she was something more of spirit than of flesh. But would they grow back? Or were the wounds dealt you by the hands of your own children like the touch of silver? Hurts that never healed.

He did as she had bid him, moving forward, though each step was a stab of pain, along the faint flickering tightrope of silver that wound through the coils of the Black Spiral.

The Eighth Circle
The Dance of Paradox

Arkady and Sarah walked a broken nine-gyred path, discontinuous in time and space. Glimpses of distant times and places rose up to meet them. But the true path, the way to the very center of the Black Spiral Labyrinth, eluded them. Somewhere in this tangle was the key that would unlock their way forward, but where? They sifted through disconcerting and rapidly shifting scenes like archeologists trying to sift some relic from drifting desert sands.

Here Arkady, as a child, stood at the outer circle of the moot. He listened to the words of Peter Twice-Whelped, the tale speaker of the sept. Words Arkady had thought he had forgotten long ago.

"As it is above, so is it below." Peter Twice-Whelped raised muzzle to the night wind. Arkady could smell the fear rustling through the assembled warriors like fire through the high grass of the steppes. Its sharp acrid tang caught in the craw of his throat—a splinter of bone he could neither swallow nor dislodge. A mouthful of ashes.

They would not break and run, these haughty champions of Gaia. They were too proud for that. These were the very teeth and claws of House Crescent Moon—the most ancient and illustrious of the Silver Fang noble houses. His house. Neither fear nor uncertainty came naturally to them. And when it did descend upon them, they did not suffer it gracefully. Arkady could sense the violence slowly building here. A warrior's credo: *In blood, there is both catharsis and redemption.*

Conscious of the silhouette he cut against the moonlit rock face, Peter straightened. His entire body was an arrow pointed straight at the moon, a single sharp line from the tip of his tail to his raised muzzle. A finger jabbed defiantly at the heavens.

The tale speaker opened his throat to the sky and let the night wind howl through him, use him. Giving voice to the atrocity it had witnessed but could not contain.

"I sing the fall of Winter's Eye, Lord of House Crescent Moon. Friend and kinsman he was to me, but fallen in a distant land. Far from kin, far from home. He tracked the Dancers to their lair and there he fell, into the darkness where even the light of his star dared not follow. I have felt his passing, and you have as well. Let the word go out to all the tribe. I sing of Winter's Eye."

The great howl was taken up by a dozen throats around the circle.

Arkady knew it was too late. What he was searching for was no longer here. But Winter's Eye was already gone, his precious relic and namesake lost with him. It had passed on, beyond his reach.

Arkady cursed and his mother cuffed him on the back of the head.

He knew if he could not trust his own senses to pick out the way forward along the Silver Spiral, he would have to rely upon Sarah to find it for him. And the wounded girl was in no condition to lead anyone anywhere. He would have to find some way to help her before she could help him.

● ● ●

The pattern shifted again and Arkady was once more jerked out of the continuity and thrust into a strange place, an unfamiliar time.

He was in an enclosed space, a warehouse perhaps. Heat radiated inward through walls of rusted aluminum, turning the air oppressive. A desert sun beat down through an open bay door.

There was a girl here before him, an Uktena lorekeeper. And she was laughing at him. In her hands, she held a peculiar sphere made of interlocking bones.

He had arrived in time.

"Then you refuse me?" Arkady demanded of her.

"Last I checked, that's what 'no' means. Or would you like to hear it in all hundred voices?"

"Very well. I am deeply disappointed."

Arkady's blade sailed through the air and lodged in her shoulder. The bone sphere went flying. Before Amy Hundred-Voices hit the floor, the artifact was in Arkady's hand.

"No, you can't," she half-mumbled.

Arkady cupped the relic in his hand and smiled in triumph. Surely here was an orb that Sarah could use to guide them. A dousing sphere attuned to the music of the Wyrm writhing in its lair. An Ariadne's thread for this most terrible of labyrinths.

But already he could see the prize slipping through his fingers. The sphere stretched outward in time, its every position over the next few minutes revealed to him. And Arkady saw that this prize, too, was already lost to him.

• • •

The pattern shifted a third time. Arkady didn't recognize the room he found himself in, but he did know the three figures who occupied it.

It was a pleasant enough room, as far as sick rooms go. The shutters had been thrown back and there was sunlight streaming in through the open rectangle of the window. The light had a faint but unmistakable greenish tinge to it, as if reflected from a forest canopy. The bird songs that accompanied it indoors reinforced this impression.

They were not in the North Country Protectorate, he was sure of that. He had spent many years living, working and fighting in the domain of Jacob Morningkill. There was not a single inch of that sept that he was not familiar with.

But they were not too far away from it, either. Somewhere in the American Northeast, he thought. New England, perhaps. Arkady stepped fully into view and crossed to the bedside, more because of his ache to be in that warm green sunlight than because of any great concern for the woman lying there.

It was another betrayal. The sunlight felt as scratchy as coarse wool upon his blistered skin. There was not an inch of his body that had not been burned raw by long exposure to the Silver Spiral. He envied the woman lying insensate on the bed—the luxury of a pleasant place to lie down, of clean white sheets, of friends around her.

Mari Cabrah thrashed from side to side, lost in some inner struggle. They had not strapped her down, he noted. That was foolish, sentimental. Even as he watched, her seizures nearly threw her violently to the floor. This could not have been the first time.

They were too soft on her, always had been. If she were awake, she would have resented it. Were their positions reversed, if it were one of her two packmates on that bed, she would never have been so weak.

Mari was their strength, always had been. For all of Albrecht's posturing and Evan's pontificating, Mari was their center, physically, spiritually. You could see it just by looking at them now, the way the fight had gone out of them. The way they hovered at her bedside like old women, averting their eyes and talking in whispers.

They were afraid to leave her, afraid to touch her. They knew they were powerless to help, powerless to do anything but watch her die. And they hated it, every minute of it. And they couldn't make it stop.

And most of all they were afraid that if they didn't keep careful watch, that it would end. And then they would be alone.

Serves them right, Arkady thought. *The both of them.* He would like to see how Albrecht would handle being alone. Being *really* alone. He wasn't built for it, not like Arkady was. He would buckle under the strain. Evan and Mari, they were more than his packmates, they were his legs, they were the only things holding him upright. This *thing* that was taking Mari away from them, it was gnawing right through one of Albrecht's legs. You could see it in his eyes. Arkady would have liked to have kicked the other leg out from under him as well.

The boy saw him first, Evan. He looked as if he had seen a ghost. At the sound of the boy's sharp intake of breath, Albrecht wheeled. He swore.

In two quick strides, he had covered the intervening distance, his klaive already out of its sheath, a deadly arc of silver streaking down through the ribbon of space between Arkady and the bedside.

"Get the hell away from her, you bastard. I don't know how the hell you got in here…"

Arkady smiled at his old rival. It was not a pleasant smile. "I am pleased to see you again as well, *cousin*," he said, spitting the last word like an invective.

"Don't give me any of that polite bullshit. You so much as try to lay a hand on her and I'll split that damned jackal grin of yours right in two."

Then Evan was at Albrecht's side, one hand laid in restraint upon the warrior's weapon arm. "Not here," Evan said. "Not now."

The line of muscle rippled the length of Albrecht's arm as he fought down the change into his Crinos war form. His eyes never left Arkady.

Arkady ignored him, turning his back and crossing to the window. The light was wrong here, too sharp. It hurt his eyes. He pulled the shutters closed and latched them. "I'm not here for the girl, Albrecht. If I'd fancied her, I would have taken her before now." He ignored the low warning growl. "There are more important things for us to discuss."

"Get the hell out of here." Albrecht's voice was a harsh whisper, but he had his anger in check.

"Soft," Arkady said. "You've grown soft, Albrecht. The Litany is quite clear in matters like these. Do you remember what it says? Suffer not the idle and the wounded in times of war…"

"Don't lecture me on the Litany! You've got no damned right. You're a Ronin, an outcast. I saw to that myself. Although if I'd thought you had the balls to show your face around here again, I'd have cut you down on the spot. Saved everybody a lot of trouble."

"Nonsense," Arkady cut in. "You weren't soft then, not yet. I'm hoping you're not so far gone

Eric Griffin

now that you can't be made to see sense. I need something from you."

"Go to hell."

"One step ahead of you. As usual. That's actually what I want to talk to you about. Hell. Malfeas. The Black Spiral. I think I must have passed the third gyre by now, but I can't—"

"What? What do you mean you must have passed the third gyre? No, forget it. I don't want to know. This is just more of your BS. I want you out of here now." Albrecht shook Evan off and took a threatening step forward.

"Fine," Arkady shrugged. "You want me out of here, it's your funeral. Or rather, it's hers. Good to see you again, child," he called to Evan in parting.

"You son of a bitch," Albrecht swore and latched on to him with his free hand to turn him back around, but drew back again with a curse. His hand came away covered in clumps of fur and long strips of dried white skin that clung to his hand.

"Geez, you been playing with that home radiation therapy kit again?" He tried, with limited success, to brush his hand clean on his pants leg.

Arkady paused. "I hadn't realized you'd taken up nursing full-time now. The boy must be rubbing off on you."

"You're the one rubbing off on me." Albrecht's face twisted into a grimace of disgust. He kept wiping absently at his pants leg. "I don't know whether to kick your ass or just put you out of your misery quick and clean. What the hell has happened to you?"

"I am walking the Silver Spiral."

"No shit? You picked a funny place for it. I suppose that means that we're walking the Silver Spiral, too, huh?"

"No," Arkady explained in his most patronizing tone. "You are walking all over your pant cuffs. I am currently in the Temple Obscura, walking the Spiral. The fact that you and the boy wonder are here should be ample proof that I am, in fact, in hell."

"Hey, that's pretty good," Evan interrupted as Albrecht fumed. "Ask him if he wants to borrow my Bat Wyrm repellant."

Albrecht mastered himself. "Let's assume," he said, "for the sake of argument, that you are in Malfeas. Walking the Black Spiral. Never mind the fact that you are here talking to us. We'll also assume that you are not just a raving lunatic…"

"A dangerous homicidal lunatic," Evan put in helpfully. "Maybe even a genocidal lunatic."

"Let's not get carried away," Arkady said.

"Still," Albrecht continued, speaking over the interruptions, "you shouldn't be here. I sent you away, remember? Invoked the power of the Silver Crown. Banished you and in front of witnesses. Falcon himself presided over the sentence. I've got every right to kill you for coming back here.

To cut you down where you stand. To do to you what you did…"

He fought for control. Even Evan noticed the sudden edge to his packmate's voice and started to say something, but Albrecht cut him off with a slash of his hand.

"You're not still bitter about that, are you?" Arkady asked.

"Oh, you don't know the half of it. You've got a lot of balls, showing your face around here. And this time, I might just cut 'em off for you."

"After all this time?" Arkady snorted. "After all that has happened? You won, remember? You're the one sitting on the throne of Jacob Morningkill. You are the one parading around in the legendary Silver Crown! I am the one stuck here in hell. There's no way to back out now, gracefully or otherwise, and at this point I'm not sure I can even go forward, not without your help."

At that revelation, Albrecht smiled. "Sounds like you're in a tough spot. But you know what, I don't care. If you burn in hell for all eternity, I just don't care. Here, maybe I'm being too subtle for you, so let me spell it out: I. Don't. Care. As far as I'm concerned, you got what you had coming to you, pal. And I, for one, ain't too broken up about it. But hey, it's been real nice talking to you and all. See you around. Or not, I guess."

"Don't be an ass, Albrecht. You don't even know why I came here, or what I was going to ask of you. Nor do you know what I am offering in return. Why, for all you know…"

"Which part about 'I don't care' were you having trouble with? I don't want anything to do with you. Never have. Do you want to go back and look at all the great things you've done for me? Let's see, you killed my grandfather. Tried to usurp his throne. Then you tried to kill me—several times, in fact. And I'm not even going to talk about what you did to me when we found the Silver Crown, but it cost me more than a few mangy handfuls of my pelt." Albrecht unconsciously wiped his hands on his jeans again. "And I've still got the scars to prove it. So maybe you'll understand when I say I don't really want any favors from you. I've had enough of them."

Arkady ignored his tirade and crossed back to the bedside. At his approach, Mari writhed and moaned, caught in the grip of some new nightmare.

"I said to get the hell away from her!" Albrecht put his head down and bulled forward, but Arkady's next words brought him up short.

"I could cure her, you know." He said it casually and shrugged. Albrecht's jaws worked, but no sound came out.

"Surely you realized that," Arkady continued. "In the European moots, they are still talking about how I quelled a Thunderwyrm with a single word. Have you heard the tale?" He could see from their looks that they had.

"Of course," Arkady said, touching fingers to forehead as if remembering something obvious. "Mari. She was there. At the moot, wasn't she?"

Albrecht was fuming and Evan was addressing him in a low urgent whisper. "Don't. It's not worth it. If something happened to Mari—in the thick of the fight—you'd never forgive yourself."

"My conscience is good," Albrecht snarled back. "I'd never forgive *him*."

Arkady looked down at Mari in mock concern, laying a hand upon her brow. Her face contorted in a spasm of pain and all the color drained from it.

"Damn it, I said don't touch her!"

Albrecht spun him around, his fist knotting in the front of Arkady's shirt. He tried to press him upward and off balance, but his only reward was the sound of tearing fabric.

"There is a dark spirit within her," Arkady said, "a Bane."

Evan pushed forward. "What kind of Bane?" He set all his weight down pointedly on one of Albrecht's feet. His packmate grudgingly took the hint and, with a snort, shoved Arkady back toward the door.

"I could order it to come out of her," Arkady said. "I could do that. Do you doubt it? I commanded the Thunderwyrm."

"You son of a…" Albrecht started forward again, and again he found Evan in the way.

"Do it," the boy said with sudden intensity, before Albrecht could chime in and blow it for all of them.

"He's not laying a damned hand on her. You hear me?" Albrecht raised his voice. "You touch her again and I'll fucking cut you down where you stand."

"You can't be serious?" Evan protested. "Did you hear what he just said? He said he can help Mari! Okay, so maybe he's a liar. But why not just put him to the test? If he is a liar, what's wrong with making him eat his words? But what if he's not? We can't afford to throw away any chance of helping Mari. Especially over something like this."

"Over something like what?" Albrecht growled. "You mean over something like my pig-headedness. Over me holding a grudge. Like hell I can't; you just watch me. I've had just about all I'm going to take from this bastard. And if he's not back in hell in about one minute, I'm going to send him back there myself."

"Albrecht, think a minute. Think about what you're saying. You haven't even heard him out yet," Evan said, trying to salvage the situation before it erupted in bloodshed. Even if he succeeded, he was afraid that Albrecht would just storm out. Or that Arkady would. And where would that leave Mari? If there were a chance in a million that Arkady could make good on his boast, they had to call him on it.

"Exactly." Albrecht said. "And I'm not going to hear him out either. That's what's bugging me most about this BS—what he hasn't mentioned. What does *he* get out of all this? I'm having a hard time believing that he just dropped by out of the goodness of his heart to help out an old friend. This is Arkady we're talking about here! Even assuming that he can help Mari—which I'm not convinced of—he's going to make damned sure that whatever price needs to be paid for that help is going to be a lot worse than anything he gives away."

"How do you figure?" Evan challenged. "What price is too high to pay to have Mari back? What's he going to do, demand your hide again? And what if he did? Is that too much to ask? Hell, he can flay the skin off my back if there's a chance it's going to help her! You're standing on principle while Mari is down—maybe for good."

Albrecht's warning growl cut him off short. "Look, kid, I know you're just worried about Mari. Hell, we're all worried about her. Even this bastard, if you believe *that* line. But you can spare me the violins about how I'm not willing to put my own hide on the line for her. I don't have to prove myself in that department anymore. Especially not to you."

"I didn't mean…"

"I know you didn't. This thing with Mari is eating you up too. I'm clawing holes in the walls and you're lashing out with words. But I'm not going to be on the receiving end of your therapy, *capice?* I've got enough crap to deal with right now."

Evan put a hand on his shoulder. "You mean, *we've* got enough crap to deal with. This isn't some matter of state; this is Mari we're talking about here. And if there's anything we can do to help her—and I mean *anything*—we've got to give it a shot."

He glanced sideways at Arkady, who was standing with his arms crossed, feigning disinterest.

"If anyone were asking me," he said dryly, "I have no interest in Albrecht's hide, such as it may be. I don't have any use for it. And I resent the insinuation that I ever did. If you gentlemen will recall it was not I who put Albrecht under the skinning knife, it was that Black Spiral Dancer. What was his name?" Arkady broke off musing to himself. "It will come to me. Anyway, it hardly matters now. You have avenged yourself upon him. Or the Silver Crown has avenged you, which amounts to much the same thing. That book is closed, gentlemen. You're not really still sore about *that* are you? Why, it has been years now. And you won! You really need to let it go and move on. I have."

Albrecht only glared at him. "Get out of here."

Evan started to protest. "But what about Mari? You promised to hear him out."

"I did not."

Arkady shrugged. "I never did think you really had any feelings for the bitch. Other than for rutting, of course. But I didn't think you'd be so blunt about it in front of the boy. He idolizes her, you know. You can see it in his eyes. He'd like to put her on a pedestal. Or at least bend her over one."

With a howl, Albrecht lashed out. He was already shifting. His klaive flashed high overhead and then descended with all the weight of Crinos warrior form behind it. It was a blow that would have carved a boulder in half. There was no way Arkady could stand before it.

Evan shouted something that was lost in the fray as Arkady sprang forward, straight into the line of the attack. He was inside Albrecht's reach, rendering the klaive and its powerful overhand swing moot. He crashed into Albrecht and barreled him over, both antagonists grappling and rolling over one another in a deadly flurry of claw and fang.

At such close quarters, there was no real way any blow could fail to find its mark. Blood spurted; fur flew. The combatants' tumble was arrested by Albrecht crashing into the foot of the bedstead. The force of the blow was nothing to him; he had already suffered a half dozen far more grievous wounds. It was the sound from atop the bed that brought him up short—Mari's groan and the thump as she was thrown violently to the floor, the bed overturning on top of her.

Black Spiral Dancers

With a great shout, Albrecht hurled Arkady off him. Surprised at the sudden change in vector, Arkady tumbled once in midair and crunched into the corner nearest the door. He was on his feet almost at once—ignoring the deep rent in his chest, the left nipple nearly severed and hanging only by a flap of torn flesh. But it was already over. All of Albrecht's attention was upon the tangle of the bed's iron struts and the small dark form thrashing beneath them.

Seeing his foe had surrendered the field of honor, Arkady threw back his head and howled victory.

"Oh, will you shut up?" Albrecht snapped. A moment later, the bed frame was soaring through the air, following the exact same trajectory that Arkady had so recently taken. He batted it aside and it clattered against the door and landed in a heap. Arkady was vaguely aware of the answering clatter of running footsteps outside, summoned by his howl of triumph.

Evan was already there, bent over the fallen Mari as Albrecht tossed the bed aside as if it were nothing more than a folding cot. "She's all right," Evan said, interposing a shoulder protectively between Mari and the rampaging Albrecht. As if that would present any real obstacle to the claw tempest. "Just give her a little space, okay?"

Albrecht ignored him and stooped to catch up Mari in his arms. It was the sight of his own inch-long claws, razor sharp and wet with newly shed blood, that brought him back to himself. He was ill equipped for any errand of mercy.

He howled in frustration and tried to force his claws back into some semblance of human hands. It was no use; his blood was up. Arkady's voice, from behind him, only inflamed him further.

"Leave her to the boy," Arkady ordered. The sound of his voice whipped Albrecht's head around. "You will now…"

"Shut up!" Albrecht snapped around grossly oversized canines. "I'll finish with you in a minute."

"You're finished already," Arkady said. "It's over. You turned tail, broke off in the middle of the fight. Went to hide among the sick and the womenfolk. I accept your surrender, of course, but I had expected more of you. No matter, you will now submit to my…"

"Like hell I did! I've had enough of this crap and I'm going to finish it. Right now."

He started forward, but Evan's bellow interrupted him. "Not here, damn it!"

The room fell silent. Albrecht fumed, shooting angry glances back and forth, to Evan, to Arkady. A caged animal becoming aware of his predicament for the first time. It was Arkady who broke the silence.

"The pup has a bark to him," he admitted. "But he is right. The time for challenge has passed. You cannot deny the girl my help without condemning her to a slow and certain death. You cannot fight me further without condemning her to a brutal and senseless one. You are bested, admit it. There is no shame in it—unless, of course, you consider your concern for the woman and this pup a weakness and an embarrassment..."

"Get the hell out of here."

"It's a fair request," Arkady said contemplatively. "And one which I am willing to grant. Personally, I thought you would hold out for the life of the girl, but...as you wish." He shrugged. "But your request comes later. As you have yielded, you must first accede to my demand. You will give me the Silver Crown."

Albrecht laughed aloud. It was not a joyful sound. It involved the gnashing of a deadly array of fangs and a spray of hot spittle.

"Let's get something straight, right now," he said. He had mastered himself at last and shrugged down to his normal human proportions. If nothing else, it made conversation beyond four-letter threats and monosyllabic grunts much easier. "One, you're not touching the girl. No matter what. You say you can help her, but I'm not buying it. Two, you're not getting the crown. I've paid for it, with my blood and my hide. As I'm sure I don't have to remind you of all people. And Falcon himself placed it here, on my head. And it's not going anywhere until He asks for it back. You get me?"

Arkady smiled. "I do. And now you will understand me. I am on my grandfather's errand." His voice was quiet, but it boomed with authority.

"Like hell you are."

"But I am. I am walking the spiral in Malfeas to redeem his lost children. Samladh stalks beside me and Grandfather Falcon wheels above me. I open my mouth and it is his cry that emerges. I need the crown, Albrecht, and I will have it."

As he spoke, wings of searing white flame unfolded from his shoulders with excruciating patience.

Evan, still crouched over Mari, looked up at the sudden glare and swore.

Albrecht squinted into the light. He remembered the glory of Grandfather Falcon's wings, not only the majesty of them, but also the all-encompassing solace. He knew their touch, what it was to be wrapped within their shelter. The memory of each feather was etched in flame, not only into his eyes, but into every inch of his flayed and exposed flesh. It was a part of him.

Staring into the glare of Arkady's wings, he knew something was wrong. There was no denying that Grandfather Falcon's touch was upon him—where else could Arkady have learned such a gift but at the knee of the Silver Fang's totem? But Albrecht could see that the majestic flaming wings were not pristine. They were ragged about the edges and shot through with pulsing black veins. Albrecht winced at each spurt and surge of blood along those unsettling conduits.

Behind him, he heard Mari whimper in her coma.

"Jesus, shut that thing off, will you?" Albrecht growled.

"I have Falcon's blessing in this, Albrecht," Arkady said. "I am doing what must be done to redeem his people. *Our* people. I don't ask for your blessing, or even your understanding. All I want from you is the Silver Crown. I *need* the crown." He started forward.

Albrecht stood his ground. "What you need is a good ass kicking."

"You used the power of the crown once to command me," Arkady said, closing. "Now I'm going to use it to command you. You will give the crown into my keeping."

"It doesn't work that way," Albrecht said, drawing himself up for confrontation once more.

"But it does. The crown compels you, Albrecht, as surely as you use its authority to command others. A crown is not some laurel wreath—an accolade to celebrate your victories— it is a covenant, a solemn and sacred responsibility. You would put on the airs of king? Very well, then act like a king! I tell you this: a king's place is not mooning among the dead and dying. It is in the front line of the battle. Your people—our people— have fallen to the Wyrm, and you will not stir from among the skirts of the womenfolk to free them from their captivity."

"What the hell are you talking about?" Albrecht roared.

"A king's place," Arkady said, "is wherever his people have fallen among their enemies. That is where I am now. On the Spiral, in the heart of Malfeas. Falcon's children languish here. He has heard their cries and has suffered me to take up their cause, because you—their rightful sovereign—would not. But I cannot win through to them without your help. I need the crown to do a king's work."

"No." It was Evan's voice that answered him. He straightened and crossed to Albrecht's side. "Don't listen to him. You were right. This guy can't help Mari. He doesn't understand."

Albrecht angrily wrenched his arm free from Evan's grip.

"A king's place," Evan shouted up at the two hulking Silver Fangs, "doesn't have anything to do with riding out at the head of an army, or undertaking some damned fool quest. It's about being there wherever even the least of his people is suffering. It's about compassion, not about heroics. It's about…"

"From the mouths of babes," Arkady interrupted. "You heard the boy, Albrecht? A king's place is where his people are suffering. I am returning to Malfeas to redeem our people. You can be a king and come with me, or give me the crown and I will do what must be done."

"That's not what I said, I…" Evan began, but was cut off.

"Save it, kid," Albrecht growled.

"But you can't be buying that BS about it being your duty to go back with him into Malfeas! Geez, of all the stupid, chest-beating, alpha-male…"

"I said save it."

Arkady's face split in a wide smile. He had him. Already he was picturing himself bearing the mightiest relic of the Silver Fang tribe into the very stronghold of the Wyrm. He felt the weight of tradition, prophesy and the old tales aligning like stars—all pointing the way forward to his own glorious destiny.

Albrecht crossed slowly to Mari's side. He bent over her and kissed her forehead in leave-taking. Without a word, he straightened and turned back to Arkady.

Evan was there, between them. He shoved Albrecht with all his strength, but the Ahroun did not budge. "No! Damn it, you're not doing this. You're not leaving her. I'll fuckin' beat you senseless if I have to. Don't think I won't do it."

Albrecht looked down at Evan, but his thoughts were clearly elsewhere. Reaching down, he put a hand on Evan's shoulder and gently brushed him aside. "You've got to let me do what

I've got to do," Albrecht said. "Otherwise I'm not only less than a king, I'm less than a man."

Evan started to protest anew, but Albrecht forestalled him. "Evan. Enough."

He turned his attention back to Arkady.

"Ready?" the fallen Silver Fang asked.

"Yeah, I'm ready," Albrecht muttered. He reached up and took the Silver Crown from his head. He turned it over in his hands, looking at it from every angle. As if the strength to do what he had to do was hidden inside it somewhere and might shake loose.

He cursed. "If being a king means leaving Mari to die alone," he said, "then fuck being the king."

The precious relic shot past Arkady's head and rebounded with a clatter from the far wall.

"Take it and get the hell out."

For a long moment nobody moved or even breathed. At last, Arkady heaved a sigh and shrugged.

"As you wish," he said. He bent and picked up the dented crown from where it had come to rest. He brushed it off and set it atop his own head. "How does it look?"

Neither so much as glared at him. Arkady shrugged again, reached out for the first tentative brush of the Silver Spiral and stepped back on to it.

• • •

Even long after Arkady had gone, neither Albrecht nor Evan moved or spoke. "You didn't have to give it to him," Evan huffed, his eyes never lifting from the spot where the crown had clattered to the ground just minutes before.

It was Falcon's most recent and most ambiguous miracle, and neither of them was quite sure what to make of it. There, gleaming on the floor precisely where it had fallen, lay the Silver Crown.

"I'll be damned if I'm going to pick it up."

"You *have* to pick it up," Evan said, crossing the room and gingerly doing just that. He turned and held it out to Albrecht. "It's a sign, you great ox. Mari would kick you right in the head to hear you talking like that. Take it." He shoved the relic in Albrecht's direction.

"A sign of what?" he snorted in disgust and turned back to Mari's unconscious form. "Like I need another 'sign' to remind me that I can't take care of my people. Hell, I can't even take care of my own pack!"

"But you are taking care of Mari. You gave up the crown, the throne, everything for her sake just now. I saw you do it. You're doing exactly what a packmate should do—what a king should do. You're taking care of your own. This doesn't change that." Evan thrust the crown into Albrecht's unresisting hands.

"A king should be wherever the greatest threat to his people is," Albrecht grumbled.

"If Falcon didn't need a king right here, doing exactly what you're doing, do you think *this* would still be here? You made a tough choice,

Albrecht. I don't know that I could have made the same one."

"Yeah, and what about the choice I didn't make? What about Arkady?"

"Maybe," Evan said, "Falcon also needs a king to walk the Black Spiral."

The Ninth Circle
The Dance of Deceit

Arkady took another step and found himself upon the Silver Spiral once more, winding his way into the very heart of Malfeas. He was exultant. He had challenged Albrecht for the Silver Crown. For the right to bear it into the lair of the Wyrm and redeem his fallen ancestors. And he had won.

But Arkady could not have anticipated the dramatic effect the presence of the Silver Crown would have here, poised between the black coils of the Wyrm itself.

The entire landscape seemed to react to the presence of the legendary artifact. The reactions were extreme and contradictory, and Arkady was caught directly in the middle of the opposing forces. Everything around him—even the walls and the floor—lurched at the same time, pitching either directly toward or away from him.

The razor-edge cliff of the Black Spiral, just to his left, twisted and reared as if shying away from the presence of the ancient adversary. To his right, the chitinous body segments of the Wyrm slid gratingly in the opposite direction. Arkady had the undeniable impression of deadly coils, each as big around as a mountain, tightening about him. Trying to grind him and the offending silver relic into dust.

He had a moment of stabbing doubt, wondering if he had been duped into bringing the crown here. An unwitting offering to the Wyrm, delivered up by hand on a gleaming silver platter. He called out for Sarah but got no reply.

A wave of vertigo hit him and he stumbled, realizing only too late the other change he had inadvertently wrought by bringing the crown here. Beneath his feet, the Silver Spiral, his tenuous lifeline, was unraveling.

No! Arkady raged silently. *This cannot be. I have come too far to fail now.* He tried to invoke the power of the crown, to command the last routed wisps of the silver path to stand their ground. And for one triumphant moment, he thought he had managed to touch the relic's hidden reserve of power, to call forth Falcon's gift from its metallic tomb.

A brilliant streak of silver light surged around him, coiling about his arm. He raised a fist, crackling with energy, toward the heavens in defiance.

It was only then that he realized, as the sizzling arc of light shot away from him, that it had not come from the crown, but was only another stand of the Silver Spiral twisting free.

Arkady howled in frustration, even as his right leg sunk to the knee into a hole that had, only a moment before, been solid ground. The touch of the path burned like fire. He scrambled to pull himself up, searing his palms in the process, but he was well past caring for such trifles. His only thought now was to find something solid, something to cling to before he again plunged into darkness. The entire dreamscape was unraveling around him and his hands could find no purchase on the dissolving path.

He felt the tremor as the ground beneath his other foot began to twist and give way. He knew there was only one avenue of escape open to him now. As much as he dreaded that option, and had spent weeks searching for some way to circumvent it, he knew he had no other choice. He pushed off the path with all his strength and bounded high, catching at the rising edge of the Black Spiral.

There. He clung there for a moment, gazing down at the last wisps of what had been the Silver Spiral, his last and best hope of reaching the center of the labyrinth. There was only one other way forward open to him now. Resigning himself to it, he pulled himself fully up onto the Black Spiral.

His first sensation was actually one of relief. Not so much the relief that always accompanies the realization that you have finally arrived at something you had been dreading for a very long time. Rather, it was a more humble relief—the simple fact that the ground here did not burn as its silver counterpart did. The soles of his feet were little more than open sores at this point, and Arkady had to be glad for what small comforts came his way.

It was only then that Arkady became aware that he was no longer alone. There was a movement off to his right, out of the corner of his eye. He wheeled to face this new threat. A streak of silver—one of the remnants that had torn itself loose from the Silver Spiral—lay crackling and sputtering just ahead of him on the path like a water droplet on a hot pan. Arkady cursed himself and his overwrought nerves.

He picked his way forward, careful not to come into contact with the still-live arc of energy. But as he approached, he saw that it grew more substantial, taking on depth and form. Arkady's step quickened.

There was the outline figure there now, lying flat on the path before him. The small, broken figure of a man encased in a nimbus of sizzling silver. Ignoring the crackling energies, Arkady reached out and took the figure by the arm. His hand seemed to pass partway through the biceps, sinking knuckle deep beneath the surface of the shimmering skin. "Are you…" Arkady began, shaken. "Are you all right?"

The figure lifted his head to face him and Arkady recoiled involuntarily at the sight. Where the man's features should have been—his nose, his mouth—was only a line of silvery glyphs, splitting his face vertically from brow ridge to chin. His eyes were gaping holes, offsetting and punctuating the cryptic markings.

There was something unsettlingly familiar in those runic sigils, but before Arkady could puzzle over them further, the figure shrugged off Arkady's grip and rose unsteadily to his feet. He took up a defiant stance and seemed to swell even more, doubling in mass until he stood head and shoulders above the exiled Silver Fang lord.

Even in his warrior form, the hulking creature was stoop shouldered, his foot-long claws dragging the ground. He was undeniably lupine, but unlike any Garou Arkady had ever seen, as the Neanderthal Glabro form was unlike a normal human physique.

The thick pelt of fur that sprouted in tufts from his skin was too long by half, too shaggy even for a Garou. The fur from his thighs cascaded all the way to the floor. And it gleamed in the darkness as pure white as Arkady's own pelt—the Silver Fang's pride and pedigree.

To see such a mark of distinction on this *creature!* It was an outrage.

Arkady forced himself to meet the challenge in those gaping dark eyes, strained to make out the unfamiliar tangle of line strokes and serifs that made up the shining silver glyphs where the other's face should have been. Haltingly, he read aloud:

When first I tore from Gaia's womb, I was called me
        Full-Moon's-Pelt,
(Although born within the House of the Crescent Moon)
For they hadn't seen a coat to equal mine
In a score of generations.

Driven from my home, denied my heritage
Amid whispers that I was Dark-Moon-Born—

Conceived in a forbidden union
Between Garou and Garou,

I turned my back on my own people,
And descended here into darkness
To carve my mark, upon the Wyrm itself if need be
And to win back my birthright.

Three things only I demand, before life is done—
A piece of land to call my own
A thatched house, swept spick and span;
Not a hut for dogs or cattle.
And three silver coins, each as round and bright
As the three moons that were
Stripped from me.

Long years I have wandered here in darkness
And forgotten the way home, if ever I knew it.
My claws have blunted, my eyes grown dim
And now I can no longer fight, nor
Even recite my own tale
With my own voice.

And there is not one single
Moon to shine
Here on the Spiral.
There is no
Moon.

Arkady could not believe the words he was
saying. They struck him like physical blows. House
Crescent Moon? This monstrosity? What could it
mean? Arkady wanted to rage at the creature, to
force him to retract his ludicrous claim.

But then a darker thought struck him. Even as a child, Arkady had known that he was the purest of his line to be born in a score of generations. They had made no secret of it. It was a source of pride for them all—a rallying point, a secret and cherished hope.

But it had never occurred to him to ask who that other may have been—his distant counterpart, the brightest hope of twenty generations gone by.

No, it simply was not possible. Arkady had not come all this way to be mocked! He had come here to…

To what?

To redeem his fallen. To buy back their memories and drag them back from the very jaws of the Wyrm if need be.

Arkady bit back the challenge that sprung instinctively to his lips. He addressed the miserable creature before him.

"Full-Moon's-Pelt," he said. "It is too long since the time you were home. You have been sorely missed."

Lines of puzzlement and then relief chased each other across his stark alien features. Delicate silver glyphs pooled in the corners of his eyes. Then, with a nod to Arkady, as solemn as any bow, Full-Moon's-Pelt bounded high and shot off into the darkness, retracing the route of the Black Spiral he had walked so long ago.

The outline of his gleaming pelt flickered and grew fainter with each step. Within three strides, the receding silver smudge had unraveled completely, his memory freed at last from its long exile here.

Now Arkady became aware of other silent figures all around him in the darkness. They had been watching his interchange with Full-Moon's-Pelt with rapt attention, waiting, hanging on his every word. And now they grew bolder, pressing closer on all sides.

They came to him to hear their stories read aloud one final time. To hear their deeds recited, their heroic struggles validated on the lips of the living. To have Arkady, Falcon's anointed king, divine the twisted thread of their pasts from the lines that time and trouble had etched into their faces. A sympathetic magic.

Arkady dutifully recited their lineages—both proud and infamous. He reveled with them in their victories, commiserated with them in defeat. He soon lost all track of their number—they were a throng, a host! It seemed to him that the entire Silver Spiral had been paved with the teeming ranks of the fallen Silver Fangs, each a stone hurled in defiance down upon the Wyrm in its labyrinthine lair. Only to miss its mark in the darkness, lose its way and clatter, aimless and forgotten, to the floor of Malfeas.

He had not even made a proper start on the epic task when Arkady became aware that something was very wrong. There was a dark mood surging along the Black Spiral; it blew through him like the first tentative finger brush of fear. The awakening of the dormant memories of the Silver Fang heroes had not gone unnoticed.

Something was stirring in response—an equal and opposite reaction. The Black Spiral's autonomic defenses rose to this unprecedented challenge with swift and brutal efficiency. An eye for an eye.

There was a howling from up ahead, a hollow sound that yanked every head toward it. It was not a sound birthed within the breast of any living creature, but rather its opposite. An inrushing of air, sucking life from all who heard it.

It was not just a sound, it was voice. And not just a voice, but a word. It was a word howled over and over again, repeated endlessly until the syllables of it were rendered meaningless.

Jo'cllath'mattric.

It was a name made up of the dark voids that lurked behind the stars and at the bottom of empty graves. It was a throbbing absence, a negation of meaning, a denial of volition. At each sounding of that name, one of the gleaming memories of the fallen Silver Spirals flickered and was snuffed out.

Here, at last, was the hidden spirit that animated the Temple Obscura, Arkady realized with sudden clarity. This was the great spirit to whom that altar was built and consecrated. The Temple Obscura was the place where stories came to die, and this Jo'cllath'mattric was the devouring spirit that obliged them.

Instinctively, Arkady shoved his way forward, fighting his way toward the leading edge of the throng. Trying to interpose himself between the dark hunger and the last fleeting memories of the fallen Silver Fangs. Already he could see the terror written clearly on the faces of the nearest Garou, the realization of what must now come.

He grabbed the man beside him and shook him, trying to startle him into some action, if only to flee. But it was no use. Already could see the story glyphs of the other's face unraveling, jerking free like pulled stitches—slowly, torturously. In their wake, the flesh of his face parted down the center in a gaping wound. A howl of agony bubbled up out of the jagged cut.

The delicate silver thread that had, a moment ago, been his last testament—the last recorded memory of his life—trailed away, spiraling out toward the distant hunger.

Arkady had to turn away, fighting down the bile that rose in his throat. He staggered forward, hurling himself toward the very source of the all-consuming hunger. And soon, he found himself stumbling through a tangled skein of identical silver strands.

It was like walking through the heart of a spider's web, but each of these strands was one of his forebears, a lost memory that Arkady had sought to redeem. Instead, he had only managed to hasten them on their way to final and absolute oblivion.

Howling in frustration, he clutched at the gossamer threads drifting past him, but they slipped through his fingers, dissolved in the intensity of his clutch.

Ahead of him, Arkady could make out something vast and blasphemous rising from the Black Spiral. He could feel the weight of the dark spirit's attention turn upon him, could feel his own sense of purpose eroding. Already he was having difficulty remembering just why he had ever come here, what he had thought to accomplish and, most important, how he had ever hoped to do so in the face of this being, this force of nature.

Up until this moment, Arkady had thought that he had already faced the worst the Wyrm had to throw at him. He had single-handedly cut his way through screaming legions of fomori, hordes of gibbering Banes, packs of rabid Black Spiral Dancers. He had quelled a Thunderwyrm with a single word and weathered the ground-rending attack of the Black Spiral itself.

But this Jo'cllath'mattric was a threat of an entirely different magnitude. It was a manifestation of the Wyrm itself in one of its most fearsome aspects. Nightmare tales of multiform and terrifying masks of the Wyrm—of the Defiler Wyrm, of Beast-of-War, of Eater of Souls—flashed through Arkady's mind. But none of the old tales could have prepared him for what he now faced.

A manifestation of the Wyrm that was battle incarnate would not have struck terror into his heart. He was intimately familiar with the horrors that the battlefield had to offer, in all of their permutations. He had lived through brushes with corruption, with eco-catastrophe, despair. He was well acquainted with the Wyrm in all these guises.

But Jo'cllath'mattric was something else altogether. It was a self-defense mechanism of the Wyrm itself, born of the Wyrm's unending torment as it shrieked and writhed, trapped within the Weaver's webs. That old Wyrm had had all of eternity to brood upon its mistakes, its failings, its might-have-beens and anticipated revenges. Time enough to drive it down into howling madness.

Jo'cllath'mattric was the Wyrm Trying to Forget.

Arkady stood between it and the last memories of the fallen Silver Fangs and prepared to exact as high a price as he could for his life and theirs.

As he drew his klaive, raising it on high to rally his kinsmen around him, there came a howl of challenge—not from Jo'cllath'mattric, but from directly behind Arkady. The Silver Fang did not turn. There was little point in it.

"The king is mine," called a cruel female voice. "You will not touch him, Jo'cllath'mattric. Do what you will with these half-men, these dim afterimages. That doesn't matter to me. But the one in the Silver Crown has been promised to me. It has been foretold. It is my destiny to slay the Last Gaian King."

At those words, Arkady did turn. His eyes went immediately to Sarah. She was kneeling there at the feet of her Dark Lady—her child and now tormentor. Sarah stared fixedly ahead, oblivious to all that was going on around her and sobbing quietly. The Dark Lady gave the cord tied around Sarah's neck a hard yank and the sobbing subsided abruptly. She let the lead fall to the floor. None of the slavering hulks of bristling fur and sinew that followed her made a move to pick it up. None of them considered the girl a threat.

The Dark Lady uncoiled a long barbed whip from her side and stepped toward Arkady. "I have been awaiting our meeting," she hissed at Arkady, "for a very long time. How long has it been, Samladh?"

Startled, the girl stammered, "Seventeen. I've waited, just like you said. And the Lady before you. And so on. Back seventeen hundred years."

"That's a very long time to wait. So mine must be considered the foremost claim. The Dark Lady will kill the Last Gaian King upon the Black Spiral. So it has been written, since long before I was born. So it will be…"

She gasped, choking on the words that were issuing from her mouth, spiraling away from her like a skein of silver thread unwinding.

"No!" she gasped. "You cannot do this. You cannot take this destiny away from me. It is my right! I demand…"

Arkady stared in horror as Jo'cllath'mattric extracted her story from her and devoured it. The tale she and all those who had come before her had waited seventeen hundred years to fulfill, torn away in a single moment. The story that had cost Sarah her pride, her eyesight and centuries of senseless abuse at the hands of her children—gone. Preempted. Stillborn.

With a howl of fury, the Dark Lady threw herself directly into the face of Jo'cllath'mattric, trying in vain to wrest back what was rightfully hers.

Her right to kill him, Arkady thought.

The Dark Lady's onslaught had provided him a moment's unexpected opening, and he had to seize it.

He wanted to call out to Sarah, to tell her that it was all going to be all right. That he had, at last, found a way to redeem not only the memories of his own predecessors but her children as well. All who had fallen to the Spiral over the centuries, forgotten and unmourned.

Arkady had thought the answer lay in releasing them, in hearing their tale one final time and, in so doing, becoming the living receptacle of their last memory. He could recite their deeds, their lineages, their sacrifices a thousand times! He could make them endure.

It was only when faced with the mind-numbing reality of this Jo'cllath'mattric that Arkady realized that even this hope was a futile one. What good would it do for them to commit their stories to Arkady's keeping, when he himself would only become the next victim of the great spirit void's caress of oblivion? It would only perpetuate the cycle.

No, to make these stories have some lasting meaning, to redeem his restless dead and not just appease them, it was not enough that Arkady remember. Even if Arkady could somehow contrive to escape Jo'cllath'mattric's clutches, eventually he too would meet his end. And then all these stories, these fallen heroes, would die with him. Again.

Arkady knew what he had to do. Knew it as certainly as he had ever known anything. He wanted to howl it at the top of his lungs. To open his throat and trumpet it in Falcon's own voice. To scoop Sarah up in his arms and whisper it to her until she laughed aloud.

No, it was not enough for Arkady to remember what had transpired here. That would not buy them their lasting impression, their immortality. He had to make the Wyrm itself, eternal and unchanging, their witness. To force it to remember—or more precisely, to ensure that it could never forget.

With a bellow of challenge that shook the spiral itself, Arkady brought his klaive flashing down. As one, a legion of Silver Fang heroes leaped forward, following him along the same path the Dark Lady had taken only moments before, hurtling themselves headlong into the teeth of the Wyrm Trying to Forget.

About the Author

Eric Griffin is codeveloper of the **Tribe Novel** series for **Werewolf: the Apocalypse.** He is the author of **Get of Fenris, Fianna** and **Black Spiral Dancers.**

His other works include the Clan Tremere Trilogy (**Widow's Walk, Widow's Weeds, Widow's Might**) as well as **Clan Novel: Tremere** and **Clan Novel: Tzimisce.** His short stories have appeared in the **Clan Novel Anthology, The Beast Within (2nd Edition), Inherit the Earth** and **Champions of the Scarred Lands.**

Griffin was initiated into the bardic mysteries at their very source, Cork, Ireland. He is currently engaged in the most ancient of Irish literary traditions—that of the writer in exile. He resides in Atlanta, Georgia, with his lovely wife, Victoria, and his three sons, heroes-in-training all.

For more information please feel free to visit the author's Web site at http://egriffin.home.attbi.com.

TRIBE NOVEL:

BILL BRIDGES

author:	bill bridges
cover artist:	steve prescott
series editors:	eric griffin
	john h. steele
	stewart wieck
editor:	philippe r. boulle
copyeditor:	jeanée ledoux
graphic designer:	allen mills
art director:	richard thomas

ISBN 1-58846-822-4
First Edition: December 2002
Printed in Canada.

White Wolf Publishing
1554 Litton Drive
Stone Mountain, GA 30083
www.white-wolf.com/fiction

World of Darkness Fiction by White Wolf

The Tribe Novel Series

Tribe Novel: Shadow Lords & Get of Fenris by Gherbod Fleming & Eric Griffin

Tribe Novel: Silent Striders & Black Furies by Carl Bowen & Gherbod Fleming

Tribe Novel: Red Talons & Fianna by Philippe Boulle & Eric Griffin

Tribe Novel: Bone Gnawers & Stargazers by Bill Bridges with Justin Achilli

Tribe Novel: Children of Gaia & Uktena by Richard Lee Byers & Stefan Petrucha

Tribe Novel: Silver Fangs & Glass Walkers by Carl Bowen & Tim Dedopulos

Tribe Novel: Black Spiral Dancers & Wendigo by Eric Griffin & Bill Bridges

The Predator & Prey Series

Predator & Prey: Vampire by Carl Bowen

Predator & Prey: Judge by Gherbod Fleming

Predator & Prey: Werewolf by Gherbod Fleming

Predator & Prey: Jury by Gherbod Fleming

Predator & Prey: Mage by Carl Bowen

Predator & Prey: Executioner by Gherbod Fleming

Also by Bill Bridges

Werewolf: The Silver Crown (reprinted in
The Quintessential World of Darkness)

For all these titles and more, visit **www.white-wolf.com/fiction**

TRIBE NOVEL:

WENDIGO™

BILL BRIDGES

Prologue

Vancouver, British Columbia, 1983

The wind blew from the north whenever Morning Storm went alone into the woods. Nobody knew what she did there, and although some thought it odd for her to leave her packmates during these times, it was not considered unusual in her tribe. She was a Garou of the Wendigo People, a werewolf with a strong tie to the land; if she wanted to seek the wilderness alone, it was a sign that she heard a call. It was considered wise to heed such callings.

She and her pack, the Thunder's Gift, patrolled southern British Columbia, sniffing out Wyrm taint wherever it hid and then destroying its source or chasing it back over the border from whence it came—whether or not the border was spiritual (the Umbra) or physical (the United States).

At first, her packmates thought little of Morning Storm's solitary wandering. It didn't get in the way of their hunting. She chose to go off only whenever their duties were fulfilled, in the rare lulls between hunts. Oddly, however, when asked, she never acted as if it were fully her choice. It was almost as if there were another who called her, someone she met on her lonely trips.

She would return to the pack tired, as if she had walked for days, but with a smile on her face that not even the most vicious ribbing could erase. It seemed then that her rage was a babe snuggled in sleep, not the usual terrifying thing to be choked back before it could gain expression. A strange thing in an Ahroun, a warrior born under the full moon. Morning Storm was the pack's lead warrior. And yet, whenever the enemy appeared, it seemed that she always had rage enough to combat it.

One day, Stutters-at-Cars chided her again for her solitary trips. "Where do you go, Morning Storm? Do you pretend you're a lupus, born to all fours?" The Ragabash smirked as he said this, for he was human born like her, but he thought his wolf brothers' wild beginnings were funny and tragic.

"What I do there is my own, No Moon," Morning Storm said, raising her hackles and staring Stutters-at-Cars straight in the eyes, threatening a challenge. "Never ask me again."

The poor trickster saved face by pretending to slip on a banana peel, thus putting himself flat on his back below Morning Storm—a sign of wolfen submission, but also clearly showing his auspice through the old vaudeville shtick. The others laughed, and so did Morning Storm, and so everyone was appeased.

But Morning Storm could not long hide her pregnancy. Her muscular build kept her packmates fooled for longer than usual, but in her fifth month, her swelling belly could no longer be attributed to a warrior's bulk. Her secrecy had gone on for too long.

Wild Tooth, the alpha, pounced on her back, knocking her to the ground, standing atop her as his snout growled into her ears. "Explain, Morning Storm! Who fathered the child in your womb?"

Morning Storm roared and threw him off with a sudden burst of fury—her rage had awoken from its cradle. She snarled and assumed the battle form, ready to assault any who came near her. Stutters-at-Cars crept away, wanting no piece of such violence. The Flint Arrow Twins looked at each other nervously, waiting to see what would happen next. Blue Sky Eye growled

low, in her native wolf form, unsure what to do, waiting for a sign from her leader.

Wild Tooth assumed the man form and sat down,
shaking his head in exasperation. This surprised everyone, even Morning Storm, whose rage left her like
the wind when a door is shut. She, too, took the human form and sat.

"Tell me that it is not a Garou's child that grows
in you," Wild Tooth said.

"It is not," Morning Star said. "The baby will not
be a moon-calf. It will be pure."

"Then I will ask no further. Your secret is your
own. But know this: a secret kept from packmates is
an evil thing. It cannot bring you the privacy you desire. It will only foster resentment, leading to your
loneliness."

Morning Storm seemed to pause then, as if she
were about to reveal the truth of her tryst, but then
grew quiet and nodded her head, accepting what fate
may come from her decision.

Stutters-at-Cars came barreling into her, rolling
like a wheel in his human form. "Hey!" he cried. "Can
I be the godparent? That kid's going to need somebody with a sense of humor in his life!"

Morning Storm smiled and grabbed the capering
Ragabash, locking his head under one arm as she
rubbed her knuckles onto his skull with her free hand.
"Want to be the godfather? Only if your head is thick
enough to handle all the smacks I'm going to give you!"

"Aiie! Let go!" Stutters-at-Cars cried as he struggled
to escape her grip. The others laughed, for they knew
the trickster could escape her grasp anytime he wanted—
it was his forte, to slip free of all bonds.

The matter was thus laid to rest, and no one asked her again who the babe's father was.

Summer arrived and the time came for her to give birth. She knew that it would be soon upon her, and told the others that she needed to deliver in the woods, "among the winds." She asked them to accompany her, and they agreed. Although they sometimes grumbled about the lost trust, they loved her deeply and would not be absent from such a holy moment as the birth of a Garou's child, even if it would be years before its true heritage—as Garou or mere kin—would be known.

Morning Storm led them deep into the wilderness, to the place she claimed she conceived the child. It was a meadow nestled within a circle of trees, pines that swayed in the wind, whispering a silky sigh. She sat in the center of the clearing, among the wildflowers, and waited. Her pack roamed in the nearby woods, seeking water and food to collect and bring back to the clearing. They soon had berries, roots and deer meat to sustain them during the wait.

Three nights later, during the full moon, Morning Storm began labor. After the contractions had come hard and fast, just as the babe's head appeared, a terrible wailing broke across the clearing, drowning out even Morning Storm's pained yells. The air sparked as if lightning had struck, but no storm was in sight. Shapes seemed to move behind the clouds, and the shadows of the trees trembled. Then, part of the sky tore open and a horde of glistening, fleshy things fell into the meadow like maggots shaken from a corpse. The pack howled a warning to one another as creatures rent the veil between this world and the spirit lands, pouring forth into manifestation, screaming across the field toward the maternity.

Wild Tooth growled and leapt at the foremost Bane, his jaws sinking deep into the thing's pulpy throat. Purple blood sprayed forth and the thing dropped, its new body dissolving into a pile of mucous. But more came on, a horde of misshapen creatures hell-bent on reaching the mother and child, who even then struggled to be born.

The Flint Arrow Twins killed two more, each with a single shot from their bows, and Stutters-at-Cars distracted another into chasing him rather than attacking Morning Storm. He ducked behind a tree and jumped it from behind as it ran past where he had been. His claws eviscerated it, leaving an oily smear across the wildflowers. Blue Sky Eye broke open her nutshell fetish with her teeth, releasing the fire spirit bound within. An instant conflagration greeted the next wave of Banes, who squealed and cried in pain as their raw flesh crisped to cinders.

Even through the wall of fire, however, a hideous, clawed thing running on three legs got through. Just as the new baby dropped fully from Morning Storm's womb, the thing opened its maw to bite it. Its teeth snapped shut, not into baby flesh but instead into a muscled Crinos arm. Morning Storm had flung forth her arm to defend her newborn, and she now snapped it back, throwing the Bane into the air. A strip of ligament tore off with its teeth, but the baby was safe.

As she bent to cradle the child, a claw swiped across her throat from behind. Her arterial blood sprayed across the baby as she reached behind and crushed the Bane's skull with the last of her strength. A gurgling rattle left her throat as her eyes dimmed. Her last sight was her baby boy, a beautiful, perfectly formed human child, his mouth opening wide to suck in a gust of air for his first wail.

The boy's cry shook the sky and rattled the earth. No crack of thunder was ever so loud as that shout, and the air violently whipped about the meadow, stirred by the wailing. It picked up Banes and flung them to the earth. Stutters-at-Cars tumbled through the air into the trees, where he clung to a branch to save himself from falling. The whirlwind slammed Wild Tooth against a rock; he felt his ribs crack. The pounding wind threw the others to the ground; they could not rise until the baby paused to suck in more breath. His next cry was normal, the healthy wailing of a newborn.

The pack rose up again to defend the child from the Banes, but only patches of stinking mucus remained. The others had fled or been blown away by that strange wind.

Blue Sky Eye shuffled over to the baby on three legs, dragging a broken back paw. She nudged him with her snout and the baby calmed down, his crying growing faint. He gurgled and opened and closed his fingers, curling his toes. The wolf bit through the umbilical cord and began to lick the afterbirth off the baby's soft skin. If her coarse tongue hurt the boy, he showed no signs of it.

Wild Tooth stood up, clutching his sides, and howled a deep lament for their fallen packmate. The others each joined in, Stutters-at-Cars howling as he climbed down from the tree.

The Flint Arrow Twins straightened Morning Storm's body and closed her eyes, each fighting back tears.

"Why?" Wild Tooth asked. "Why did they come? How did they know we were here? It is as if they knew the child would be born."

"We must ask my mentor, Raven Mask," Blue Sky Eye said, assuming human form and cradling the baby in her arms. "He will know."

The packmates gathered up the body of their fallen comrade and carried her back to their sept. They knew they could not care for or raise a child. Since the boy was homid, he would best be raised by human Kinfolk. Stutters-at-Cars remembered that Morning Storm's mother was Kinfolk, a member of the human Kwakiutl tribe. They agreed that it would be best to leave the boy with his grandmother.

They took him first, however, to Raven Mask, the oldest Theurge in their sept, a spirit-seer long in wisdom but considered crazy by many of the younger Garou, for he often spoke in riddles that were rarely ever answered.

"I have been waiting to see the boy," the old man said, sitting in his dark lodge house amid the smoke of a smoldering fire. "I heard his howl from here. A mighty voice has he."

"Who is his father?" Blue Sky Eye asked. "Morning Storm would not tell us."

"Then I cannot say," Raven Mask said. "I would not anger her spirit. It will be revealed soon enough, however. Until then, the boy must have a name. From which way did the wind blow when the boy was born?"

The pack members looked at one another, puzzled.

"I don't know," Wild Tooth said. "I was too busy fighting Banes to notice."

The Flint Arrow Twins both shrugged their shoulders. Blue Sky Eye shook her head; she did not know.

"Wait a minute," Stutters-at-Cars said. "I think it came from the north."

"How do you know?" Raven Mask asked, smiling.

"When I was thrown into the trees, I distinctly remember the branches swaying in one direction, toward the stream beyond the meadow, which was to the south. So, the wind must have come from the north."

Raven Mask nodded, as if it only confirmed what he already knew. "Then he will be called John North Wind's Son."

The pack members each nodded. It sounded to them as good a name as any.

"Take him, then, to his grandmother," Raven Mask said. "She does not know her daughter's true heritage, though. You must not tell her. She must raise the child as a human. This will protect him and help to hide him from the Banes who feared his birth."

"Feared?" Blue Sky Eye said. "Why? Is he destined for greatness?"

"That is for him to say, when he becomes a man. They do not fear him so much as they do his father. They dread to see his power handed to his son." Before anyone could say anything more, Raven Mask pulled on his feathered shawl, covering his face. "Go now, and deliver the boy. Watch him from afar now and then, to see if he one day becomes one of us."

"Should we not give him a Kin Fetch, to warn us of his progress?" Blue Sky Eye asked.

A low chuckle escaped from under Raven Mask's shawl. "No. Others already watch him. They will warn us if the time ever comes. Go."

With that, the old Theurge turned his back on them and began to hum an old tune, the words of which nobody seemed to understand in these times.

The pack left the lodge and took John North Wind's Son to his human kin, and so left him to be raised a human. It would be many years before his true heritage as Garou became known to him. Even then, however, he still did not know who his father was.

Chapter One

Finger Lakes Caern, New York State, now...

Albrecht ran. He had walked the Moon Bridge from the North Country Protectorate to the Finger Lakes, but as he approached the end, his patience ran out and he bolted forward. He had been anxious for the past two days—his nerves like barbed wire pulled taught—ever since leaving the Night Sky Sept in the Balkans by an even longer Moon Bridge route than this one. Once home, he had to bring his council up on the news about the pseudovictory in Europe, where he and others had stopped the summoning of Jo'cllath'mattric, but only after the Night Sky Sept had lost dozens of prime warriors in a sudden assault. He cut things short, however, and almost immediately jumped onto a new Moon Bridge to come here, where his packmate may have already died.

Evan's message, calling him home to Mari's side, was abrupt and cut off by typical cell phone transmission problems. He had no idea what had occurred over the following thirty-six hours since they had last talked. He hoped it was good news, but his heart feared it was bad. He didn't know how much more misery he could take. He'd kept it together well enough over in Europe, but that was easy when he hadn't lost any of his own people. Konietzko, on the other hand, had lost too many septmates and allies. The old warrior still kept going, though, chin held high. Albrecht would have to do the same.

He had barely admitted to himself just how much Mari meant to him. Not as a lover or any of that soap opera crap, but as a friend, almost a sister. Sure, they fought like cats and dogs most of the time, but it was only a mutually agreed upon façade to keep from having to admit mushy emotions to one another. Evan had seen through that a long time ago and came to accept their typical—for Garou, anyway—way of relating to one another.

The lunar light of the bridge gave way to a deeper indigo of night as he landed on solid ground, pulling himself up short to keep his momentum from tumbling him into the clearing, a foot-pounded meadow set away from the caern center expressly for the purpose of admitting visitors.

"Ho!" a gruff voice cried. "Who dares enter this caern uninvited?"

"Uninvited?" Albrecht said, unable to keep the anger from his voice, looking around for his questioner. "You opened the bridge for me. Who the hell're you?"

"Your worst nightmare!" Someone leapt on Albrecht's back from behind, wrapping arms around his neck and dropping him neatly to the ground with a judo throw before he could even think about reacting.

He growled and almost shifted into Crinos form before he saw his attacker grinning down at him. He stared in shock and stammered.

"Well?" Mari said, bending over Albrecht, her hands on her hips. "Aren't you going to apologize for entering a Black Furies caern without so much as a 'may I please?'"

"Oh, I'm sorry all right," Albrecht said, grinning from cheek to cheek. "Sorry I wasn't here to keep you in line when you woke up. You've obviously picked up a chip on your shoulder since I saw you last."

"Oh?" Mari said. "And I wasn't like this before my coma?"

"Correction. You were. How could I have ever forgotten?" He put out his hand. "Aren't you going to offer a king a hand up, especially since you're the one who put him on his back?"

Mari grasped Albrecht's arm and tugged him up, catching him in an embrace as he got to his feet. She gripped him strongly for a moment, silent, and he returned the hug. For once, he knew when to keep his mouth shut. She released him and pointed down a pathway.

"Alani wants to see you, Albrecht. Everyone's curious about what's going on in the world. Evan said you've been in Europe." She shook her head. "I certainly hope you didn't insult anyone while there. If there's anyone who lives up to the ugly American moniker, it's you."

"Hell," Albrecht said, "of course I insulted folk. But they got over it. Now we're the best of buds. I'm king, remember? That makes me a real people person."

Mari threw back her head and laughed as she walked, Albrecht following alongside her. "Oh, yeah, a real people person. That'll be the day.

Albrecht, if you didn't have Evan to look after you, there'd be a trail of corpses as testament to your diplomacy skills."

"Well, there were corpses, but they were Black Spiral Dancers…"

Mari's eyes darkened and the smile left her face. "Was it bad?"

"Yeah. Lots of good people dead. But we've got something to show for it. A whole hive of Spirals destroyed before they could summon up Jo'cllth'whatsisname. But hey," Albrecht stopped and put his hand on Mari's shoulder, "What about you? Are you really all right? How the hell did they wake you up?"

"I'm fine… or I will be. I'm weak, but getting stronger."

"Weak? You just threw me to the ground!"

"Leverage. That sort of move requires little muscle power, especially against a surprised and pissant foe like you."

Albrecht chuckled and shook his head. "I'll let you have that shot. Take all you want for now; you've earned them. Come tomorrow, though, don't expect the kid gloves."

"I don't need them, Albrecht. My spirit may have been trapped in recurring torment, but I'm over that."

"Jeez, what the hell was it? Some sort of Wyrm realm?"

"No, it was my own darkness, my own untold and denied story. We repress a lot from our pre-Garou days, I guess. It came back to haunt me."

"Albrecht!" a voice cried from ahead, near the first of the cabins built to house the sept.

"Evan!" Albrecht yelled, waving. "Get over here. Where were you when I was coming in?"

Evan jogged up and punched Albrecht in the arm. "Mari wanted it to be a surprise. She figured she'd have to put you in your place as soon as you got here, or else you'd be pulling the whole 'I kicked butt in Europe' routine."

"Hey, I'm still planning to pull that routine, kid. I deserve it. It wasn't easy over there."

"No, I'm sure it wasn't. I'm glad you're back. I'm glad we're all back."

Mari smiled and tussled Evan's hair. He was a lot older now than he'd been when she first helped him through his Change and the ensuing dangers, but she still had a big-sister affection for him. "C'mon, Alani has been waiting."

They turned the corner together to see a group of women of all ages gathered on the steps of a cabin, this one larger than those around it. Bright lights poured from the windows onto the porch, highlighting the features of the eldest among them, an old black woman.

"Greetings, King Albrecht," said Alani Astarte, leader of the Hand of Gaia Sept. "I am pleased that you returned whole and hale."

"Hello, Alani," Albrecht said. "Thanks, and thank you for healing my packmate."

"I did not heal our tribe sister. You have the Silver River Pack to thank for that. It was they, the Third Pack of Antonine's prophecy, who returned with the lore needed to see her through her darkness."

"Yeah? Where are they? I'd like to give them my best."

"They wait inside, with other visitors, eager to hear news from abroad."

"Okay, let's get inside then so I can spill the juicy details." Albrecht motioned to Alani to precede him. She smiled and nodded at his politeness. As a king, some would say he was entitled to enter before others, but this was Alani's sept, and she had been a Garou elder far longer than he. It was just such considerations that made him popular among the other tribes, who might otherwise scoff at the notion of a Silver Fang king with any degree of sovereignty over them.

Inside, the room was filled with tables and benches, resembling some sort of camp mess hall. Smells of cooking wafted from a kitchen in the back. Women and men were gathered on the benches, talking among themselves. Women far outnumbered men, and the genders tended to keep to their own groups. These were the Furies who lived here. Mixed among them were Children of Gaia, who also shared the caern but did not take on as strong a role in leading it.

All talk quieted as Alani entered, followed by the Silver Fang king and his pack. The Silver River pack, sitting together to the right of the entrance next to a women who looked like a middle-aged hippy, stood up out of respect for them. The woman did the same, smiling and waving at the group.

Albrecht looked surprised to see her. "Pearl River? I haven't seen you in a while."

"It has been a while, King Albrecht. My tribe's work with the children wounded by the Seventh Generation goes well, thanks to you."

"No, that's your glory to earn. I can't say it enough. Somebody needs to heal those kids, and you Children of Gaia volunteering worked out just right. I'm glad you're here. I would have had to send a messenger from the North Country to you and True Silverheels otherwise. I've got something to announce."

"I look forward to hearing it," she said.

"And you," Albrecht said, addressing the Silver River Pack. "I can't thank you guys enough for what you did. I don't know the story yet, but Mari says it was you who helped her out."

"Oh, it was nothing," Julia said, straightening her suit. It was perfectly ironed, but her packs' adventures of late had so often wrinkled it that she couldn't break the habit of straightening it anyway. She continued on in her cultivated British accent: "I mean, once we found out about the lore spirits trapped inside the Lore Banes, we had some clue as to how to help her."

"Nothing?" Carlita said, exasperated, her eyes large beneath a knit cap pulled tight over her brow. She stood with arms crossed, her long, baggy pants hanging well below her heels. "Don't listen to her! She risked her own spirit to drag Mari out of that vicious circle she'd been in. We could've lost her, too."

"Then I'm doubly impressed," Albrecht said. "And doubly in your debt. You guys ever need anything, call on me."

"Hey," Carlita said. "Don't forget the Black Spiral Dancer and Banes that attacked. And Cries Havoc's finding out about the secret of the Lore Banes in the first place. And the caern we found underwater—"

Hush, Storm-Eye said, growling in her Lupus form. *Enough*. The scar over her eye gave her short bark a degree of menace she didn't intend.

"Don't worry," John North Wind's Son said, "there will be time enough to tell our story again." As he sat back down, his icicle necklace made a hollow clack as it knocked against his spear, held loosely in his hand. He certainly fit into some people's stereotype of a Native American, complete with a raven tattoo on his chest, but it was a role he was proud to fill.

Cries Havoc, joining the rest of his packmates as they sat down, shook his head and smiled at their attempts to jockey for acclaim. He hadn't said anything, too nervous to draw attention to himself. His cap hid his metis horns, but he still worried how strangers would take his wearing a hat around everywhere. He preferred to feel out the tenor of a group before stepping up before it. He was a Galliard, a lorekeeper and tale singer, and liked to know his audience before he hit the stage.

Alani Astarte clapped for attention. She had continued to the far side of the room, to a podium up a short flight of steps. "It's time we heard King

Albrecht's tale," she said, motioning to Albrecht to take the podium.

He walked briskly past all the other Garou, all of whom looked at him curiously, and turned to face them once he reached the top of the steps. "Thanks, Alani. As you all surely know by now, I've just returned from Europe. A lot happened. There are Galliards better fit to tell the tales of heroism and tragedy we experienced there. I've invited some of those who witnessed the events to come and tell these tales at my court soon, once all this is over. We can revel in them then.

"For now, we've got to act. When I was at the Night Sky Sept's caern, it was attacked by a hive of Black Spiral Dancers. We rallied the troops and slaughtered them, but not before losing a number of damn good warriors. Margrave Konietzko and I managed to stop their summoning rite, to keep them from freeing Jo'cllath'mattric."

A murmur spread throughout the room at the mention of the Wyrm beast's name.

"He's out there, chained for now in an Umbral subrealm of his own, stewing in whatever juices he sucks from others through his Lore Banes. But the chains are weak and he's damn angry at our stopping up his food source. He could break through into our world any day now, unless we get to him first.

"I want to convene a moot of spirit-seers and lorekeepers at my caern to work this over, to figure out how the hell we're going to find his realm and lead a war party to it. It's the only way we're going to keep one step ahead of him. He's got the advantage of eating all sorts of memories, so he knows a lot about us. We know next to diddly-squat about him.

"In three days, I'll convene the moot. I'm asking you to send whatever representatives you think can best help us puzzle this mess out. Also, please tell the other tribes. My tribe is sending out a call right now, but there're a lot of folks around here who won't listen unless the invite comes in person. If you're on good terms with some of them, do me a favor and get them involved. I'd go to everyone personally, but I just don't have time. That's it. Any questions?"

A young Fury stood up, smirking. "I will tell the Get. As strange as it sounds, I have befriended one among them. He can get them to send at least one Theurge seer."

A middle-aged man stood up. "I'll tell the Shadow Lords. We're neighbors. They don't like us—the Children of Gaia—but they won't be so foolish as to miss hearing anything about Konietzko's sept."

"And I will tell the Fianna," Pearl River said, standing and readying to leave. "But we must all go now, if we are to make it in time."

"Please do," Albrecht said, stepping down from the podium. "The sooner the better. I've got to get back to the North Country and prepare."

The room exploded into noise as every Garou stood up and began heading for the exit, talking among themselves strategies for how they were each going to participate. The Silver River Pack waited until most of the room had cleared before it rose to go.

"Wait a minute," Albrecht said, coming over to the pack. "You're all invited, of course. I know you're not all Theurges, but you've been in this from the start, so there's no reason to keep you out now."

"Thanks," Cries Havoc said. "I want to see this through." Carlita kicked him in the hamstrings. He turned and gave her a hurt look and then noticed her expression. "Uh, I guess we should talk it over first. We've been through a lot lately."

"You guys probably need a good, long rest," Albrecht said. "But I do hope to see you there." With that, he walked out to join Alani and Mari, who had already left. Evan, who had loitered behind him, came over to the Silver River Pack.

"It's okay to turn it down, you know," he said. "Nobody would fault you after what you've been through."

"We are tired," Julia said. "And I'm sure Big Sis misses Tampa."

"Well, yeah," Carlita said. "I haven't been back since all this started. You got to see your homies in London, at least. And poor Storm-Eye here, she ain't seen wolves in who knows how long."

Don't speak for me, Storm-Eye said in the wolfen language of gestures and growls. *I wish to see this through.*

"As do I," John North Wind's Son said. "We were chosen by Uktena for this. Who can say our part is done just because we healed Cries Havoc and Mari?"

"And killed a bunch of Banes and Black Spirals," Julia reminded him. "But I suppose you're right. We should see it through. I would like to see a moot at the North Country. I mean, it is the seat of the North American king."

"Sheesh, you monarchists!" Big Sis said. "America ain't got no king. Only the Garou do."

Julia rolled her eyes. "Have it your way. You're all just rebellious subjects of the British Crown anyway."

"Not me," John North Wind's Son said. "My people were here before your king ever heard of America. Or Storm-Eye, for that matter; wolves recognize no king but their own pack alpha."

"Okay, okay!" Julia said. "Point taken."

As they talked, they left the cabin. Once on the porch, they saw some sort of altercation taking place not far from the building. A short, broad Native American stood arguing with a group of Black Fury caern warders, obviously trying to get into the cabin. He wore a tattered denim jacket, and his long black hair descended in two braids on either side of his head. Underneath the jacket, he wore a T-shirt with a picture of a howling wolf. His belt buckle was huge, a large pewter wolverine head, snarling. His shoes were brand new Nikes, sparkling white. When he saw the Silver River Pack, he perked up.

"There!" he cried, pointing at John North Wind's Son. "That's the guy I've come to see.

Tribal business, ladies. You can't stand in the way of that, can you?"

"Do you know this… person?" one of the Furies said, addressing the young pack.

Everyone looked at one another but nobody responded. John looked at Evan. "I've never seen him before," he said. "Have you?"

"No," Evan said, walking up to the man. "Hello, I'm Evan Heals-the-Past, of the Wendigo. You said something about tribal business?"

The man brushed past the warders and shook Evan's hand vigorously. "That's right! Call me Hairy Foot! I was sent by Aurak Moondancer to fetch this cub here." He nodded toward John North Wind's Son.

John looked puzzled. "I've heard of him. He is lorekeeper for the Sept of the Hawk, in Ottawa. But I've never met him. What does he want with me?"

"He didn't tell me," Hairy Foot said, stepping forward and offering his hand to John. When John took it, there was a loud crackling noise, and he jumped back, startled, his hand tingling. Hairy Foot bent over laughing. "Ha! Always works! The first handshake is normal, so nobody suspects nothing, but the second one's got the buzzer." He revealed a joke buzzer in his palm, the kind you'd buy in a magic novelty shop.

"Oh hardy har har har," Carlita said. "What kind of moron are you, anyway?"

He shot her a wicked glance. "Hey, I haven't been able to use that for a long time, sister, so cut me some slack. It's not everyday…" he stopped speaking, as if he were about to say something he shouldn't. "Anyway, I need to take John here to meet the lorekeeper. Something about the tribe's involvement in this Umbral storm thing."

"Why don't I know anything about this?" Evan said, looking concerned.

"Beats me. Like I said, they don't tell a lowly Ragabash like me nothing. All's I know is that Cries-in-the-Wind preferred that Aurak get John here rather than you. Oh, yeah, I hear them talk about you up there. Kreeyah likes you, and he's got respect, but he don't lead the tribe. No, that's Cries-in-the-Wind, and I heard him say 'I have no desire to heal a past that has been stolen from us.' He was talking about you, I think."

Evan looked hurt. John put his hand on his shoulder. "Do you know these Wendigo well, Evan?"

"Not really. I've dealt with them a bit and Kreeyah at least is a friend, but he's among the few that recognize what I do among the other tribes. Old Cries-in-the-Wind is bitter, and he has a long memory about past slights. He thinks my mission to soothe past wrongs is a waste of time."

"Then I won't go. You were the one who found me after my Change. You taught me the Ways. I owe you a lot besides friendship. If they aren't friends of yours, then they're no friends of mine."

Evan smiled but shook his head. "We can't keep living that way. They're tribemates, John. They may not respect all that I do, but I respect their position. You should, too. I think you need to go with Hairy Foot here and see Aurak. You may be able to convince him to come to Albrecht's moot. We could really use his wisdom."

John looked at Hairy Foot, who had been scowling but now smiled at Evan's words. "All right, Hairy Foot. I'll come with you, as long as I can be back in the North Country three days from now."

"Sure!" Hairy Foot said. "We're not going all the way to Canada. Aurak'll meet us at the Mohawk rez upstate."

We will come, too, Storm-Eye said.

"What?" Julia said. "But we've been invited to the moot!"

"You heard Hairy Foot," Cries Havoc said. "We can be back in time."

"Uh… I don't know about this," Hairy Foot said. "I was just told to bring John."

"My packmates come with me or I don't go," John said, stamping the butt of his spear on the ground.

"Okay," Hairy Foot said, "but they'll have to ride in the back of my pickup. I don't have no high-falutin' SUV to fit them all in."

Fine, Storm-Eye said. *Let us leave now.*

Hairy Foot smiled and cackled. "Hell, yeah! The sooner we're there, the sooner I can get you back! C'mon!" He took off running toward the parking lot the sept maintained for guest vehicles.

"Be respectful, John," Evan said. "Don't let them anger you with talk of war between the tribes. If Kreeyah is there, you can count on him to be an ally."

"Thanks, Evan," John said. "I'll tell you all about it in three days, at the moot."

"Come on!" Hairy Foot yelled from off in the distance.

Storm-Eye loped forward, and the rest of the pack followed. John clasped arms with Evan and then turned to join them. They heard the revving of an old engine before they saw the pickup. It was a 1969 Ford, rusted almost to the frame. It would be an uncomfortable ride.

Hairy Foot sat in the driver's seat, gunning the engine to keep the idle from dying. "Well, get in already. I swear you white folk got no sense of urgency!"

"Oh, that's rich," Julia said. "I thought Indians were supposed to be the lazy and shiftless ones. At least, they are in those old John Wayne cavalry movies."

Hairy Foot cackled. "Whatever you say, kemosabe!"

"I'll ride in back," John said. "Julia and Cries Havoc can fit up front with Hairy Foot. Storm-Eye and Big Sis will be fine in back with me."

"Hell, yeah," Carlita said, climbing into the rusty bed. "I ain't sitting up there with his skanky ass, anyway. Let's go!"

Once they were all in, Hairy Foot threw the truck into gear and they lurched forward, barreling down a gravel driveway toward the main road, watching the distant silhouettes of Garou prepare for a major gathering without them.

Chapter Two

The sun rose over the trees by the time they entered the Akwasasne Mohawk reservation boundary in the rattling, bumpy pickup. John, Carlita and Storm-Eye huddled in the truck bed, grunting with each lurch the truck made—it seemed to leap upward at least a foot every time a tire hit even the smallest piece of gravel.

"Doesn't this guy know what shock absorbers are?" Carlita had asked early on in the trip. Now, like the others in the bed, she had retreated to a sullen silence, waiting out the rest of the jarring ride with teeth gritted.

Inside the cab, it wasn't much better. Julia had asked Hairy Foot at least ten times to put out his smelly cigar, but the Ragabash just cackled and kept puffing away at it.

"You gotta respect tobacco," he said.

"That's not tobacco, you idiot," Julia said. "It's a bunch of dried chemicals masquerading as a natural plant. Do you know the kinds of filler tobacco companies put in those things?"

"Don't know, don't care. If it smokes, I smoke it." He cackled again and blew out a noxious cloud.

"Are we almost there?" Cries Havoc asked, his head turned to catch what breeze he could from the window Julia had cracked open. The air was frigid, but they figured it was better to freeze than choke to death.

"Just crossed the border. We're almost there. Don't get your horns in a curl."

Cries Havoc winced at the reference to his metis deformity. He was way past getting angry at their mention or whenever someone taunted him about them, but he still didn't like being reminded of his difference. He looked out the window, wondering what a modern Indian reservation looked like, but saw a scene similar to the rest of rural upstate New York: rows and rows of trees along the back roads, with occasional homes hiding down lanes, signaled by roadside mailboxes.

The car suddenly lurched to the left as Hairy Foot made a sharp turn off the road and onto a tight dirt lane leading out to a wide-open field. It looked like some sort of crop had once grown there, but it had been at least a few years since the field was last cultivated. Frost clung to the thin, short shoots of grass and the wind whistled as it blew across the open space.

The truck came to a quick stop as Hairy Foot yanked on the emergency brake. Julia's forehead almost hit the windshield, but she stopped herself just in time. "No thanks to seatbelts or air bags," she muttered in response to Cries Havoc's look of concern. "Is this it? Where are the Wendigo?"

Hairy Foot leapt out of the cab and loudly slammed the rusty steel door behind him. "Oh, they'll be here soon enough. C'mon." He started walking out across the field.

John and Storm-Eye jumped out of the back and stretched their legs, while Carlita carefully climbed out, looking worn and tired. "Can't we stop for coffee or a Coke first?"

"Too late," John said as he jogged to catch up to Hairy Foot. The others took their time falling in behind them, creating a loose line across the field. Hairy Foot whistled a tune, something nobody recognized. As John caught up to the Ragabash, he tapped him on the shoulder. Hairy Foot turned to look at him but didn't slow his pace.

"Yeah? Something on your mind?" he said.

"Why are we here?" John asked, motioning to the emptiness around them. "There's no lodge, no shack; not even a lean-to."

"There're also no people. It's never a good idea to do Garou business in front of others."

John nodded. "True, but surely there's a warmer place for this, away from prying eyes."

Hairy Foot looked at him with a frown. "You afraid of the cold? You're a Wendigo."

"I don't feel the cold," John said. "Never have since my Change. It's my pack I'm worried about." He motioned back to his packmates. Hairy Foot looked back and saw that each of them, except for Storm-Eye in her wolf form, shivered as they walked, arms wrapped around themselves in a poor attempt to stay warm.

"Oh, don't worry about them," Hairy Foot said. "If they think it's cold here, wait till… Well, they'll be fine here. They can always take to all fours to get a coat of fur. Whoah," he said as he came to a stop, looking down at the ground. A surveyor's stake jutted from the hard dirt, with a red tag dangling off it. "This is it. The place."

"I don't understand," John said, staring at the stake. "What sort of meeting site is this?"

Before he could fully react, Hairy Foot jumped on him. Within seconds, he had him in a full nelson, tugging him to the ground.

Storm-Eye, a few yards behind them, barked a warning howl to the others and bolted forward to help her packmate. Before she got there, however, she saw a glistening shimmer as of sunlight on a babbling brook, and the two Garou disappeared.

Cries Havoc, running as fast as he could to reach them, stopped. "What happened? Where did they go?"

Umbra! Storm-Eye barked. *We must step across!*

"Grab my hands," Julia cried. The others ran to her and grasped her arms. Storm-Eye wrapped her wolf body and tale around her leg. Julia yanked her PDA from her coat pocket, thumbed it on, and stared at the pulsing light glowing from its screen. Looking beyond the light, she began to shift them across the Gauntlet separating the worlds. They all felt the familiar lightness seep into their bodies, as if gravity were suspended for a moment, but then weight came lurching back.

"Why aren't we across?" Cries Havoc cried, reeling a bit with the sudden dizziness.

"I... I can't pierce the Gauntlet," Julia said, a look of complete surprise on her face. "It's as if the barrier thickened when I tried to step across. I've never felt anything like it. There's no way the wall should be so wide in an empty field in the middle of nowhere. But it's thicker than it was in New York City!"

Each of us must try, Storm-Eye said. *Hold out your fetish!*

Julia shook her head. "It won't work, I'm telling you! The Gauntlet is too thick."

Storm-Eye growled low in response. Julia sighed and held forth her PDA for the wolf to look into. After a few moments of concentration, in which Storm-Eye stared intently at the shimmering, pulsing light, trying to gain sympathy with the spirit world and her own body, she grunted and looked away.

"Told you," Julia said, putting her PDA away. "We can't get over. What are we going to do? What kind of trap is this?"

Storm-Eye howled in frustration and Cries Havoc joined her. Their cry reverberated across the field but was then lost in the whistling wind.

• • •

John hit the ground, his face plowing into a snow bank. The sudden appearance of the wetness surprised him and he halted his struggling. Hairy Foot's weight on his back suddenly lifted, and he leapt up, ready to attack the Ragabash. Snow and wind hit his face with a fury, forcing him to squint.

He stood in the middle of a raging snowstorm, the wind biting into his bare chest like tiny daggers. He stumbled backward, unsure what to do. He had never felt a painful cold like this before in his life. *No, that's not true*, he thought. *I felt like this once before, when I was a boy, before I became a Garou. What's going on? Why do I feel the cold now?*

Even after his First Change, it had taken him a while to realize that he always felt less bothered by cold weather than other people. As a boy, he was renowned in his neighborhood for rarely wearing a coat in winter, but even he felt cold once in a while, during the worst temperature drops. But after his Change, he rarely felt even those frigid temperatures anymore.

At first, he thought all Wendigo were like him, but he soon realized that most of them faked it, pretending stoically that they felt no bite from the icy chill. It was a matter of willpower for them, though, not an absence of pain.

But now… now he felt the full force of the coldest storm he'd ever experienced, and he had no shirt to warm him. His icicle fetish necklace seemed frozen to his skin, and he was afraid to touch it lest his fingers also stick to it.

He heard a voice over the whistling wind and immediately tried to trace its source. It sounded like Hairy Foot, but John couldn't hear the person he talked to. He thought he heard the Ragabash laugh, but then silence, only the whine of the wind.

"Hairy Foot!" he cried. "Explain yourself!"

No answer.

John couldn't see more than an arm's reach in front of him. The snow came down fast. It had already collected about his ankles in the time he had stood still. John realized that, were he to keep standing there, he would eventually be buried.

He brought his spear to his face and turned the flint blade over and over, trying to catch a glint of light, a gleam by which he could traverse the Gauntlet. He realized now that he was in the Umbra, for no natural storm could blow this hard and fast. But what light he saw could not mesmerize him enough to break through. It was as if a door had been closed and he couldn't find the knob to open it.

I will die here if I cannot find shelter, he thought. *What sort of Wyrm trap is this, to freeze me to death?* He shifted into Lupus form and instantly felt better. His thick coat kept out much of the wind's bite, but it still hurt, and he felt the numbness working its way deep inside him.

He threw back his head and howled for his packmates, listening to the howl echo off into the distance. He waited quietly, ears pricked to hear even the slightest response. Nothing.

He dug his nose into the snow, trying to reach the dirt below, but when his nose pounded against it, he knew it was frozen and too hard to dig into. Even if he shifted to Crinos form, he might waste too much of his precious energy trying to make a deep enough hole. *To what end? If I stay here, I die.*

He loped off in the direction he believed the main road had been, unsure what to do next. He only knew that he had to keep moving.

Chapter Three

"Nothing!" Carlita yelled in frustration, kicking at the frozen ground. "There's nothing here!"

The Silver River Pack had fanned out across the field, searching and sniffing for any kind of clue whatsoever to the thickening of the Gauntlet or the Wendigo's reasons for stealing John away into the Umbra.

"I thought for a moment that there was a weak spot over there, by the trees," Julia said, returning from a jaunt to the edge of the field, "but it seemed to disappear the closer I got, like a mirage."

There must be an answer, Storm-Eye said, casting about across the field for what seemed like the hundredth time.

A distant, metallic thud came across the field. All eyes turned back to the pickup truck, still parked where Hairy Foot had left it. The Ragabash now sat in the driver's seat, having just shut the heavy door. He revved the engine up, grinning and waving at them.

The pack shot forward, each shifting into their Lupus forms for speed, vaulting as fast as they could at the truck. Storm-Eye called upon the Rabbit's power, and each pumping of her legs sent her farther than the others. But even this could not get her to the truck in time. She had been too far away when they heard the truck door shut.

Hairy Foot gunned the engine and roared out of the field, back onto the road and down deeper into the reservation territory.

Cries Havoc roared in frustration and began to slow.

Storm-Eye yelped an admonishment at him and kept running. *We must catch him!*

The others picked up their pace again and set off after Storm-Eye, chasing a truck that had already disappeared around the bend.

● ● ●

Hours had passed since John first walked away from where Hairy Foot had left him. He had seen no sign of even a pine tree since then. The field seemed endless. In the physical world, trees and houses bounded it. Here, there were no boundaries. Only snow, wind and chilling cold.

Now and then, he thought he heard voices whispering around him, but when he stopped to listen, they grew silent. He believed once that his pack had called for him, and he howled back to tell them where he was, but heard no answer.

He kept going. His strength faded and his belly rumbled with hunger, but he dared not stop in the open, in the raw, blistering wind. He forced his paws onward.

Once more, he thought he heard a howl in the distance, a packmate, perhaps Storm-Eye, calling. He howled back, but his cry was weak and would not carry the distance.

Something answered. A croaking roar came from somewhere off to his left. He peered through the wildly blowing snow and saw a shape moving there, growing larger. It was not a wolf shape.

He backed up, trying to remove himself from where he had been when he made the howl, hoping that the shape sought the source of the sound rather than his scent, and was perhaps blind in the snow. It changed course to follow him.

He stood his ground and shifted into Crinos form, hefting his fetish spear as it formed from raw spirit substance. The shape paused, as if sensing his rage. But it came forward, stumbling through the snow at him.

For a moment, the wind shifted and blew away from him, opening a window in its wall of whiteness, revealing the thing that moved toward him. The slim, skeletal giant stood nearly twelve feet tall. It looked like it had once been a human, but had devolved into… something else. Bare ribs poked from its torso's flesh in awkward angles, revealing a frozen but still beating heart, encased in ice but pulsing with red life.

Its fingers stretched into long, jagged claws, resembling the crooked row of jagged teeth jutting from its maw, open and groaning with hunger. Its eyes had no whites, only black pits that seemed all the darker in the white snowscape.

John's courage shriveled as he took in all these details and recognized them. He knew the stories his granny used to tell, old Indian tales of the north. The Garou Galliards of his tribe had confirmed them after his Change, and they added details Granny could never have known, the kind of details only first-person eye-witnesses could impart.

He knew the Atcen, the terrible cannibal spirit that now approached him. It served his tribal totem, the Great Wendigo, but it was no friend to men. The hungry creature cared nothing for warmth or human kindness, or even the laws of the Garou, for it ever sought only the meat of humans. It would not eat the flesh of animals or even lupus Garou, but John was a homid, human born. He was a ready meal.

The wind shifted again, this time blowing from John's direction toward the Atcen, delivering John's scent to the creature's nostrils. It paused and sniffed deeply of the smell, and then put on a sudden burst of speed, lurching so fast at John he could barely react.

John thrust his spear forward, slicing into the thing's thigh. It howled but did not relent, knocking the spear aside with its thin but powerful arms, tearing the fetish from John's grip with the suddenness of its strength. The spear fell into the snow.

The Atcen reached out with both arms and grasped John in a bear hug. Its strength was like iron; John used all the power he could muster—formidable in his Crinos form—but could not budge the thing's limbs. Sharp, serrated teeth sank into his left shoulder, rending muscle and ligament. John howled in pain, his eyes swimming, barely seeing anything now but snow and Atcen bone. The thing reared its head back and tore away a chunk of flesh, swallowing it whole without chewing.

John's left arm was useless without the shoulder muscles to lift it. He dug his snout into the thing's grip, hoping to reach its throat. He could see the Atcen heart within its open ribcage, beating stronger now, the ice beginning to thaw as his own blood coursed through it. He also noticed that, thanks to the tight grip the thing had him in, his right hand was almost next to the heart. He opened his fingers and closed them upon the cold thing, feeling both the searing cold of its ice and the burning pain of its heat. He yanked it out.

As the heart came free, the Atcen halted. Its arms loosened and John fell from its grip, tumbling into the soft snow. The thing stared into its empty torso and seemed confused. It looked about and saw the blood from its still-beating heart, clutched in John's hand, spraying out into the snow, staining it red. It reached forward, grunting angrily, to snatch back its heart, but then toppled forward, dead. Its body hit the snow hard and sunk deep. Almost instantly, the storm covered up the hole its shape had made.

The ice around the heart in John's hand melted, revealing the juicy, warm meat. Its smell was agony to John's stomach, which strained and rumbled at the sound, desperate for sustenance.

But John remembered what created the Atcen spirit: any who eat of Atcen flesh become Atcen themselves. Weak and in pain, his shoulder growing numb with blood loss, he tossed the heart away. It, too, sank into the snow, leaving only bloodstains soon covered by the falling mantle.

He picked up his spear and shifted back into Lupus form. The spear, a thing of spirit, merged with his new form, appearing as a spear-shaped whiteness on his fur. He stumbled off, away from the stench, the pain of his open wound now numbing his mind.

Chapter Four

Storm-Eye sniffed at the road, walking in circles. Julia, Cries Havoc and Carlita stood nearby, panting, tired from the long run. They had followed the truck's scent over the road for what must have been three miles now. There had been little change of scenery. At a four-way stop sign, they lost the trail.

Carlita shifted back to human form and sat down by the side of the road, huffing and out of breath. "Shit. That bastard got away."

No, Storm-Eye growled, still frantically sniffing the asphalt. *Many other scents, but his truck is still here.*

"You'll never pick it out among all that gasoline stench. Face it, he's gone. And so is John."

"No," Cries Havoc said, also shifting into human form. "Don't think that way. We'll find him. His truck has a... unique scent."

"Unique?" Julia said, joining them by the curb in human form. "Pungent more like. I don't know how Storm-Eye withstood it on the trip over here from Finger Lakes. If we'd been in Lupus form, I suspect we'd have been retching all the way."

You judge smells too much, Storm-Eye said, pausing. *Smell is just smell. Not good or bad. Except Wyrm smell...*

"Not to us humans, sister," Carlita said. "Some stenches are downright gross. And Hairy Foot qualifies. Why the hell do the Wendigo hang out with that guy, with a smell like that?"

"I suspect they don't," Julia said. "We've been set up. I doubt Hairy Foot is a Wendigo at all. Or if so, he's probably a renegade."

"You think so?" Cries Havoc said. "He seemed to know a lot about the sept he mentioned, and Evan fell for it."

"Anyone can research a Garou sept. Given enough time," Julia replied.

This way! Storm-Eye yelled, running off down the road to the right.

They all shifted back into Lupus and joined the chase. They each smelled the truck again, its pungent stench like a lingering cloud of gas passed by a human fond of spicy foods. That the truck could be so inundated with the smell said much about its source's ripeness. Hairy Foot probably hadn't bathed since before any of them were born. Why they hadn't noticed it when in human form, none of them knew.

Storm-Eye turned down a muddy lane, a rusty mailbox marking it as a residence. The ramshackle houses stood closer together here. The area had the look of a rural tenement. Storm-Eye slowed to a halt, and the others stopped with her.

There, she said, pointing her nose down the lane. *Our prey*.

The truck sat parked by the side of a small house with cheap aluminum siding. Tires lay scattered over the front lawn, as if someone had begun some mechanical work and abandoned it long ago.

Julia perked up her ears. *Somebody's laughing inside*.

They all heard it. Mixed sounds of giggling and moaning.

Come, Storm-Eye said, leading them forward, creeping low and quiet down the lane to the truck. The sound of tires on gravel suddenly crackled behind them, and they all scattered into the trees bordering the lane, leading to the forest stretching out behind the house.

Another pickup pulled into the lane but halted as it faced the house. The driver, a young Native American man, stared perplexedly at the truck in the driveway before him. He rolled his own truck slowly forward and stopped, killing the engine. He climbed out of the cab, staring at Hairy Foot's truck as if it were a UFO or some equally strange manifestation that did not belong here.

He walked up the front steps and opened the screen door. It squeaked on its hinges. The laughing from within stopped. The pack members crouched in the brush, waiting to see what would happen.

The man opened the front door and went into the house. A few moments later, they heard a yell.

"Hey! That's my wife! Who the hell are you?"

The back door slammed open and Hairy Foot leapt down the steps, struggling to pull up his pants. He had nothing else on, not even a shirt. He cackled and laughed as he stumbled about, tugging the jeans up his legs.

A Native American woman stuck her head from a nearby window, wearing nothing but a bedsheet. She looked angry. "Get back here, you bastard! You said you weren't afraid of Scott!"

The man who had just entered the house, presumably named Scott, came out the back door and hurled a beer bottle at the fleeing Hairy Foot. It crashed into splinters on his head and he paused for a minute, licking up the foamy spray, along with a few glass shards, before running hell-bent toward his truck.

Storm-Eye leapt out of the woods and intercepted him before he could reach the cab. Hairy Foot skidded to a halt, genuine surprise on his face. "Oh, shit!" he cried. "Hi ho, Silver River Pack!" He turned and bolted for the rear woods.

The wolves ran forward, hurling themselves after the Ragabash.

Scott cried in fright at the sight of the pack and leapt back inside the house, slamming the door behind him. The woman likewise cried out. "Scott! Ohmigod Scott! There's wolves in the yard!"

The pack ignored them. Hairy Foot had reached the woods and was proving himself quite adept at leaping over roots and branches. They each hunkered down and poured on the speed, determined not to lose their prey again.

• • •

John shivered, a four-legged icicle. He felt very little pain anymore. The wound had finally closed, but only after he'd lost a lot of blood. The cold had stolen away all feeling, except for a pervasive numbness. He couldn't even feel his legs moving, but he saw them stepping ever forward. He wondered where they got the will to keep going; he didn't think he had enough energy left to even tell them to stop.

They thumped into something in the snow and he almost stumbled. Only an instinctual shifting of weight kept him balanced and standing on all fours. He looked down. A deer carcass lay before him, its blood on the snow nearly dry. He cried out in relief and dropped his snout to bite into the cold but good meat.

The deer jerked its head away, turning so its eyes met John's. He stopped, shocked. How could it still be alive?

Wendigo, the deer said, speaking the language of the spirits. John did not know that tongue, but somehow understood the being's meaning. *You cannot eat of my flesh. Only those who earn it through sacred hunts may so gain my power. Go, and leave my body whole.*

John stared at the being, torn. His hunger was almost a living thing, tugging at him, bidding him to bite the flesh before him. His mouth watered at the thought and his wolfen instincts battered at his numb mind, bidding him ignore the spirit's command.

I beg of you, oh deer spirit, John said in the wolf tongue, *I am starving. Give me your meat and I shall perform whatever task you demand.*

The deer did not respond. John sniffed and saw that it was truly dead. He whined and backed up a few steps, and then stepped forward again, sniffing at the meat.

If I do not eat soon, I will die. Surely the spirit will understand that and not hold me responsible. But John knew the stories of his people, told to him by his grandmother and the Garou Galliards. Only those who respectfully slay their prey have right to their flesh. To violate the pact made between Garou and the Animal Elder spirits was to curse all Garou to hunger.

John bowed his head and dropped to the ground. *I will respect the spirit's wishes, and so sustain the bonds between my people and the spirits. I will die here, but my people will live on.*

He closed his eyes and felt no more.

When he opened them again, he smelled burning wood and saw light playing off the snow around him. He weakly lifted his head and saw a roaring fire with a spit turning upon it, rolled by the gentle wind. The deer's carcass roasted over it, its steaming fat dripping into the fire, sending sizzling spouts upward. He whined again, the hunger too much to bear.

Eat, a deep, rich voice said.

John did not hesitate. He crawled over to the fire and knocked the spit from its frame. The carcass hit the ground and he tore into it, eagerly devouring its warm, beautiful meat. He did not care who spoke. He only knew that he must eat, and that this was the greatest meal he had ever tasted.

Later, once he had eaten all he could, he sat beside the fire in his human form, warming his hands. Once his mind had thawed and he could think straight again, he looked about him.

"Who are you?" he said. "Who do I have to thank for my meal?"

You earned your own meal, the voice said, seemingly all around him, carried by the wind. *You have passed my test.*

"Test? What am I being tested for? Who are you?"

The wind blew fiercely for a moment, gathering in a whirlwind beyond the fire. It took shape, formed from snow and ice. A great bear stood before John, looking down at him with stern but kind eyes.

I am the North Wind. I am your father.

Chapter Five

Hairy Foot tripped over a log but was immediately up again and running. The momentary pause, however, allowed Storm-Eye to vault over him and land in his path. As he stepped forward again, his foot met her jaws. They clamped down hard.

"Aaawooo!" he cried, falling to the ground. "Let go! Let go! God, it hurts!"

Storm-Eye loosened her grip but did not let go. The rest of the pack appeared and surrounded the Ragabash, who began cursing.

As he did, his shape shifted, melting into something larger. This didn't surprise Storm-Eye, for she expected him to assume the Garou battle form. His final form, however, so shocked her that she lost her grip.

Hairy Foot pulled his foot away and nursed it with his hands, rocking back and forth while gritting his teeth with the pain. "Damn, bitch, that hurt!"

The rest of the pack had also shifted forms, into Crinos, but they stood staring slack jawed at their prey.

"What… what are you?" Julia asked, staring at what appeared to be a half-man, half-wolverine. His short, stubby snout was clearly that of a wolverine, as was his broad-shouldered torso.

Hairy Foot held up his hands for a truce. "Okay, okay, you got me. You bastards are persistent, I'll give you that."

Cries Havoc peered at him as if he couldn't believe his eyes. "But there're no such things as were-wolverines!"

"No, there ain't," Hairy Foot said. "You can call me Kwakwadjec." He stood up and lifted a hairy leg.

A wet trumpeting noise heralded the rank smell that assaulted their noses. Hairy Foot sighed with contentment, as if he'd been holding it for a while.

"Blech!" Carlita cried, spitting as if clearing her mouth might wash away the stench. "You are one ripe asshole. And what's that name supposed to mean, anyway?"

"Mean?" Hairy Foot said, indignantly. "I'm Kwakwadjec!"

"So?" Carlita said. "And I'm Big Sis, who's about to get Pleistocene on your ass if you don't explain where the hell John is!"

"Idiot cubs! Nobody remembers the old ways! I'm Wolverine, you jackasses!"

"What a minute," Julia said. "I get it now! You're a spirit! One of Wendigo's brood! But that doesn't make sense. How can you be running around here physically?"

Hairy Foot scratched his behind with a hairy claw. "Ya-oh-ga, the guardian of the North Wind, lent me some of his power. As long as John North Wind's Son remains in the Umbra, I can stay physical here in this world. And boy did I! That gal was hot!"

Storm-Eye growled. *Bring him back!*

"I can't," Hairy Foot said, shrugging his shoulders. "That's for his father to decide."

● ● ●

John stood up and faced his father. The ice bear towered over him, a pillar of strength, but he did not seem threatening. His eyes looked upon John with appreciation.

"Is this true?" John asked. "I… I always thought my name was a… metaphor. That it meant I had the strength of the north wind. And you… you tell me you're my father?"

I am, the bear said.

"Why did you bring me here? I assume Hairy Foot was doing your bidding. Where is Aurak Moondancer?"

I brought you here to test you, the bear said, dropping to all fours and hunching its shoulders. It was no longer the loving father, but a menacing animal. *A mighty task is set before you, my son. The River Snake has given you a powerful destiny, one that has brought you great glory so far.*

"Uktena? Is that who you mean?"

All that has passed is as nothing to the danger to come. The bear moved forward, its paws like giant trees uprooting themselves. *I love you too much to risk you to such a fate. If you fail, your spirit will not survive.*

"I don't understand," John said, stepping forward himself, to show the bear that he did not fear it. "Is this why you starved me and nearly left me for dead?"

Garou of greater rank than you will fail at the coming doom. It is better for you to have died here than in the enemy's realm, far from your people. But you survived. You bested the cannibal spirit and your own hunger. You held to honor and kept pact with the spirits even at the cost of your own life. You are stronger than even I had dared to hope. I am proud of my son.

John did not know how to reply. His anger grew as he realized he had been used, thrown into a deadly test just so his father could save him from a more dangerous task. He had been tricked by Hairy Foot and separated from his pack, starved and attacked, and refused food, all to appease his father. His father, the North Wind, who knew no physical deprivation or suffering.

And yet, his father had said he was proud of him. Ever since he was a little boy, he had yearned to know who his father was. His grandmother said she did not know him personally, but knew he was a great soldier who had died fighting for others. John thought for years that his dad was some sort of special ops commando, killed in a secret mission defending world freedom. The older he got, the more he knew this to be untrue. His father was likely an alcoholic nobody who knocked his mother up and ran off before she even recovered from some drug-induced haze.

His grandmother refused to believe his mother died a crack addict or whore, but the complete absence of any information about her, except that "she had died bravely," left him with little else to believe. Until after his First Change.

Once he had become Garou, the story was told to him. His mother had died giving him birth, sacrificing herself that he might live. He wept long and hard and asked her spirit to forgive his doubting her bravery, but he still never discovered who his father was.

And yet, here he finally stood, the wind itself claiming to be his dad.

The scar you bear on your shoulder will remind you to strike at your enemy's heart, the bear said, *for that is where he is weakest. Do not forget this, for its truth lies on your skin.* The bear turned to go, looking back over its shoulder at John.

"Wait," John said, stepping forward, hand out, beckoning. "You can't leave now! I… I have so much to ask you!"

I have stayed away from the Gates of the North too long. I must tend the winds. At that, a whirlwind rushed through him, breaking up his form, returning it to snow and ice, scattered on the eddies.

"No!" John cried, falling forward. He clutched his spear and bowed his head. "I finally know you, and you can't stay to speak to me? Am I so pitiful you abandon me again?"

A hand gripped his shoulder. Real flesh, not ice or wind. It squeezed him reassuringly, and he looked up to see a Native American man in his midtwenties, dressed in traditional Kwakiutl garb.

"It's not you, John North Wind's Son," the man said. "You father has great responsibilities, duties he neglected long ago to woo your mom. He can't stay to chat just now. He sent me instead."

John stood up. "Who are you?"

The Indian offered his arm. When John took it, he said, "I'm your godfather, Stutters-at-Cars."

John swallowed, fighting back tears. "But I heard you died. My mother's entire pack, the Thunder's Gift, all died fighting the Wyrm. This is what they told me when I became a Wendigo."

"I am dead. Sort of. I escaped the bonds of death so I could be here, to see you and make sure you're okay. I'm what you might call an ancestor spirit."

"You did this for me?" Tears now streamed down John's face, stinging his cheeks as they froze in the chill wind.

"Hey," Stutters-at-Cars said, "hey now, be strong. Of course I did it for you. I made a promise to your mother before you were born. Pack bonds are the one thing I can't escape, and I have no desire to. I realize being an orphan wasn't easy, but we're Wendigo. We've eaten far more bitter meals than loneliness."

John wiped his tears. "I know. It's just… I haven't really dealt with any of this before. I've always put it in the past."

"If we always live in the past, we will have no future. That is what our tribe needs to learn. This is what you need to teach them." He began walking away from the fire. "Come on, let's go someplace a bit warmer."

John nodded and followed. "Are my packmates all right?"

Stutters-at-Cars smiled. "I think so. They didn't make it into the Umbra, if that's what you mean. They're chasing Hairy Foot down, trying to get some answers."

"Who is that guy, anyway?"

"Let's just say that too many people think us Wendigo are a bunch of humorless soldiers. Our legends, however, are full of trickster tales, some a lot bawdier than any you'll hear about Coyote. Heck, a Ragabash like me thrives on that kind of stuff. How do you think our ancestors got through the cold winters? By staring at each other in silence over the fire? Hell, no. They told lots of jokes."

"Yeah, I've heard some of the stories. The ones about Raven, and even Whiskey Jack. So Hairy Foot really is a Ragabash from the Winter Wolf Sept?"

"No. But don't worry about him or your packmates for now."

John noticed that the winds had died down and the snowfall was lighter. The bitter cold had let up, and he felt normal for the first time since he had entered the Umbra. He noticed a set of animal tracks before them. It seemed that Stutters-at-Cars was following them. He couldn't identity the animal, but he was sure it was some sort of large cat or skunk.

"Whose tracks do we follow?"

"A wolverine's. Follow them and we'll find Hairy Foot, and where he's at, your pack is surely near."

As they continued after the tracks, the snow grew thinner and thinner. Clear patches of ground could be seen here and there, with brown grass poking up out of the wet, melting mantle.

"I've got to warn you about something," Stutters-at-Cars said. "That's what I was sent for. You remember that weird storm that's been haunting the Umbra? The one with all the black birds?"

"How could I forget?"

"Well, it comes from Jo'cllath'mattric's realm."

At the mention of the Wyrm beast's name in the Umbra, John swore he heard the cawing of birds off in the distance, sounds that sent a shiver up his spine even though the cold had left him.

"All those people and things it snatches," Stutters-at-Cars said, "it takes back to its realm, blowing them there like a tornado."

"King Albrecht is trying to find that realm. You're saying that if he follows the storm, he'll get there?"

"No, he'll be torn to shreds. Nothing can easily survive it. Not without help. That's where your father comes in. He's granting you a boon. Think of it as a coming of age present, and an apology for what he put you through. He was mighty impressed with how you handled yourself, especially with that deer. Hell, I would have dug in and had a fine meal. Many people would have starved because of that, not just folk who live on deer way up north, but lots of meat would have gone bad. You piss off one of the Hooved-People and they can start a whole boycott going with all of them. But that wouldn't have mattered to me, not when I was alive. I wasn't too smart that way. But you passed that with flying colors."

John smiled, swelling with pride at the notion of his father's respect. He wondered just how close he could ever get to a spirit who guarded the northern winds, and realized it probably wasn't too close, at least, not in this lifetime. The divide between spirits and humans was too great these days. That they still had trysts with even Garou nowadays was a rare thing. He hadn't heard such a tale in years, and here he was, the product of just such a myth.

"Of course," Stutters-at-Cars said, "it's not just for you. Your father owes a debt to Uktena, your pack totem, and he's calling it in."

"I see. So what is this boon?"

"Your father's spirits, and those who serve all the Gates of the Winds, can navigate the storm and protect people who are carried along by it."

"That's great!" John cried. "Albrecht can lead an army there and we can finally confront Jo'cllath'mattric!"

"That's the idea. But… it's no guarantee. Jo'cllath'mattric is greater than you can imagine, John. It's not a simple raid on a Wyrm caern. It's a war party straight into a monster's maw. You can't let yourself get cocky about this. You earned your father's trust and aid here, but he can't just wave his hand and let the winds take care of everything. Things aren't like they used to be in the old days. The world has forgotten our tribe's spirits, and they can't easily return, especially to a Wyrm realm. That's what us wolf-changers are for. We can go places most spirits can't, because we are flesh and spirit."

"But with his winds, we can at least get there. Our claws and fangs will do the rest."

"That's the spirit! And don't forget that spear of yours. You might want to take a look at it, after all it's been through."

John held up his spear and noticed a layer of ice coating the flint blade. The increasing warmth they now walked through had not even begun to melt it. He chipped at it with his fingers.

"I'd leave that on for now," Stutters-at-Cars said. "Think of it as another boon, this time from the Animal Elders, for your keeping the ancient pact."

"I don't know how to thank you," John said, looking up from his spear.

But Stutters-at-Cars was gone. So were the snow and wind. He stood in a small meadow surrounded by trees, once more in the material world.

Chapter Six

Storm-Eye shook with anger, her hackles raised, her eyes squinted and her lips drawn back to reveal a row of sharp teeth. Her growl grew louder in volume. She was clearly about to lose it to her rage.

"Uh…" Hairy Foot said, taking a step away from the wolf, "can somebody calm her down?"

"Why should we?" Carlita said. "Hell, I'm almost as pissed at you myself. Why shouldn't we all just rage on your ass?"

Hairy Foot stopped and spread his feet, taking a stand. "'Cause you wouldn't like me when I'm angry, girls. And boy, can I get angry…" As he said this, his own eyes sparked with fury and his mouth overflowed with spittle. He began to bark at Storm-Eye, and that was the final trigger. She leapt at him, slamming into his belly and knocking him down. But he was ready for it—his claws dug into her back and began raking furrows from neck to tail.

"Somebody stop them!" Cries Havoc said. "We'll never get John back if we lose him!" He rushed forward and reached for Storm-Eye's pelt to try and yank her from the wolverine's grip. Before his hands could touch her, Hairy Foot began to fade away, like a ghost in the movies when daylight came.

He stopped the attack, seemingly oblivious to the wolf snapping her teeth at his immaterial jaw. "Oh, for crying out loud!" he cried. "Well, it was great while it lasted…" He faded completely from view.

Storm-Eye stopped short and shook her head, as if trying to dry it after a drenching. She looked confusedly about, unable to figure out what just happened.

"He dissolved back into the Umbra," Julia said, "although not by choice. If what he said was right, that means John must be—"

A howl echoed through the woods, from not too far away. They instantly recognized it as John's. They each raised a throat and howled back. John returned their howl, with a note of exaltation and relief, and they began triangulating locations with one another through a series of howls.

Carlita was the first to see him, standing in a small field somewhat less than a mile from where they last saw Hairy Foot. She ran up to him and wrapped her arms around him in a hug. She might have knocked a normal person off his feet with the force of her welcome, but John barely shifted balance to meet it. He hugged her back.

"What the hell happened over there?" Carlita said. "What's this about your father?"

"It was a test," John said. "I passed."

The others came into the clearing and all ran up to him, joining into a group hug. A few weeks ago, such open show of affection would have been awkward for them, but not after the fierce bonding they had in fight after fight across the real world and the Umbra.

John looked up at the sky and the lowering sun. "How many days have I been gone? Has the moot started yet?"

"Days?" Julia said. "It's been about eight hours, at best. We've spent the time chasing down Hairy Foot and trying to beat answers out of him, for what little good that did. He wasn't even Garou! Some sort of wolverine trickster spirit."

John seemed shocked to hear the news about the time. "I wandered for days. I know I did. No way could it have been hours."

"Time works weird in the Umbra," Cries Havoc said. "Whatever realm you were in must operate on different principles of day and night."

"And I'm curious to know just what realm you were in," Julia said. "What the hell happened?"

"Holy Mother of Mary!" Carlita cried, loosening her hug and staring at John's left shoulder and the ragged teeth mark punctures running across it. "Something took a bite out of you! It's amazing you're alive." She delicately pressed the wound with her fingers. "Does it hurt much?"

"Not at all," John said. "Believe it or not, it's fully healed. It won't get any better than that. But there's no loss of function. It doesn't make sense, but I think it has something to do with my besting the beast that did it. Since I won our struggle, its power over even my wound grew less. It's a nice battle scar, though. Something to show off around the fire."

"You're telling me," Cries Havoc said. "That is, you better tell me all about it! There's a great story here. I can't wait to develop it to tell at the moot!"

John looked surprised at that. "So soon? I don't know… this moot isn't about me."

"Don't get humble on us now," Cries Havoc said, "it's not a strong Garou trait. Besides, it seems to me a little story about spiritual victory might really be the thing to cheer the troops, or at least win the respect of all the Theurges there."

John nodded, somewhat embarrassed, although he didn't know why. He'd always wanted a great story of honor, glory and wisdom to tell, and here he had it. It had the added attraction of a mythical birth and parentage. But for some reason, it seemed too private to share with the whole Garou nation. At least, not this soon.

"Look, I'll tell you all about it," John said, "but not here, in the woods at night, when I can tell you guys are cold. Besides, we've got to get to the moot."

"Oh shit," Julia said. "How? We don't have a car."

"Well," Cries Havoc said. "Hairy Foot's car is still there, I bet. It couldn't have been a spirit. He probably stole the thing once he materialized."

"Ugh," Carlita said. "That piece of shit on wheels? Isn't there a better way?"

"We can at least use it to get us to a car hire agency tomorrow morning," Julia said, "in whatever the nearest big city is."

Then we go, Storm-Eye said, eager to get the pack moving again and to the moot before something else could get in their way.

They made their way back through the woods to the small house. Hairy Foot's pickup was still there, but so was the Native human's. It was getting dark by then, so they crept up to the pickup as quietly as they could, each of them in wolf form, except for Carlita, who stayed in human form. She was the designated driver.

The wolves climbed into the rear bed, while Carlita opened the driver's door as quietly as she could. It still let out a loud creak.

A voice came from inside, through an open window. "Shit! That bastard's back! I'm gonna pound him a new one!" The voice grew louder and closer as it spoke, seemingly heading for the back door. But Carlita was already in the truck and boosting it. She knew how to hotwire a car in fifteen seconds. She had the pickup engine revving in eight.

"Hey!" the young Native American yelled, coming out the back door with a baseball bat, ready to swing it. He halted when he saw Carlita throwing the car into reverse, and his jaw dropped when he saw the wolf pack in the rear bed. The truck shot back down the lane, fishtailing onto the front lawn just before it hit the other pickup. Carlita then threw it into gear and shot past the parked car and onto the main road, heading in a direction John had earlier told her probably led to some sort of town center. She heard no more from the man in the driveway, who was probably too confused to figure out what to tell the cops.

A few blocks away, she pulled over, and Julia and Cries Havoc joined her in the front cab, taking human form again. Julia cranked the heater up. After about ten minutes of arguing directions as they drove, they finally wound up at an all-night diner.

Gathered in a rear booth in a corner of the diner, John told them about his father's test.

"That's damn intense," Carlita said, stuffing her face with steak and eggs. "You Wendigo guys are serious shit."

"I can't believe our luck about the wind spirits," Julia said. "It's almost like a puzzle where all the pieces fall together at the right moments. First the prophecy and now your father's appearance, giving us reinforcements just when we need them."

"They may not be enough," John said. "The spirits can get us there, but they won't be able to help us take down whatever's in that realm. Besides, it all seems too little too late to me. If the spirits could really help here, surely others would have stepped in. Why hasn't the Shadow Lord's Grandfather Thunder dealt with the storm? He's supposedly king of all storms."

"Not Wyrm storms," Storm-Eye said, eating ham in her human form. "We do not know what power constrains the totems. That they help us at all is a powerful sign. Their ways are old and the earth no longer sustains them."

Everyone was quiet for a while after that, eating and thinking about how much worse things were probably going to get before they got better.

"So what's up with this Hairy Foot guy, anyway?" Carlita said. "He didn't seem at all like a Wendigo spirit. They're regal, stoic and cold. This guy smelled and was a real ass."

John smiled. "I don't know a lot of the stories, but I do know that Wolverine was one of the crudest tricksters in any Indian tale. They mainly knew about him in the northeastern part of Canada. I guess he used to roam there. Labrador, places like that. He did keep the people laughing most of the time, though. He mainly caused trouble with other spirits rather than humans, but he could certainly mess things up for everybody now and then. Of course, they always learned from the mistakes. Like Ragabash, tricksters have their sacred roles."

"Sacred?" Julia said, scrunching up her nose. "More like stench ridden. I mean, I like a good joke as well as the next, but bodily emissions humor is so grammar school."

"Try living in a frozen world for nine months out of the year," John said, "stuck in dark, seal-fat smelling shelters. If you can't laugh at your neighbor's cruder acts, you're probably ready to kill them."

"Oh, I suppose that's true," Julia said. "But that doesn't excuse Quackwaddle, or whatever his name was. I think I figured out how he materialized. He must have used his own power at first, but once he'd delivered you to that realm, your father lent him enough power to materialize again as long as he wanted to—or until you returned."

John nodded. It sounded as good a theory as any. When the pack had eaten its fill of diner food and coffee, it paid for the meal with Julia's credit card and walked back out to the truck.

"Hey," Carlita said, "isn't there a casino or something here on the reservation? We could try to make some money so Julia doesn't have to always pay for everything."

"How's gambling going to make us money?" Julia said. "Those casinos are rigged to win money from us."

"I think there is a casino around here," John said. "But I don't know if it's still open. All sorts of legal problems with the state, I heard, which doesn't like the idea of Indians making more money than they. The Mohawk kids used to run cigarettes over the Canadian border, fighting it out with mafia types who wanted a monopoly on the biz. The casino gave them safer employment, until it was shut down. The kids went back to smuggling and getting shot at. I don't know if the issue was ever resolved or if the casino's back up and running."

"I don't want to waste any more time," Cries Havoc said. "We need to get to Vermont for the moot."

"And get a real car," Julia said, staring at the pickup as if she were reluctant to get back in it. "The sooner we find a car hire, the better."

They got back into the car and drove to the nearest city. Gas station attendants directed them to Utica, and they found a rental car agency there easily enough. By the following evening, they were more comfortably stretched out in a Ford Explorer SUV.

"I thought these things destroyed the environment," Cries Havoc said. "Should we really be contributing to gasoline waste by driving it?"

"Oh, and you think that pickup was spitting out clean emissions?" Julia retorted from behind the wheel. "We've got a moot to get to. Once we take care of the Wyrm, then we can worry about CAFE standards in vehicles."

They drove in silence for a while, until Carlita reached up past the front seats to turn on the radio. After flipping dials, she settled on a station playing rap music. She sat back and rolled her shoulders to the rhythm. Julia rolled her eyes.

"Look," John said, "I realize now that I have to take up this final leg of the quest against Jo'cllath'mattric. None of you have to follow me. You can each go home and take a well deserved rest."

"Buzz killer," Carlita said, trying to tune him out and concentrate on the music. Nobody else said anything. It was as if they hadn't heard John.

"Somebody answer me," John said. "You can't all want to actually do this thing. I'm telling you you don't have to anymore."

"Did somebody hear something?" Julia said. "Like the buzzing of a very annoying fly?"

"Ignore it," Cries Havoc said. "It's just the voice of a twisted conscience."

"But…" John began to say.

Quiet, Storm-Eye said, lying in the back in her Lupus form, low enough so passing cars couldn't see her. *We have clearly made a choice. No more words.*

John nodded. He didn't want his packmates to risk themselves in what was surely the most dangerous part of this whole prophecy yet, but he was proud that they wouldn't even consider discussing the possibilities otherwise.

As he sat back, wondering what lay ahead of him, he realized just how tired he was. His second wind, so to speak, had run out, and he suddenly felt exhausted. He closed his eyes and was asleep within minutes.

He dreamed that he was back in the snow, by the fire with the deer. The fire had almost gone out, mere embers smoldering for only a little while longer. He heard something on the wind, a cawing sound, as of a flock of birds. Suddenly fearful, he crouched down low and threw snow onto the remains of the fire, extinguishing the last of it.

A flock of black birds appeared in the sky on the horizon, coming in his direction, cawing madly. He heard a soft thumping in the snow grow louder and noticed a white winter hare rushing by, fleeing the cloud of birds. It saw him out of the corner of its eye and stopped, speaking: *Son of the Wind, you must seek shelter.* It then bounded away and was lost in the snowscape.

John leapt up and ran, heading in the direction the rabbit had gone. Falling snow already covered its tracks. He saw dark shapes ahead, unmoving, and realized they were trees. He plunged into the pine forest with relief, just as the cawing came nearly over his head. He heard the birds flapping back and forth above the trees, as if confused by having lost their prey.

He ducked under a tree and snuggled up tight against its trunk, hoping the pine needle branches would hide him. He did not understand what made him so afraid, but he felt like the birds exuded it, the pall of fear. His instincts told him to hide, but his mind now wondered at that. Were his instincts false? Should he not face his enemy squarely?

A loud screeching noise appeared near his face, and he saw one of the birds land on a branch. It stared right at him. Before he could think, he thrust his spear into its breast. The bird flapped its wings in surprise, staring at the spit, and then flopped over, dead.

The rest of the flock moved on, its cawing growing weak with the distance. When he heard them no more, he crept from under the tree and placed his spear point on the ground. He slid the carcass off the shaft with his foot. It left a trail of black blood on the wood.

He suddenly felt dizzy and almost fell, but he leaned against the tree to catch his balance. He noticed a weight on his left shoulder and looked to see another bird, this one sucking on his blood from a now-open wound.

He swatted at it, but it refused to move. He grew weaker with every second, and tried to remember what to do. He could not even remember his name or why he was here.

A voice spoke from the base of the tree. The hare huddled there, shaking its head: *Fool. You forgot what your father told you, and you have wasted the gift of the Animal Elders.*

He wanted to respond, to cry out for his father's help, but he could not even remember who his father was. The bird cawed contentedly as it continued feasting on his shoulder.

John started awake as Carlita shook his shoulder.

"Whoa!" she said, removing her hand as if he were about to bite it. "That must've been some nightmare. Wake up, man. We're almost there. Cries Havoc wants to know if you want anything while we gas up here."

John looked around and saw that they were stopped at a gas station. It was pitch black outside. Cries Havoc stood by the front door, looking concerned. "You look like you've seen a ghost."

"Uh... bad dream is all," John said. "I guess days of deprivation in the Umbra don't heal so quick in the real world. Yeah, uh, get me some water, will you? And maybe some jerky?"

"Sure thing," Cries Havoc said, heading for the food mart within the gas station.

Storm-Eye placed her paws on the back seat, by John and Carlita's shoulders. *You are safe here*, she said. *We will not lose you again.*

"Thanks," John said. "I believe you."

When Julia and Cries Havoc came back, they handed out a bunch of drinks and munchies.

"Not far now," Julia said. "We just entered Vermont. We'll probably get there just as dawn hits."

The rest of the trip was spent in silence, except for the chewing, munching and gulping noises as they devoured their snacks. John wondered at their appetites. They'd had a large meal only a few hours ago and here they were eating again. He suspected that their bodies, grown used to long periods without food, had decided to stock up while it was plentiful.

A few hours later, as a pale light appeared on the horizon, they pulled up into the driveway of the Morningkill Estate. That's what the sign read, something to satisfy humans about the occupants of the vast acreage. Garou knew better; to them, it was the court of the North American Silver Fang king.

At the gates, Julia pulled up next to a speaker post. She froze before her hand could hit the window button. A line of faces had appeared peering over the wall, pointing rifles straight at them. The gates opened just wide enough to allow a group of five men and women out, each dressed in what looked like SWAT uniforms.

They fanned out around the car and pointed guns at the windows. One of them held a magazine of bullets in her left hand, waving it to get their attention and pointing with her index finger to the lead bullet. They could all see it was silver.

"State your names and business," one of them said, his gun barrel thumping against Julia's half-open window.

"This don't look good," Carlita said.

Chapter Seven

"Names and business," the guard repeated, this time leveling his gun at Julia.

She held up her hands and slowly moved her left hand to the window control button. The guard didn't respond negatively, so she pressed the switch and rolled down the driver's side window.

"My name is Julia Spencer, and we're here to see…" she tried to remember King Albrecht's real name, in case they had pulled into the wrong driveway. She didn't want to start babbling Garou secrets around to ordinary, everyday security guards. The silver bullets, though, did seem to show they had the right place—or that it had been taken over by a paramilitary squad of werewolf hunters. "We're here to see Jonas Albrecht."

The guard nodded. "Why?"

"He invited us. We just saw him at the Finger Lakes."

The other guards circled the car, peering in at the pack members, who looked back at them nervously, except for Carlita, who scowled. Storm-Eye scrunched down in the back, trying to look more like a family dog than a wolf.

John whispered to the rest of them. "See their arm patches? That picture looks like a dragon with a sword stuck through it. I think it's some sort of House Wyrmfoe symbol. That's Albrecht's house. These guys have to be Silver Fangs."

"Your pack name?" the guard said.

Julia let out a sigh. Definite confirmation that these people were in the know. "The Silver River Pack. And who are you?"

"Court security." He lowered his weapon and gestured with a free hand toward the driveway. "Follow the road to the parking lot at the end. You will be directed to a space. Park only in that space. Do not stop the car until then, and do not get out of the car unless bid to do so by security. Do you understand?"

"Yes," Julia said. "But why? I've never seen anything like this before. What's the high security for?"

"All will be explained inside. Move along." The guard waved his gun, a gesture for them to quit talking and move on through. The iron gates swung open, clearly given a signal from one of the guards. All this time, the other guards had kept their guns leveled at the pack. As Julia eased the car forward down the winding driveway, the guards followed them through onto the grounds, then took up places along the wall again.

"Holy shit," Carlita said. "You'd think this was the goddamn UN or something. What the fuck's going on? It's just a moot, isn't it?"

"Obviously, something's happened since we last talked to Albrecht," Cries Havoc said. "Some breach of caern security that's got them all on high alert."

"You think those guys were Garou or Kinfolk?" Carlita asked.

"I don't know. Maybe a mix of both," Cries Havoc said.

Look there, Storm-Eye said, her eyes following something in the woods that lined the driveway. The others looked but didn't see anything except passing trees.

"What is it?" John North Wind's Son asked.

More security. Wolves. They hide well.

"Well, here's the parking lot," Julia said. They had reached the end of the drive, which swept around in front of a mansion and culminated in a large parking lot. There were other cars there, but the lot was no-where near full. A security guard, this one a woman dressed in a black suit, directed them toward an empty space. She held a walkie-talkie in her hand.

"This one looks more like Secret Service than those SWAT guys at the gate," Carlita said.

After Julia brought the car to a halt and killed the engine, the suited woman came up to her window.

"Greetings, Silver River Pack. I apologize for the cold welcome. All will be explained at the court. If you'll follow the stone path around the mansion to the open field, you will see the throne. The court awaits you there."

"Thank you," Julia said, getting out of the car. "Is there any imminent danger? Should we be looking out for anything in particular?"

"The incursion has been neutralized. The security is simply to ensure that no further incursions interrupt the moot." She nodded curtly and went to stand in the middle of the lot, waiting for more cars to arrive.

"Well, I guess she said all she had to say," Cries Havoc said. "We're to proceed on our own, I suppose."

"Come on," Julia said. "I want to find out what happened."

The pack followed the directions it had been given, walking on a path of stones, each flat, smooth stone separated by a wide swath of grass. It led the group around the large, New England mansion. As they turned the final corner, they saw a large field.

"Whoa," Carlita said. "When they say 'court,' they mean it."

Tents were lined up in rows surrounding a huge oak tree, ancient enough to have been old when English colonists first arrived here. Tables and chairs underneath the tarps made it clear that these were where guests would sit during the moot. Only household retainers moved among them now, placing plates, cups and silverware at each setting. It looked like it would be a feast also.

At the base of the oak, a throne had been carved into the bole, the Silver Fang pictogram painted clearly above it. King Albrecht sat there—lounged there, really—talking to a well-dressed gentleman with a clipboard. He looked up and saw the pack. He smiled and waved it over.

"Now, that's not something you see everyday," Carlita whispered to the others as they approached the throne. "It's sorta like that John Goodman movie, *King Ralph*."

"What do you mean?" Julia said. "Albrecht's not some distant hick relative suddenly made heir to the throne. He wears the Silver Crown, for Gaia's sake."

"Yeah, but look at him: blue jeans, Doc Martens. Everybody else here's in finery. Sort of a funny contrast, don't you think?"

"A very American one, I suppose," Julia said. She gestured for Carlita to quiet down as they reached the bole of the tree. The well-dressed gentleman next to Albrecht, who Julia surmised was some caern official, examined them with an upraised eyebrow but said nothing. "Greetings, King Albrecht," she said, offering her hand to the king. "I hope we are not too late."

"You're early," Albrecht said, standing and taking her hand gently. Regardless of his brusque look, he knew his manners. "The moot starts tomorrow night. Did you have any trouble up north, with the Wendigo? It looks like Aurak Moondancer is coming, so whatever you did, it sure helped."

The pack members looked at one another, each wondering what to say. John spoke. "We did not meet with Aurak. He hadn't summoned us at all. The spirits called. Our journey became a test of my worth."

Albrecht was silent for a moment, looking them all over. "Spirits, huh? Yeah, I see that huge scar on your shoulder now. I don't remember that being there when I saw you last. Strange times. What did they want from you?"

"To know that I could carry my duty until the end."

"Duty? You mean this Jo'cllath'mattric thing? I think you guys have proven your worth in this many times over. The spirits weren't convinced?"

"My father had to be convinced for himself."

"Yeah? Who's your father that he'd get the spirits involved in this? Why didn't he just address you himself? Or was this some sort of Wendigo ritual thing?"

"My father…" John paused, unsure how to say it. "He is the North Wind. He summoned me to task."

Albrecht just looked at John, not saying anything. He seemed to approve, though, because a grin slowly widened on his face. "You guys are something else. Really. I think I now understand our little incursion earlier."

"What happened?" Cries Havoc asked. "Security's so tight, they wouldn't tell us anything about it."

"I think I can get them to stand down some now. We had a Penumbral incursion. A bunch of spirits shaking things up, blowing things around like a storm. Evan was convinced they were wind spirits, but we all assumed it had something to do with the Umbral storm. Warders set off into the Umbra to find out what it was about, but they couldn't find any clues. For all we could tell, a bunch of spirits flew in, took a look around and flew out again. No explanation. What you said about the North Wind, though, that makes me wonder if this isn't tied in somehow."

"My father swore to help us travel through the Umbral storm," John said, "to reach Jo'cllath'mattric's lair."

"You're shitting me!" Albrecht said, stepping away from the throne as if shedding its formality. "That's a major development. Solves a whole load of problems. Hell, yeah, that'll look real good for the Theurges when they get here, too. But why would a bunch of wind spirits show up here, and then just leave?"

"I don't know. Maybe they were making sure the place was safe for me. Or readying themselves to aid us later."

"I want to know everything that happened with you and your father. Evan's going to want to hear this, too. We'll wait till he gets back from patrolling the bawn. Antonine wasn't kidding when he opened his mouth back there at the Anvil-Klaiven. The Third Pack is proving itself to be quite pivotal. You guys are going to have eyes on you for the rest of your careers."

Julia blushed, while Carlita smiled and put a swagger in her stance. "Damn straight," Carlita said. "We're getting more than our fifteen minutes."

"We haven't even told you about Jo'cllath'mattric's real name yet," Cries Havoc said.

Albrecht's eyebrows shot up and he stared at the metis as if he had just announced he were a long-lost Garou hero. "Its name? How did you get that?"

"From one of the freed Lore Banes," Cries Havoc said. "It's an odd name, and I'm not sure I should say it freely. I guess I could whisper it."

"No, not just yet," Albrecht said. "I want you to tell it to Loba. She's been doing some spirit research on this thing. It might do a world of good for her. It looks like you've brought yet another zinger for the moot. I'm officially giving up being surprised at your resourcefulness. With as many bull's-eyes as you guys have hit, it's going to be hard for you to keep topping your act. Feel free to go on into the mansion. Evan and Mari set a guest room aside for you. Crash out for a while. This moot's going to go on all night tomorrow."

"Thanks," Carlita said. "We are pretty tired."

"Just ask anyone in there about the room; they'll point you the way." Albrecht waved them on and turned back to continue his discussion with the gentleman, perhaps arranging the logistics of the moot.

The pack walked to the mansion and entered through the wide-open rear doors. A butler-type Kinfolk immediately came to usher them to their room. It was on the second story, with four beds and a couch. Storm-Eye immediately curled up on the floor under the window, while the others each staked out a bed of their own. They took turns using the adjoining bathroom and shower and were soon dozing away even though sunlight peeked through the drawn curtains.

• • •

A hand gently shook John North Wind's Son awake. He opened his eyes and saw Evan standing by his bed, his finger placed over his mouth in the traditional "shhh, be quiet" gesture. John nodded and sat up, looking around. His packmates were still asleep. Carlita snored. By the lack of light coming from the cracks in the curtains, he realized it must be after dark.

Evan gestured for him to follow and left the room. He stood up, grasped his spear from the bedside table and followed. Once in the hall, he quietly closed the door behind him. Evan waited by the stairs.

"I tried to let you sleep awhile," Evan said. "But curiosity got the best of me. I have to know what happened."

John smiled, glad to have a powerful story to tell his former mentor. "It'll take me a while to tell it right. Are you sure you don't want to wait till the others are around? They've got their own part to tell."

"I want to hear them tell it, too, but just give me the gist of it. Albrecht is expecting you to tell the whole thing at the moot, to show the Theurges that the spirits are with us." He began to walk down the stairs, toward the kitchen. "I've been looking for signs of the spirits that swept through here, and they were definitely wind spirits. When I heard about your experience, it only cemented it for me. I think they're still out there, nearby in the Umbra, keeping a watch over the caern, but they don't want to interact with us. At least, not yet. Maybe they're waiting for Aurak to arrive."

"I guess he does have some role to play in this," John said, following along, his stomach rumbling as he caught the scent of roasted meat from the kitchen. "I was led to believe, though, that Hairy Foot had just used his name without permission."

"He may not have known about Hairy Foot, but your father may have alerted him afterward. If he's going to let his wind spirits help us out, somebody's got to direct them. You're not a Theurge, John, regardless of this incredible lineage you've discovered. I think Aurak is coming at the spirits' bidding, but he'll be the one bidding them once we set out."

"That makes perfect sense," John said, entering into the kitchen after Evan. It was a huge room, obviously designed to feed large dinner parties. Apparently, dinner that evening had already taken place. Evan grabbed some bowls from a cabinet and handed them both to John.

"Dig into that stew for us there. I'll get us some bread. The others ate already. Most of the solid food is reserved for tomorrow night."

John went to the stew pot and pulled out a ladle heaped with meat and vegetables swimming in a thick, brown broth. He poured it into the bowls and joined Evan at the table, offering him one of them. He thanked John and slid a loaf of French bread at him, along with a butter tray.

"Man," John said. "I didn't realize how much I miss downtime until I actually get some of it. You forget how nice it is to just sit down and eat a simple meal, with no Banes biting at your heels."

"Yeah," Evan said, "it's easy to forget when times are slow. But once the shit hits the fan, life's little pleasures seem all the more important."

They ate in silence for a while. John relished the meaty stew and fresh-baked bread, chewing each bite slowly. He wasn't as hungry as he'd been yesterday, but he really enjoyed tasting each bite this time, when there was no rush for him to fill his empty stomach or finish quickly.

"So," Evan said. "The North Wind, huh? How cool is that? Uh, no pun intended. What did he look like?"

"At first, he was just an icy whirlwind," John said. "I could only see him because of the snow he kicked up. But then he used the snow to form himself a body, so I could actually interact with him. It was a large bear, like what a prehistoric cave bear probably looked like. Except made out of snow."

"Makes sense. One of the North Wind's images in Garou myth is Ya-oh-gah, the bear that guards the Gates of the Winds to the north. That's a powerful destiny you've got there, John. I knew there was something different about you when I found you after your Change, but I had no idea it was so… legendary."

"That's up to me to earn, I guess. Just having a spirit for a father doesn't give me special renown. If anything, people are going to expect more out of me now, and judge me by a higher standard. I don't know if I'm ready for that."

"Nonsense. The past weeks have proven your status. Your pack's heroism in Hungary is becoming known, and your role in discovering the lore spirits is also on everybody's lips. You'll stand up well to whatever is expected of you."

"I hope so."

They sat a while longer, just eating and not talking. The kitchen door opened and Mari Cabrah came through.

"I thought I'd find you here," she said to Evan. "Hello, John North Wind's Son. I hear you're behind that little storm we had earlier."

John frowned. "I didn't cause it. It's just that my father, well, he's sent spirits to help us. I guess no one was here to guide them properly. Evan's not a Theurge."

"And I'm not a Wendigo," Mari said. "Otherwise, I would have been in the forefront of the investigation."

"Hey," Evan said. "I specifically kept you out of it. You're still weak, Mari. Just admit it and save us all the nightmare of convincing you out of doing foolish things before you're ready to handle the consequences."

Mari just grimaced at him. "That'll be the day. I'm perfectly capable of handling myself. I may not be up to full speed yet, but I'm still more than a match for most Garou."

Evan sighed and took another sip of stew. John smiled and did the same, hoping not to be drawn into the debate.

"I came here to tell you that your tribemate just arrived," Mari said. "That Aurak Moondancer elder is about to exit the Moon Bridge."

Evan looked at John. "I guess this is when we find out if our theories are correct. Come on, let's go meet him. He's been around a long time and knows an awful lot. Even if he wasn't somehow involved in this affair, he'd be worth meeting."

John nodded and picked up his spear. "Which way do we go?"

"Follow me," Evan said and stood up and headed out the door, but then stopped and turned to look at Mari, who had taken his seat. "Make sure you eat, Mari. You need to get back your strength, and I don't want to hear anything about you not having an appetite."

She just waved at him annoyingly and looked away. He shook his head, but with a smile on his face, and opened the door, gesturing for John to proceed him. He then led John out the back door and across the field to a small grove hidden from the mansion's sight.

A young Theurge stood there, concentrating on something only he could see. Two security guards stood nearby, their guns slung down but ready to bear at a moment's notice. A few minutes later, a gleaming, silvery radiance filled the grove, sparkling off the birch bark around them. A spiraling hole of light appeared in the air, and shadowy figures moved within it, walking forward. As they came, their features grew sharper, as if they gained form the closer they got.

The lead figure was an old Native American man dressed in ancient style regalia, his long gray hair tied into braids that ran down either side of his face. He clutched a walking stick hung with feathers and beads, and he clearly needed its support to walk. But his eyes were sharp and met John's before he had even left the Moon Bridge; they seemed to size up the young Wendigo. The old man nodded as he stepped off the bridge, followed by three Wendigo companions, all of them clearly warriors, two male, one female. The glowing light waned and went out, and the grove was still and dark.

"Greetings, Aurak Moondancer," Evan said. "Welcome to the North Country Protectorate and throne of the Silver Fang king."

Aurak approached Evan and nodded to him. "I know you, Evan Heals-the-Past. You bring honor to our people in the eyes of the other tribes."

"Thank you, lorekeeper," Evan said, and motioned to John. "This is John North Wind's Son, whose name is no lie. I believe you know something of him."

Aurak turned to face John and met his eyes again, as if he were looking for some sign deep within them, seeing past John himself toward some symbol or image that hid within him. "I do indeed. Two nights ago, his name was unknown to me, although some in our sept had heard of his deeds. My dreams, however, speak of his father. I have been asked by the winds of the north to guide them in aiding this boy."

"I am glad to hear it," Evan said. "This is an incredible help to us."

Aurak looked away from them both and marched out of the grove. "We shall see, young one. Before I do what I have been asked, this boy must prove his right to such help."

"Prove?" Evan asked, following behind him, looking annoyed. "Is this the will of the spirits?"

"No. It is my will," he said, stopping to look at Evan. "If I did everything the spirits asked without judgment, I would be dead many times over. Do not think that just because a spirit asks for something that you should give it. Was there not a trickster feigning power in my name? A wolverine spirit at that! I respect my spirit brethren, but I keep my own council. I will do as the spirits say, but only if this boy's tale proves worthy of their request."

Evan shot John a worried look. The last thing they needed was to lose Aurak's favor. The success of the entire moot might depend upon it.

Aurak turned to look at John, gripping his staff tightly. "I know not what deed you have done to send the spirits to me, but tomorrow you will reveal it." He turned and walked away, toward the mansion, his warrior entourage following close behind.

Evan looked at John. "I think you'd best wake the others. Cries Havoc is going to have to practice some tale telling. He's got quite a chilly audience."

John leaned on his spear, looking up at the sky. "Bad pun. It looks like I'm going to have to start living up to those high expectations pretty quickly. I just hope there's a good wind at my back."

Chapter Eight

Albrecht convened the moot at sundown the following evening. All that day, Garou had arrived in small groups, Theurges with their pack members or entourages. They came mainly by Moon Bridge, but some arrived by car. Others slipped onto the grounds from the Penumbra, after confronting the Caern Warders who patrolled there. They came by moon path from caerns across the Northeast. At least one member of most of the Twelve Tribes was present. Only the Silent Striders were absent, for the Striders had few representatives in the region. Antonine Teardrop also could not return from his own journey in time to make the moot, so the Stargazers—no longer full participants in the Garou Nation—also remained unrepresented.

The Silver River Pack, minus Cries Havoc, wandered about the grounds, looking to see whom they recognized among the eminent Garou. From the Black Furies, there was Nadya Zenobia, the healer who first tended Mari in her sickness. They were all pleased to see Mother Larissa again, from the New York City Bone Gnawers. Pearl River represented the Children of Gaia; she had sat next to the pack at the Finger Lakes caern when Albrecht first announced the moot. The pack did not know the strange and unnerving Theurge she brought with her. She called him Wyrdbwg, of the Fianna; he acted like he didn't understand English, and his mind seemed to be roaming elsewhere, but the reverence the other Garou displayed toward him spoke of his power.

They also did not know Gnarled Fingers, the scary runecaster of the Get of Fenris, or the cold and intimidating Sylvan-Ivanovich-Sylvan of the Shadow Lords, sharp in her expensive suit and ever surrounded by an entourage of what looked like Mafioso thugs. Five Paws, a Theurge of the Red Talons, sulked well away from the homids, roaming the edge of the bawn with his wolf pack until the time of the moot drew nearer.

The Glass Walker Theurge representative was typically everything you would not expect in a shaman. Kleon Winston wore modern, New York City street clothes and had an easy, sociable manner. Also kind to the pack was Robert Kinsolver, from the Uktena, a Native American from the Tuscarora Reservation near Niagara Falls. He was eager to meet John North Wind's Son and told them all how he admired the tale of their pack so far.

Loba Carcassone represented the Silver Fangs, a gruff woman in her fifties or sixties who had gained much renown by exposing a Wyrm plot hiding under everybody's noses for years. She still made it her job to protect children harmed by such conspiracies. When she met the pack, she drew Cries Havoc off with her, trying to find out everything she could about Jo'cllath'mattric's true name. She then left to finish her own preparations, which she claimed had something to do with summoning a spirit.

The Silver Fangs did very well at accommodating the fractious group, keeping them separated for the most part until the moot itself began that evening, at which point they were all given seats under the tents, each facing the throne and a small platform that had been erected next to it, where the speakers would stand to address the gathered shamans. The first speaker was, of course, King Albrecht. His packmates, Evan and Mari, sat behind him, near to the throne.

"First off, I want to thank you all for coming here under such short notice," Albrecht said. "I think your presence shows how seriously you take this threat. Europe has been pretty ravaged by it. We've gotten off easy. For now. That won't last. We have to take action, to hunt down this Wyrm creature from the past and kill it before it can manifest and destroy everything we love best, namely, the world.

"While I was over in Europe, we discovered some important things about old Jo'cllath'mattric. I'm sure you've all heard about him. The stories about the Anvil-Klaiven conclave have been all over. Basically, this creature is something real old. So old, nobody remembered it. At least, not at first. You see, it devours memories. That's how it hides itself. Even its own servants only call it the Forgotten Son."

There was a snort of derision in the audience.

"Sylvan-Ivanovich-Sylvan," Albrecht said, addressing the source of the interruption. "Figures you'd be the first to speak. Something on your mind?"

"We've heard the stories of the Silver River Pack's journey into Bosnia and how they faced memory eaters," the severe Shadow Lord woman said. "This is nothing new."

"Except for one thing. Thanks to one of the lies that bastard Arkady used to trick his own people, and some information others brought to the table, we were able to locate the caern where the Dancers were going to free Jo'cllath and stop them."

Sylvan harrumphed but said no more.

"Tell me," Nadya Zenobia said, "why is it that this creature eats memories? What is its story?"

"Glad you asked," Albrecht said. "And you asked exactly the right question. 'Story.' That's what it's all about. You see, there were once a bunch of lore spirits, tasked with remembering all the stories of the world. They *were* stories, living stories. But then things went bad. The Wyrm turned. Jo'cllath'mattric was some sort of balance spirit. It couldn't deal with the horror of what happened to the Wyrm, so it did what a lot of us do all the time: it tried to repress the whole thing, to forget the bad stuff. Like a kid sticking his fingers in his ears, shutting his eyes and blathering to shut out what he doesn't want to hear. Like the Wyrm, it went mad."

"So it not only forgot what it was, it tried to make others forget what it was?" Kleon Winston, the Glass Walker Theurge, said. "Excuse me for saying it, but isn't this all just a little too Freudian?"

"Foolishness is what it is," Gnarled Fingers, the Get of Fenris Theurge, said. "How do you know these things? Because a Fang traitor said so?"

"The background actually came from Third Pack from the Anvil-Klaiven prophecy." Albrecht indicated the Silver River Pack as he said this. All eyes shifted to them. The packmates simply kept their eyes on Albrecht. "And a whole lot of supporting evidence has been dug up lately. Thanks to them, we know about the lore spirits. Once freed, they've told us all sorts of lost stuff."

The assembled Garou returned their attention to King Albrecht. "You see, one of Jo'cllath'mattric's defense mechanisms is the Lore Bane. These bat-vulture things suck parts of a person's spirit away, taking memories of his life with it. The thing we didn't know until recently, thanks to Cries Havoc here, is that the Lore Banes were made up of captured lore spirits, tangled and tied together so tightly no one could see them past the Bane wings and feathers."

"This sounds incredible," Robert Kinsolver said. "I would think that my people, the Uktena, would have known about these things."

"Nobody knew about these things until recently. They seem to have been dormant until Jo'cllath'mattric's binding rites grew weak. He then sent them out to scour the world of memories, to bring back to his realm. He somehow gains sustenance from them. At least, that's what I suspect. He grows more powerful with every stolen story."

"You say you stopped the summoning," Sylvan-Ivanovich-Sylvan said, "then why are we here?"

Albrecht took a moment to swallow back his rising rage. "This thing is still out there, somewhere in a spirit realm, and as far as we can tell the wards that were holding it back are either broken are breaking. We stopped the Dancers from summoning it, but if we just sit back it'll get free soon enough. Then we'll all be hip deep in Lore Banes."

"If such spirits are real," the Shadow Lord spat back, "then show one to us. As one who can see the Spirit World, I only believe what is before my eyes. Rumors are just that, rumors."

Cries Havoc groaned, low enough for only his pack to hear. "I didn't think about this. Lots of these guys want any excuse possible to avoid helping Albrecht. We should have brought a spirit back with us from England."

"Can't think of everything," Carlita said. "Let it play how it plays."

Albrecht smiled. "Well, I would have hoped that the fact that your own tribemate Margrave Konietzko supports the idea would have been enough to convince you, but I do have more to say on the subject."

He motioned to Loba Carcassone, who stood from her seat and took the stage. The silver-haired woman looked tired, as if she had been through some sort of recent ordeal. She pulled a book from her satchel, an old, leather-bound tome, looking like something from the early nineteenth century or older. She held it up for all to see.

"This is the *Book of Thrones*," she said. "It's an ancient Silver Fang tome that has been in our library for generations. It was once used by Theurges to record the names, offices, titles and ranks of spirits from the Umbral courts so that Silver Fang diplomats would know how to properly address them."

"Oh, good God," Wyrdbwg said. The pack members looked at him, startled. He'd feigned not knowing English earlier. His accent, however, sounded very Welsh. "Can't you Silver Fangs ever just let spirits be what they be? Do you always have to assign rank and title to everything? I bet you've got ranks and heraldic crests for these chairs we're sitting on!"

Laughter rose up from the gathered Theurges, but it seemed good natured. Even Loba smiled.

"This book only ranks those spirits who claimed such ranks," Loba said, "and who seemed to deserve them. I show it to you now because I used it for a ritual this very day. I summoned a lore spirit, one of those recently freed in Europe, and bound him into this book so that he might tell his tale to you today."

The Theurges murmured to themselves and nodded, seemingly impressed by Loba's forethought.

"The missing key I needed to gain its aid came from the Silver River Pack." Once again, all eyes were on the pack, until Loba again. "You will understand the value of it soon enough. If no one has any objections, I will release it. We will all then be engulfed in its story. It's sort of like virtual reality." She stopped and reconsidered her choice of metaphor. Many of the Garou there didn't understand the term. "You will live the story as if you were there, an observer who can watch but can't participate."

She looked at the crowd and waited to see if anyone had anything to add, but they were all clearly impatient for her to begin. "All right. Here we go." She opened the book and read from a page toward the end. "In the olden days, when the world knew not the horrors it has since birthed…"

As she spoke, the stage faded away and a new landscape appeared, a primeval forest. It seemed to everyone there that she, and only she alone, were in this landscape by herself, watching. The words came not so much as sounds but *knowings*, images and thoughts that occurred to their minds as if they themselves witnessed or thought them…

• • •

The mighty, plumed dragon soared in the sky, its shadow below sweeping over the forest, ever following behind but always managing to keep up. The animals of the woods looked up in awe when they saw the majestic beast, and they cried out to it, hoping it would answer their call and come to hear their plea, for all knew it to be a good judge and noble mediator whose rulings were seen as wise by all parties. None felt wronged by its advice, and all grew in understanding whenever they heeded him. All honored the great dragon Macheriel.

Even this peerless one, however, answered to a greater power. He soared high so that he might espy his master, the Great Wyrm That Binds the Earth. When this elder being's scales could be seen, Macheriel would gyre downward to earth and alight upon them. He would snuggle his head and neck under the warm, metallic scales and listen to the beating of blood in the elder serpent's heart. Such drumbeats hid messages, wisdom to all who could hear it, ways in which its servants might maintain the Balance of the world and keep the forces of chaos and order coupled in loving embrace rather than fractious dispute.

But the day came when Macheriel saw not his master's scales, but a silken cocoon wrapped about them, suffocating the Great Wyrm. The elder serpent writhed in its bonds, but the Weaver Spider who spun them did not heed its cries. Macheriel dove downward and raked his talons at the Spider, but she moved quickly and rolled to the side. As Macheriel shot upward again, she spun forth a web, snatching his tail. The dragon struggled against the web, but it would not break. The Spider yanked her silky cord and pulled the dragon to the earth.

He plummeted and smashed his head against a stone, and ceased to move. The Spider went back to her weaving, ignoring the dead dragon. But he did not die. He arose later, shaking his injured head, looking about with blurry eyes. His master was gone. In its place he found a huge cocoon, impossible to penetrate.

Macheriel wailed in despair, for he could not reach the drumbeat of his master's heart. He crawled upon the ground for leagues, crying and roaring in fear and anger. He had forgotten how to fly. As he crawled across the hard, sharp rocks, his feathers fell out, leaving only black, leathery skin. When he finally reached the woods where the animals who knew him dwelt, they could not recognize him. They screamed in horror at this strange new beast that now came at them, moaning in misery.

Their fear angered him. Had he not served them well all these years, solving their disputes for them? How dare they run from him now, in his time of greatest need! He lurched forward and gnashed at the slowest among them, digging his teeth into the poor creature. He liked the taste of it.

"I take back that which I freely gave," he cried, and withdrew his judgments so that no one who had resolved a dispute through him could remember how it had been solved. Old enmities arose, angers and wrongs committed that everyone had once thought were behind them. Macheriel took back his rulings and swallowed them like tiny fish, nestling them deep in his stomach where none could consult them.

The animals fell to fighting among themselves, forgetful that their disputes could be harmoniously resolved. Macheriel laughed, for his revenge was sweet. But it brought him no relief. He remembered his master and felt the pain of its confinement. He bashed his head against a rock, seeking once more the oblivion that the Spider had given him. With each blow, he forgot more and more about himself. Eventually, his own name was lost to him, and the animals called him Jo'cllath'mattric. Even his shadow left him, floating away into the woods, never to be seen again. He slithered into a deep cave and slept, his dreams empty of image and meaning.

• • •

The darkness of the cave gave way once more to the lamp-lit stage before the throne. Loba closed the book and looked at her fellow Theurges, her eyes old and tired. Hushed murmurs spread throughout the crowd as each shaman turned to another to seek confirmation that they had all shared the same story. The details they quietly shared with one another were the same. The lore spirit had delivered a single tale to them. They turned their eyes back to the stage.

"It was an old spirit who lived that story," Loba said, "one who had been bound for many ages. It was freed by Albrecht and Konietzko in Europe, and the secret of Jo'cllath'mattric's true name, brought to us by the Silver River Pack, allowed me to summon it." She bowed her head and left the stage.

Albrecht stepped up once more. "This creature— this ancient dragon—must be put down. It's not a matter of healing it. It's been too long for that. If it could be healed, it would have happened by now. The only conclusion is that it doesn't want to be healed. It's bad to the bone and it's our job to kill it."

"I agree," Sylvan-Ivanovich-Sylvan said. "The beast must die. But where is it? How do we track it down, when so many do not even remember it exists?"

"We have a clue there, thanks again to the Third Pack, the Silver River Pack. I'm going to let them tell the tale of their latest exploits."

Albrecht motioned to the pack, and Cries Havoc stood up to take the stage. The others followed him but stood to the side, more as witnesses than storytellers. They had practiced that morning what they would say, and all of them decided that Cries Havoc would do the talking. If necessary, the others would pantomime their actions now and then to add emphasis to the story.

They told the gathered Theurges about their assault on the Black Spiral Dancer's club in London and their killing of a host of Lore Banes, freeing dozens of lore spirits. They told of the healing of Mari Cabrah and explained just what such a Lore Bane could do to a Garou, trapping her in her own memories. Then they told of John North Wind's Son meeting his father, and the promise the spirit had made to them, to lend his wind spirits to aid their cause, taking them through the Umbral storm to Jo'cllath'mattric's lair.

Many of the Theurges seemed skeptical at the beginning of the pack's tale, but Cries Havoc had regained all his Galliard skills since besting the Lore Bane that beset him, and he eventually won them over. By the end of the story, they grinned and cheered at the pack's victory. Most of them, anyway; Carlita noticed that even scary old Gnarled Fingers at least nodded in satisfaction at the tale.

As the pack left the stage, John North Wind's Son lingered, seeking out Aurak Moondancer in the audience. "I care nothing for the glory I may receive for my deeds if they cannot stir others into action." He turned and joined his packmates, leaving the stage.

Aurak arose. Albrecht offered the stage to him, and he ambled forward with his staff to stand before the others. "I have been approached in dreams by the wind spirits, asking me to accomplish this thing John North Wind's Son tells about. To travel through the Umbral storm to an ancient Wyrm lair from which none of us may return. I myself have great duties at my sept. There are young Theurges who need my wisdom to come of age and assume their tasks for my tribe. I would risk much to take this journey for others."

John gritted his teeth. He felt his rage rise, embittered by Aurak's words. The shaman clearly felt that the needs of his sept were more important than the fate of the world.

"And yet…" the old shaman said, looking at John, "I choose to undertake it, knowing that I may never return. I deem the quest worthy. I deem it necessary." He left the stage and took his seat.

John closed his eyes and asked the spirits to forgive his anger, to forgive his wrongfully judging the shaman before he was done speaking. Cries Havoc punched John in the arm.

"You did it, man," he said.

John nodded and looked at Evan, who smiled back at him, giving him a thumbs-up.

Albrecht took the stage once more. "Thanks, Aurak. That means an awful lot. I don't expect the rest of you to join us. It's going to be dangerous. Once we get there, it'll be warrior work. No time to appease spirits then. What I am asking of you is some guidance. Put your heads together and figure out what sort of game plan we need to assault this place. We'll have the wind spirits to get us there, but we can't count on them inside the realm. The other thing I'd like to request are some fetishes. Summon up some friends and put them to work in weapons for us, things that'll take down Lore Banes. Claws work, but long range arrows or guns might work better."

"Phah," Gnarled Fingers said. "I thought you sought our wisdom, but you clearly want our power. You want us to make weapons for the Silver Fangs? Why arm those who may not support us?"

"Because this isn't about tribal differences, Gnarled Fingers, and you know it. Those fetishes probably won't last the whole battle. Hell, we may not even come back from this battle. We're about to throw ourselves into the fire. If you want to sit back and watch without helping, feel free. But we all know what the other tribes'll say about you then."

"Do you think we care about the prattling of others? You plan an expedition to win glory for yourselves, leaving the Get behind!"

"If you feel that way, join us! Come on, call up a bunch of warriors. They're welcome to come along!"

"I will! By tomorrow, I will have a pack of warriors here to ensure that you do not fail us all!"

"Oh?" Sylvan-Ivanovich-Sylvan said. "I will not let either the Silver Fangs or the Get take the telling of this tale from us. Where there is storm, there are Shadow Lords. Let come the storm, we will ride it!"

"And we!" said Wyrdbwg. "The Fianna will come! And we will be the first to sing the tale afterward!"

No! Five Paws of the Red Talons growled. *To the wolves shall go that glory!*

And so it went, with each tribe promising not just fetishes and wisdom, but warriors besides.

"He's doing a good job feigning annoyance at having the sole glory stolen from him," Evan whispered to Mari, nodding at Albrecht. "I think he's finally learning subtlety."

"For now," Mari said. "I'll give him this one. I told him he'd never get them to commit to the war party, but playing on their lust for glory seems to work. No one wants to see the Silver Fangs actually earn their reputations."

"Hey, the more the merrier," Evan said.

By the morning, the Theurges had dispersed back to their homes to gather a war party the likes of which North America had rarely seen.

Chapter Nine

They spent the following week in preparation. Albrecht wanted to leave sooner, but the logistics of gathering warriors from across the region wouldn't allow it. In addition, Aurak reported from the wind spirits that the Umbral storm had lulled, but that, like a tide going out to build a stronger wave, it would return all the stronger. They would have to wait for it. So the Theurges spent the time summoning spirits and binding them into weapons, as short-term talens or longer-lasting fetishes: bows, arrows, guns, bullets and klaives.

In the end, as the last of the promised warriors gathered, King Albrecht's war party totaled nearly fifty Garou, a nearly unprecedented number in modern times. Each tribe gravely risked its caern by lending such warriors to this cause in a faraway realm. Should Wyrm minions hear of it, they could take advantage of the weakened defenses and destroy everything generations of Garou in the region had fought and died for. What's more, most knew they would not return from this fight. Their septs would be left weakened, and new cubs would have fewer elders to learn from. And yet, the warriors had still come, knowing that, should Jo'cllath'mattric become free, all their defenses would be for naught.

Albrecht would lead them, along with Evan and Mari, who could not be convinced out of coming no matter what. Along with them would be Loba and seven other Silver Fangs, one of them a Galliard but the rest all Ahroun warriors.

Five Get of Fenris came, along with three Shadow Lords and four Red Talons. Two Fianna arrived, accompanied by two Children of Gaia, who intended mainly to heal any wounded along the way. From New York City came one Bone Gnawer and two Glass Walkers. That any had come at all from either faction was a surprise; the Gnawers were not known for war and the Glass Walkers normally stayed out of such affairs.

Four Black Furies came from the Finger Lakes Caern, and two Uktena arrived soon after them, one a warrior, the other a Theurge. Five Wendigo warriors arrived, large, muscled men and women, guarding Aurak Moondancer, who would lead the wind spirits.

With the Silver River Pack, that brought their number to forty-seven. Julia was convinced they didn't have a chance.

"Look, I'm not trying to be negative," she said to the others. "It's just that we're going into a huge, unknown Wyrmhole with only forty-seven of us. I doubt we're going to come out."

"Only forty-seven?" Carlita said. "That's forty-seven damn good warriors. Are you forgetting that Albrecht is leading us, or that Loba and Aurak are with him? And did you see that Hurls Rocks guy from the Get? Whooee, girl! If we Garou could get it on, I'd be doing the nasty right now."

"You're so disgusting," Julia said, rolling her eyes and shivering at the image. "I'm not downplaying the war party's members. I'm just emphasizing the opposition."

"We have no idea what awaits us," John said. "It may be as you fear, an endless realm of hellish beings. But it may also be an empty place, housing only Jo'cllath'mattric. For all we know, he may be weakened by his attempts to manifest, or maybe he's still bound in chains in the Umbra, and that's why he wants to manifest here. If he's still bound, we can make quick work of him."

"Oh, I suppose you're right," Julia said. "We don't know what's there. Maybe it will turn out for the better. But ask yourself this: What in this whole mess has turned out better for us? It's all been unremitting nastiness."

Stay, if you wish, Storm-Eye said, with no anger or pity in her voice. *Perhaps one of us will then survive.*

Julia looked at the wolf, shocked. "I would never abandon you. You know that, don't you? I was just venting, I suppose. I'll shut up now."

Cries Havoc hugged her and the matter was put to rest. The next morning, the expedition set out.

The Theurges led the group in stepping sideways, and they all moved away from the Penumbral caern and bawn. On the horizon, the sky was dark, flecked with lightning flashes. The air stirred, blowing in circles around them.

"The storm comes," Aurak said. "Everyone prepare. Tie your fetishes to you and hold tight to a partner. The spirits will keep us alive, but they cannot guarantee to keep us whole."

John North Wind's Son locked arms with Julia, while Cries Havoc and Carlita did the same. Storm-Eye had shifted into Crinos form, and she locked arms with Earth Stained Red, a lupus Shadow Lord. The two had met during the preparatory week and found a sort of kinship across tribal boundaries.

The rest of the war party did the same, except for Aurak, who stood alone, his hands gesturing to the wind spirits as he whispered strange names at them. Albrecht and Mari stood together, Evan and Loba nearby. If they were separated by the storm, at least both of the pairs had a Theurge among them. The wind whistled in all their ears and ruffled their hair and fur. Those that had not done so before now shifted to Crinos form, ready to take on whatever opposition came with the storm.

In mere moments, faster than anyone had realized possible, the storm moved in from the horizon and swept over them like a tidal wave. Just before its black, roiling mass touched them, it was repulsed by an invisible force. The wind spirits had wrapped themselves around each Garou and provided a shield between them and the storm. All this did, however, was to buffet them in its violent cloud. They were flung to the sky and around in circles, like twigs caught in a tornado.

John clung to Julia with both hands, more fearful for her sake than his. He had a sense that the wind spirits were especially strong around him, and that might help her. But if they were separated, he doubted he'd easily find her again.

The roaring in their ears grew unbearable. It sounded like a mad marching band pounding cymbals and drums in their ears. John winced as a cloud smashed into him like a granite slab. The wind spirits took the main force of the blow, but it still hurt. There would be a bruise.

Julia likewise yelled as something unseen punched her in the gut. Again, the benevolent wind spirits turned away most of the force, but she now gasped for breath.

The storm carried them along, throwing them high and then low, dragging them along the ground and then zigzagging them through its lightning-shot interior. They managed to survive that unscathed only by dint of quick reactions. Even the wind spirits could not turn aside all the searing bolts.

Over the deafening rumble, they heard a new sound: the croaking and cawing of the black storm birds. Shooting into the black cloud mass, the birds dove for any Garou they could spy. The wind spirits threw themselves at the birds and managed to knock some of them off course, but not all. The birds swooped onto their prey and raked their talons across fur or pecked at faces. They met claws and fangs in return. The warriors were soon bloodied, but every last bird had been torn to shreds, their carcasses flung from the storm.

John slammed up against a wall and Julia slammed into him. The storm had let them go. He realized that the wall was the ground. He gently shoved Julia aside and stood up, watching the storm funnel into a whirl-wind, squeezing its bulk into a small, tight cave entrance on the side of a hill. They were at the edge of some sort of realm.

Other Garou rose from the mud and mire around them, also flung there by the wind spirits, who could not follow the storm into the realm proper. The spirits swirled over them, keeping away the worst effects of the storm until it disappeared, like ink sucked down a drain, into the cave entrance. All was suddenly silent.

Albrecht yelled to the designated tribal leaders, the captains, to perform a head count. The Garou gathered with their tribes, and John and Julia scanned the area for their packmates. They soon saw Cries Havoc and Carlita and called to them. They heard a howl from nearby, and Storm-Eye bounded to them, after having guided Earth Stained Red to a fellow Shadow Lord.

Albrecht walked around, reviewing the troops. After getting them lined up into a close group, he addressed them: "It looks like we've lost three of us. Two of my own tribe are missing, and Alexei of the Shadow Lords lost his partner, Dani. That either means that they fell out of the storm, and are somewhere else in the Umbra, or they're in there." He pointed to the cave. "Either way, that's where we're going. If we see any of them, we'll help them out however we can. Now, let's go!"

He drew his klaive and marched forward. The gathered warriors fell in behind him. They climbed the short, scree-scattered slope to the cave mouth and peered within. It was a large enough to fit a standing Crinos Garou and appeared to widen not far within.

"Let me test the way first," Aurak Moondancer said. He whispered something no one could hear, and a wind arose, flowing into the cave. In seconds, it flowed back out, smelling of rot and decay. "The winds cannot go far; there is a ward against spirits. But there are no enemies in sight, only signs of recent death."

"Let's go," Albrecht said, stepping forward and entering the cave. Mari followed behind him, and groups of Silver Fang warriors behind her. They all followed behind, one by one, spreading out once they were within. They stood in a huge cavern that stretched out before them beyond sight, numerous stalagmites and stalactites rising to or falling from the ceiling.

A layer of mud covered the floor, dead bodies mired within it. They appeared to be animals and even human carcasses, recently killed, but there were no obvious signs of Garou among them. The detritus of the storm. The war party moved on, slipping quietly through the maze of pillars, looking for signs of Jo'cllath'mattric.

"There's a light ahead," Evan said, pointing toward a faint glow. It looked like a light reflected onto the cave wall from another room. "It looks like a bend in the cavern. There's something on the floor between us and it, though. I can't make it out."

"Anyone see it?" Albrecht asked.

A few Garou shuffled forward and peered ahead. Alexei of the Shadow Lords nodded. "It looks like treasure. Mounds of ancient treasure, flowing from chests. Gold, jewels and scroll cases. The sort of thing you'd see in the hold of an ancient pirate ship."

"What the hell's that doing here? Junk brought in by the storm?"

"Remember," Aurak said, "the storm brings memories it steals here. These are not real things, but the memories of them. Perhaps they are not what they seem."

"Perhaps it hides clues to Jo'cllath'mattric's weakness," one of the Get of Fenris said. "We should investigate it."

"I'm not sure that's a good idea," Albrecht said. "It could be hiding more than clues. We should avoid it. Nobody touch anything, okay? Just walk around it."

There was some grumbling among the warriors.

"Want to question my orders?" Albrecht said. "Now? In the middle of a Wyrm caern? Well, forget about it. I'm the leader in this time of war, so I can't be questioned. I'll say it one more time: stay away from the stuff." He looked to make sure they were all complying and then moved forward. "I think it's time for some light."

One of the Silver Fangs opened a satchel and began distributing what looked to be lightsticks. He shook one and bent it in two. It burst forth into a lantern-bright brilliance, far stronger than any human-made lightstick. "These should last for about three hours apiece," he said. The other sticks were handed out to each member of the party, and most of them activated theirs; some kept theirs for later. The room was soon as bright as day, as each warrior clutched a lightstick talen bound with a sun spirit.

They could all see the treasure mounds now. The muddy floor was covered with ancient doubloons and other coinage, scattered here and there with gleaming gems in all the colors of the rainbow. They marched around these mounds, staying to the mud, heading toward the distant bend in the cavern.

"Dani!" Alexei yelled and ran for his fellow Shadow Lord, who had been lost in the storm. His feet scattered the coins and he fell to his knees by the body of his comrade, buried among the gold as if stashed there among the treasure. He was clearly dead, his body torn by numerous gashes—the talons of the black birds. "Oh, my brother!" Alexei cried, hugging Dani's body to him, rocking back and forth with grief.

Albrecht stepped forward. "Leave him, Alexei. Walk very carefully back to us. Do not disturb the treasure again."

Alexei looked up at Albrecht in shock and anger, and then looked around himself. He seemed only then to realize that he stood amidst the things they were ordered to avoid. He lowered Dani's body, whispering, "May Grandfather Thunder reward you for riding the storm." He then stood up and walked slowly, carefully back to the rest, avoiding moving the treasure in any way.

Albrecht moved on. The others followed. As Storm-Eye passed the area Alexei had walked upon, she halted, sniffing. She heard a slight clink as one of the coins settled. Her hackles raised and she growled, warning the others.

Suddenly, a black shape leapt from underneath the coins and onto Storm-Eye. Its leathery bat wings wrapped around her arm and its tail whipped behind her to slash at her neck. Before it could fully land its blow, however, Cries Havoc fell on it, tearing its grip and slashing it from neck to groin. The Lore Bane screeched in pain and fell into tatters. Lore spirits, freed, fled to the cave entrance, escaping into the Umbra.

Everyone stood ready to receive an assault, but no more Banes appeared. Albrecht sighed and shook his head. "I expected more opposition than this. Where the hell is everybody?"

"Perhaps they scour the Umbra for us while we sneak into their lair?" Loba said.

"That'd be rich. I don't buy that for a second. Come on, let's keep moving." Albrecht led them to the light, and as they peered around the bend, they could see a long hall leading to another cavern, lit with torches. Painted figures and scenes filled the length of either wall, resembling the famous cave paintings from Lascaux. The beasts depicted on them, however, were mythical. If they ever existed on earth, no human had ever seen them. Perhaps they were from a time long before man.

"I wish I'd brought a camera," Cries Havoc said. "These deserve deciphering. Who knows how old they are."

"Who cares?" Carlita said. "Let's just keep moving and find this thing we're looking to kill."

"Wait a minute," Julia said, stepping back from examining the wall. "This doesn't make any sense. This is us!"

"What are you talking about?" John said, leaning to look at the section of wall she pointed to.

"There! Those stick figures. They're clearly Garou. Not just Garou: us. Our war party. See, there's Albrecht, the one with the grand klaive leading us, and there's you, with the spear and wind spirits, the squiggles in the air next to you."

"But the wind spirits didn't follow us in," John said. "You're reading into it. Stop being paranoid."

"Look here: Silver Fang warriors. See the pictogram?"

"Yes, but there are far more of them pictured than came with us."

"Who's this?" Julia said, pointing to a stick figure leading the Silver Fang warriors. It was glowing, marked by white chalk lines. "Some sort of king?"

"But you said Albrecht was over here," John said, pointing to the first figure with the grand klaive.

"I don't understand this at all," Julia said.

"What's going on?" Evan Heals-the-Past said, coming back down the line to see what the commotion was. Julia pointed out the painting and her theory about it. "It seems unlikely, but if you're right, what does it say about our task?" They traced the painting down the wall, looking for signs of their fate, but the wall appeared to have been smudged. Nothing seemed clear.

"If this is our fate, I have no idea if it's good or bad," John said, frowning and squinting at the wall.

"Wait," Julia said, her voice quavering. "Look here." Amidst the smudges, one portion of the picture seemed clear. The stick figure with the spear—John, according to Julia's theory—lay on the ground, red ochre paint dripping from him, a huge, black dragon perched over him and feasting on his heart.

"That is not a good omen," John said, gripping his spear tightly and scanning the ceiling overhead for any sign of flying creatures.

A howl broke out ahead, where the tunnel entered into a larger room. It was immediately followed by a cacophony of howls, one of them clearly that of King Albrecht. From John's place in line, he couldn't see what happened, but one thing was clear: the battle was joined.

Chapter Ten

John hefted his spear and joined the group howl, a roar of rage and anger meant to chill the blood of any enemy. He edged forward against the press of warriors ahead of him, looking over their shoulders to see the battle. He could now hear the twang of bows and the whistling of arrows, along with the meaty *thwack* of klaives sinking into flesh.

The group of warriors immediately ahead of him made steady progress forward. The whole band moved out of the tunnel and fanned into the larger cavern, making way for more warriors to join them. Once John cleared the tunnel walls, he stepped to the right, looking over his shoulder to make sure that Julia stayed near to him. She did, but her eyes watched the air above them. John followed her gaze and saw a flock of Lore Banes plummeting from perches in the high, dark ceiling, swooping down at the mass of warriors.

Around the cavern walls, lore spirits sought refuge in the nooks and crannies. Apparently, the first wave of Banes had been defeated, freeing the lore spirits. He now witnessed the second wave.

Loba Carcassone stood nearby and opened a satchel painted with all manner of strange glyphs, and seemed to howl to the sky, but John could hear no sound. The lore spirits, however, seemed to hear her, and some slipped from their new cliff havens to glide down and slip into her bag. No matter how many swooped into the satchel, it grew no larger, as if it held more space inside than out. John realized that she was collecting the spirits, trying to salvage the past. The tales these freed spirits could tell might prove powerful to the Garou septs—if they got out of here alive.

John steadied his spear and stood firm in the face of a Bane diving straight for him. At the last moment, the Bane banked to the side to avoid the spear, zipping in toward John's face. But John had anticipated the move and expertly swung the point around. He didn't have to do anything else; the Bane impaled itself on the spear with the force of its own momentum. Its flesh flew past in tatters, like a shirt thrown into a high-powered, industrial fan. As the tatters settled to the ground, they unraveled, becoming lore spirits. The confused spirits spiraled around, looking for escape, before fleeing down the now-open tunnel, toward the entrance to the realm and freedom.

John examined his spear point; its ice encasement was still intact. He didn't know what sort of power it had, but it clearly hadn't activated yet. He looked around to see if others needed his help, but they had already dealt with the second wave. The Children of Gaia medics tended to two warriors, both of whom had terrible-looking wounds on their chests and arms. The victims teetered as they stood, seemingly confused about their predicament.

"Looks like the Lore Banes got a bite of them," Julia said. "They don't remember where they are. The medics will bring them up to speed."

"Fan out!" Albrecht yelled, visible to John now, waving his grand klaive, now smeared with some of the Lore Banes' remains. Apparently, not all their substance was made from lore spirits.

The warriors followed his orders and spread out across the new cavern in a line. They stood along a beach overlooking an underground lake. Their lights were not powerful enough to cast across the entire distance, but enough could be made out in the dim gloom across the way to see an island of some sort, marked by ancient ruins. Behind them, other tunnels led into new passageways, dark and unknown. Warriors turned to guard against any incursions from these places.

"Aurak?" Albrecht said. "Can you send your scouts?"

Aurak spoke to two of his Wendigo entourage and they each leapt into the air. Instead of falling, they walked across the air as if it were solid, although their steps left a wake of chill frost behind them. As they flew over the lake, their lights cast down so that the others could see. The ruins looked Grecian, mixed with Egyptian motifs.

"Atlantean," the Uktena Theurge, Cloud's End, said. He stepped to the edge of the shore and peered across, squinting. "I saw it in a tale from one of the freed lore spirits. It passed through me on its escape, and I caught a glimpse of its ancient song."

"You've got to be kidding me," Albrecht said. "Atlantean?"

"I do not lie," the Uktena said, disdainfully. "I saw it clearly, as if I lived there before its sinking. Those are Atlantean columns. Do you see the shell and kraken motif?"

"No. Not from here, but I believe you. It doesn't matter. These are just memories; ignore them and concentrate on our goal: Jo'cllath'mattric."

The scouts circled the island and began running back to the group, skipping across the air like rocks across a pond's surface. They stepped back down onto the sand. "There is something there," one of them reported. "A snake of some sort, coiled among the ruins. I could see its breathing scales."

Albrecht looked at Aurak and Loba. "Is this him? Do we swim out to kill the thing?"

Loba shook her head doubtfully. "I don't know. That water could be full of Banes. The snake may be a mirage, a memory. Who knows if it's really Jo'cllath'mattric?"

"All right. What if we send a small expeditionary force, to get a better look on the ground?"

"That would be wise," Aurak said. "We would not commit our entire strength in case the real beast waits elsewhere, down one of the nearby tunnels."

Albrecht turned to face the group. "Any volunteers for investigating the island?"

A number of hands went up. John raised his hand and grasped Julia's to raise it also.

"What are you doing?" she whispered. "We're not qualified."

"Better than any of them," John said. "We've got more underwater fighting experience after the troubles we've been through, and besides, our totem is Uktena. This was meant for us."

"Silver River Pack," Albrecht said. "I'm glad you're stepping up. It's a good omen for us."

John noticed that Cries Havoc had also raised his hand, as had Storm-Eye. Carlita held up her own, but reluctantly.

"You'll have to swim," Aurak said. "My warriors cannot walk the sky while bearing others."

"That's okay," Cries Havoc said, stepping to the water's edge. "We've done this before. You guys ready?" He turned to his packmates, looking in their eyes to make sure they were up for it. Julia and Carlita nodded, but not without a sense of resignation. John and Storm-Eye marched up to the edge and into the water, standing ankle-deep while waiting for the others to join them. They all splashed out into the lake and walked until the water engulfed their chests, at which point they began swimming.

The Wendigo scouts, still held aloft by their wind-born gifts, hovered over them, holding out their lights to mark their way. Nothing rose up from beneath the waves to hinder them. John took a deep breath and submerged his head, opening his eyes to see if there was anything below them. He saw only a deep murk. Dark shapes seemed to rest on the lake bottom, about twenty feet below them. They looked like extensions of the island's ruins. Perhaps the temple island was the highest point in an ancient city. *Memory of a city*, John told himself, rising above the waters and taking a fresh breath.

They soon reached the shore, crawling up onto its jagged rocks, the broken arm of some former ship dock. They shook off as much water as they could from their wet, Crinos-form fur and set off into the interior. John led the way, followed by Storm-Eye and then Carlita, Cries Havoc and Julia. Their lightsticks made strange shadows as they moved them about from right to left, examining the ruins. The Wendigo's lightsticks cast an ambient radiance from above.

"It was over there," one of the Wendigo gestured. John followed his pointing to a large, black wall blocking the way between two columns. Its surface gleamed with a wet oiliness, but with a scaled pattern across it. As they watched, it slowly expanded outward toward them and then retreated back, before slowly expanding once more.

"That's breathing, all right," Carlita said. "That thing's alive."

"Let's trace it to its head," John said. He moved off to the right, stepping over fallen pieces of walls and pillars, following the line of the black scales.

He stopped short at a sudden howl from across the lake. He spun and looked across the water to the shore. A flood of Banes poured from three of the tunnel entrances and into the massed warriors. These creatures weren't flying, but running on four legs like animals. But they didn't resemble any animal John had ever seen.

"What the hell are those?" Carlita cried. "Rhinos?"

The things did have fierce-looking horns on their snouts, which they used to gore the front line of warriors. Two Garou went down, but the rest ignored the horns impaling their legs and torsos and lashed out with claws and fangs. Some swung klaives, slicing the horns off their aggressors.

The two flying Wendigo warriors shot off across the sky, heading back to help their comrades. John headed toward the shore, looping his spear into its back sling.

No, Storm-Eye said. *We have a mission here. If they cannot handle the enemy, we cannot help.*

John growled in anger but knew she was right. He gritted his teeth and went back to the path he followed. "Damn it! Let's find this thing's head and chop it off!"

"I'm with that," Cries Havoc said. He stepped over a marbled rock, following after John, but then yelped with pain as his right foot shattered the loose scree on the other side and he sank hip-deep into a hole. He struggled to lift himself but could not budge his leg.

"I'm coming," Carlita said, rushing up to him. She wrapped her arms under his and yanked with all her strength. Part of his leg came free, but in doing so, more ground collapsed. What little surface was holding Cries Havoc up gave way, and he tumbled into the hole, taking Carlita with him.

Storm-Eye bounded to the edge and looked down. Her packmates were sprawled across the floor amid the fallen stones, ten feet down. They both shakily stood and regained their balance, looking around them with curiosity.

What do you see? Storm-Eye said.

"Uh… I think we found it," Cries Havoc said.

"Holy shit," Carlita said. "It's looking at me."

• • •

Albrecht roared a howl of attack, and the line of Garou surged forward, pushing back the army of pre-historic beasts that had charged from the caves. These were some sort of Lore Banes; they unraveled into lore spirits like the birds, but they were much harder to beat down into their constituent spirits. Their tough hides were like armor.

Most of the warriors had fetish weapons of some sort, and these proved somewhat better than claws at penetrating the Banes' skin. Arrows went flying and bullets (mainly from the Glass Walkers and Bone Gnawer) pounded into flesh. The front-line Garou sliced at them with klaives or smacked them with hammers.

Nonetheless, five warriors were down. Some of them seemed lost in confusion, their memories wiped by the Banes, but others were clearly dead, gored to bloody ribbons. One of them was a Silver Fang.

Evan bit into the neck of a beast that broke through the ranks, almost colliding into Albrecht's leg.

"Thanks, kid," Albrecht said, and then vaulted through the opening the creature had made, slipping past their line before spinning to attack them from behind. Two slices from his klaive released a horde of lore spirits, which scattered for the high ceiling, trying to get out of the way of the battle. He heard a grunting sound behind him and saw a fresh pack of Banes rushing from another tunnel.

Calling upon his spirit powers, he ignited his fur into a silvery flame, spreading his arms wide and howling with rage. The Banes skidded to a halt, their eyes wide with fear, and then stumbled over one another trying to back away from the shining Garou warrior.

Albrecht advanced on them and thought he saw another light from out of the corner of his eye. He glanced over and saw a line of shining warriors advancing with him, their fur the purest white. These were not his warriors; they had not come with him. They stepped past him and sliced their klaives through the air, some of them at invisible targets, but others sunk their blades into the fleeing Banes.

The warriors howled their acclaim, and Albrecht froze, staring at them. Their particular howl was a Silver Fang song, one reserved for lords and kings. Who the hell were these guys? Moments later, they disappeared, and Albrecht's band rushed forward into their place, as if they had never been there.

Albrecht looked at Evan and Mari, but they were occupied with finishing off the last of the Banes. He looked to Loba and saw that she was shaken. She met his eyes and nodded. He ran over to her.

"Did you—?" he started.

"Yes," she said. "I saw them. Silver Fang lords, fighting alongside us. What does it mean?"

"I don't know," Albrecht said. "Our ancestors are with us. This thing is even bigger than I thought."

• • •

John leapt down the hole, landing next to Cries Havoc and Carlita, who stood still, staring at something off to the side. He looked in that direction and froze himself. Two huge, glowering red eyes stared back at him.

The dragon's head rested on the floor at the far end of the room, looking straight into their eyes. Its mouth cracked open, expelling hot steam, but its eyes never closed. The thing was no mere serpent; only the term dragon did it justice. It seemed to be part bird; its mouth was lined with fangs but somehow looked more like a beak than a snout. Meeting its eyes, John felt mesmerized, unable to move, as if the weight of its gaze pinned him down. He wondered why it didn't lurch forward and swallow them with one bite.

He then noticed the chains around its neck. Large, golden chains stretched tight in loops around its neck just behind its jaw, anchored to large pins on the floor. The flagstones were covered with magical-looking glyphs. Scattered across the floor, however, were broken lengths of chain; it had clearly snapped through some of the links that bound it.

"It can't move," John said. "It's still bound here, although barely. It hasn't burst all its chains yet."

"Good news," Carlita said. "But I can't move, either."

"Neither can I," Cries Havoc said. "It's got me paralyzed."

"Don't come down," John cried up to Storm-Eye and Julia. "It's trapped us in its stare. Try to work around to the hole over there—I can see where its neck comes into the room. If you can distract it, it may look away, freeing us."

"Okay," Julia said from above. He heard her footsteps leaving the hole.

"If they do distract it," Cries Havoc said, "what do we do then? It's damn big. I doubt we can take it down ourselves."

"We get out of here and call the others over," John said. "An entire war party should be able to chop it up."

"Something don't seem right," Carlita said. "If this is really Jo, it's pretty damn wimpy. I mean, I thought he was supposed to be scary just to look at."

"It looks like the dragon from the lore spirit's tale," John said. "He has been here a long time. That sort of stay would make anything emaciated."

"It doesn't seem weak to me," Cries Havoc said. "If its stare could do this to us, I'd hate to see what it can do when it's free. Besides, it's clearly been wounded recently."

"What are you talking about?" Carlita asked.

"I see it now, too," John said. "There, on the floor below the chains: dried blood. It's got loose scales hanging from its neck there. Something hacked away at it recently."

"Who the hell's been here before us?" Carlita said.

The sound of crumbling stone echoed from across the room, from behind the dragon's head. The dragon shifted in place and turned its head to look, breaking the spell. John immediately turned away from it and grabbed Cries Havoc and Carlita, spinning them around to face the wall, away from its gaze.

"Whew," Carlita said. "I think we can crawl back up this hole. There're a lot of rocks to climb on."

"You guys go first," John said. "I'll wait till you're done."

The two Garou scrambled up the slope and reached for the lip of the hole. As Carlita's hand wrapped about it, a black-winged Lore Bane landed and pecked her hand, taking out a small chunk of flesh.

"Ouch!" she cried, losing her grip and falling back into the room. She groggily stood up, turning to face John. "What the hell happened?"

"No!" John said, rushing to block her view of the room behind him. She had clearly lost memory of the last few minutes. Too late. Carlita looked over his shoulder and froze, pinned in place by the dragon's stare.

Cries Havoc cried out. He slashed at the Lore Bane, which was now airborne and trying to peck at his head. John thrust his spear forward and pinned it to the wall. Cries Havoc slashed at it, tearing it to pieces, which quickly flew up out of the hole as freed lore spirits.

"What's that noise behind us?" Cries Havoc asked, afraid to turn to look into the room.

"Oh, shit," Carlita said. "It's Julia! Jo's got her in some sort of spell. She's moving toward him! God damn it, girl! Stop it!"

"I can't," Julia cried from across the room, her voice echoing off the walls. "It's making me do this. I can't fight it!"

"Where's Storm-Eye?" Carlita yelled.

"She's frozen like you!" Julia said.

"You gotta do something, John," Carlita cried, desperation in her voice unlike anything John had heard from her before.

John backed into the room. "Guide me," he said.

"More to the left—my left!" Carlita said. "You're almost on him. Don't get to close! He's got fangs!"

John shuffled across the floor, walking past the pin that anchored the chain. He could see the glyphs under his feet, although what language system they were wrought from, he had no idea. His steps smeared some of them, as if they were written in chalk rather than carved into stone.

"Don't walk on those!" Julia yelled, her voice very close now to John's ear.

Suddenly, the chain moved, tugging at the pin. The stones where the glyphs had been smeared buckled and shattered. The pin shot through the air, free, whipping the chain out and across the room.

Before any of them could react, the dragon launched itself into the air, free of its bondage. Its neck slammed into the wall as it rose up, sending chunks of stone into the room. One of them barely missed Julia as she felt the paralysis lift. She dived to the side, knocking John out of the way of a huge block that slammed to the floor where he had just stood.

The dragon roared, causing the very air to tremble. It rose up and away from the room and shot out across the waters. Jo'cllath'mattric took flight.

• • •

Albrecht had gathered the war party in a circle, ready to defend against any more waves of attack, but no more Lore Banes showed themselves. A total of eleven Garou were dead from the Bane hoard's assault, members from many tribes. The Get, Red Talons and Silver Fangs had suffered the most, but the Glass Walkers were down to one. Albrecht turned to consult with Aurak on their next move, when a bloodcurdling roar shattered the air.

All heads turned to the island and saw Jo'cllath'mattric rise from the ruins. His long, black body stretched out, batwings flapping to keep his bulk aloft. His face looked like a vulture's, and his arms and legs flexed their talons. He shot threw the air straight at them, roaring.

"This is it!" Albrecht said, raising his grand klaive high.

The dragon swooped over them and circled, looking for an opening. He flapped his wings to hover above the war party, staring down at them with malice. His eyes glowed like burning coals and his tail traced elaborate circles in the air. He opened his mouth and hissed, a long, slow, sibilant sound that seemed to take form in the air and crawl into each Garou's ear, infecting their eardrums, thrumming into their brains.

Albrecht weakly lowered his grand klaive, staring at it. Where the hell did he get this nice piece of work? He didn't remember owning a klaive. He looked around him and saw a group of Garou, none of them known to him. What was he doing here? Why were they looking at him?

Evan sat down on the sand, exhausted. He didn't know who any of these Garou were, but he didn't want any of whatever agenda they were pushing. He was tired of bearing everyone else's burdens.

Aurak Moondancer wept, remembering his lost cubs but forgetting the identities of the warriors standing next to him. They forgot who he was and laughed at the old man, his tears a sign of weakness to them.

Loba forgot her satchel and the allies it now held within. She grimaced and grit her teeth, growling low at the unknown Garou around her. She couldn't trust any of them. Who knew which ones were really working for the enemy? The Wyrm was subtle and corrupting and could hide its intentions in the hearts of any Garou. She turned in a circle, wary not to keep her back exposed to any warrior for long.

Every Garou had forgotten why he had come and who his comrades were. Even packmates' bonds were lost before the dragon's mystical assault on their memories.

Only Mari had a glimmer of their true purpose. Her ordeal had strengthened her against Jo'cllath'mattric's power. She looked around her and realized what was happening, although she was unsure just who everyone here was. She remembered, though, that she hunted Jo'cllath'mattric, the creature that had nearly killed her spirit. She did not know who the dragon hovering above them was, but she suspected it was the enemy himself.

The dragon ceased his song and dove into the mass of Garou. His talons tore into them, scattering them and killing four Garou in one sweep. He caught two more in his jaws and rent them to pieces with a shake of his neck. Their bodies disintegrated as if they had never existed. As the dragon rose to make another dive, he felt a terrible pain in his tail. Looking down, he saw one of the Garou, a black-furred female, clinging to him, rending his scales with her claws. She tore into the already open wound below, the one he had suffered recently from that cursed white wolf, from before this new menace arrived to free him.

Jo'cllath'mattric recognized the Garou who now clung to him. No matter how hard he tried to forget, he knew everything that the Lore Banes retrieved, every memory snatched as a meal. And he remembered that he hated this one, this Mari Cabrah.

He weaved violently through the air, trying to shake her, but the Garou's grip was too strong. He bent around and brought his teeth to bear, puncturing her side. And yet, she did not lose memory. Her sense of identity was too strong. She had suffered his judgment before and had escaped the verdict. Jo'cllath'mattric screamed in rage at her effrontery and snapped his tail with all his strength.

Mari could not hold on, not after the thing had bit her ribs. She fell to the sand, landing hard. She growled in pain but ignored it and stood again, readying to launch herself at it once more if it came back.

Jo'cllath'mattric swooped far above, circling around, gaining momentum for a massive dive.

● ● ●

John climbed out of the hole, helped by Storm-Eye and Cries Havoc. He was the last one out. Julia and Cries Havoc were staring at the far shore, witnessing the slaughter going on there. The Garou scattered and ran, obviously confused about something. Albrecht wandered about in a daze as if he had no idea he was their leader.

Only Mari fought the thing, and she had just been thrown to the ground. Cries Havoc cheered when she got back up.

"What the fuck do we do?" Carlita cried, running back and forth along the shore. "We can't swim there fast enough."

John measured the distance and realized that there was no way he could throw his spear so far. But in doing so, he noticed the ice still clinging to his spear's blade. "Get its attention. I don't care how, just get its attention!"

The dragon reached the apex of his climb and aimed his nose down. He fell, a living rocket, a controlled dive at incredible speed. Straight toward Mari.

"I have an idea," Cries Havoc said. He cupped his hands around his snout and yelled out to the dragon. "Hey! Macheriel!"

The dragon lurched in the air, wheeling out of his dive, mewling loudly as if he had been hit with a sledgehammer in the face. He shook his head and cast about, seeking the source of the sound.

"Macheriel!" Cries Havoc yelled again.

The dragon whipped around and headed straight for the island, his eyes burning with anger. The wolf-creature on the island had said his name. His hated name. He could not bear to hear the badge of his failure again. He must snuff out the source. As he swooped in at Cries Havoc, he opened his talons wide.

John drew back his spear, ready to fling it at the beast's heart, but it was too quick for him. It snatched Cries Havoc into the air and flung him hard against a wall. It released the broken Garou and climbed high into the sky, preparing another dive. Cries Havoc feebly tried to crawl, but his shattered bones screamed in pain and refused to move.

Julia jumped over a rock and landed next to him, reaching over to touch him gently on the chest. She whispered low, calling upon the spirits' teachings, and began to heal him, mystically reknitting his bones. Before she could finish, however, a dark thing landed on her shoulder and bit into her ear. She immediately forgot everything she was doing and stared off into empty space.

John ran forward and knocked the Lore Bane away with the haft of his spear. It tumbled through the air but righted itself and flew at his face. He snatched it aside with his claws and crumpled it up in his fist like a piece of paper. Its shredded body dissolved, freeing lore spirits to slip away into the ruins.

"It's coming back!" Carlita cried.

John saw Jo'cllath'mattric descending straight at them from above, this time heading for Carlita. John ran to stand at her side, aiming his spear at the dragon's heart, but he pulled up at the last minute and vomited at them. Instead of partially digested food, what came out was a living mass of black ichor. It splashed upon the ground and immediately slid up Carlita's leg, engulfing her. She slashed at it, but her claws went through it like water.

"Jesus, it burns!" she cried. "I can't get it off!"

John tried slashing it, but his hands also went right through it with no effect. "Julia," he cried, "what is this?" There was no answer. He looked over and saw that she still had a vacant stare; the Lore Bane had taken too much from her. Cries Havoc writhed on the ground, trying to stand, but he was barely able to move, as most of his bones were still smashed.

Storm-Eye appeared, leaping into the black ichor, but she roared as it began to burn her, too. Nothing she did had any effect on it. She leaped about in its ever-widening puddle, and John could now smell her scorched fur.

He looked up and saw Jo'cllath'mattric wheel about, his intention now drawn to the far shore, where the Garou warriors milled about confused, some of them dying. The dragon obviously thought the pack was no longer any threat.

John looked to his spear and the ice-glistening tip. He knew it could probably affect the ichor; whatever power the spirits had put in it could surely harm the liquid thing that burned his packmates. But if he used it to save them, his only weapon against Jo'cllath'mattric was gone.

Carlita collapsed to the ground, gurgling in pain. John looked to the far shore, seeking some sign that Albrecht and the others had rallied and could take down Jo'cllath'mattric. He saw only Mari and Loba standing firm. Loba stared at the incoming dragon, her hand in her satchel. Did the lore spirits she kept there give her clarity and courage?

He looked up and saw that Jo'cllath'mattric was almost out of his spear's range. He had to choose. He remembered his dream and heard again the voice from that dream: *Fool, you have wasted the gift of the Animal Elders.*

Storm-Eye howled in pain and collapsed panting next to Carlita, the steaming ichor now climbing up her neck.

Tears welling in his eyes, John drew back his arm and launched his spear at the dragon. It sped straight to the beast's heart but glanced off the scaly armor, the throw not strong enough. Then the ice on the blade's tip suddenly gleamed bright, and the spear pierced the scales, sliding through flesh and into the dragon's breast. The tip burst out from the beast's spine.

Jo'cllath'mattric gargled and fell. He tried to right himself, wheeling through the air in circles with violent spasms of his wings, but they were too weak to hold him aloft. He crashed onto the island's shore and lay there twitching. From the spear point jutting from his back, a host of spirits unraveled from the melting ice. Animals appeared in the air and floated down before the dragon's eyes, a menagerie of beasts from the time before time.

It was agony for the dragon. The animal spirits whispered at him, reminding him of the judgments he once rendered for them, in the time before his master was bound, in the time before he had failed. He sobbed and tried to shut out their growls, bleats and chirping. It did no good. He could not shut them out or the memories they awoke.

He reared back his head and roared in pain and anguish, and then beat his head against the ruins on the island, shattering the stones and marble pillars in a desperate attempt to destroy his own mind, to end all memory. As the rocks broke off, he opened his maw and devoured them, swallowing them whole and then snapping his jaws shut on more scenery. The island began to disintegrate.

John vaulted toward the beast, flexing his claws to finish it off. A horde of Banes descended from the sky, trying to defend their wounded master. John smacked three of them from the air with both claws and leapt over two more that tried to sweep in low behind him. Just as he reached Jo'cllath'mattric and drew his hand back to strike, a Bane crashed into his left shoulder and clamped down with its fangs. John howled in agony. But instead of blacking out or losing himself to the loss of awareness, he stayed sharp and focused thanks to the pain.

The Bane had bitten his wound, the one the Atcen spirit had made, a sign of his father's test. He remembered his father's words: *strike at the enemy's heart*. John gripped his spear and pulled it out of the dragon's flesh. He saw through the open wound that he had not pierced the heart like he thought, but had only torn its edge.

Jo'cllath'mattric writhed about, his torso twisting to and fro. As the Bane gnawed into John's shoulder and the pain became nigh unbearable, he aimed his spear again. The twisting torso made it hard; if he missed the open wound, there was no way he'd pierce the scales. He waited, trying to time the dragon's turning. The Bane bit deeper, and he felt dizzy, as if it had finally touched some layer of his spirit, draining it of vitality.

He clung to his father's admonition and thrust the spear forward. It slid into the open wound just as

Jo'cllath'mattric stilled his thrashing. It ploughed straight into the heart.

Jo'cllath'mattric tumbled over, splashing into the lake, sinking deep below the surface.

The black ichor dissolved into the air like mist. The Lore Banes screeched and fell apart, their lore spirits freed. The tattered spirits shot forth, bounding into the pack members, restoring their spirits and suffusing them with memories from long ago. They shook their heads and scrambled to stand, trying to focus on the here and now, shutting out the voices from old stories.

Julia placed her hands back on Cries Havoc and completed the healing. He sighed with relief, still in pain but able to move.

"We've got to get out of here!" he cried, standing unsteadily on the crumbling ground, which still quaked from the dragon's thrashing. He grabbed Julia's hand and they both ran for the shore.

Storm-Eye, her fur singed all over, nudged Carlita up. She stood wearily, alive but weak. Storm-Eye edged her to the shore and into the water. *Hold on to me*, she said. Carlita grunted and wrapped her hands about the wolf, and they swam toward the far shore.

John dived in, grabbing Cries Havoc around the waist to help him stay afloat. The Garou was weak but still capable of swimming. Julia, uninjured and her senses restored, swam faster than the rest of them.

They felt the water tug backward, and turned to see the dragon sucking it in, slurping it up. They were pulled back with it but fought harder now to reach the far shore.

Garou on the shore ran out into the water to reach for them. They seemed to have all their memories back and a keen awareness of where they were and what was happening.

"It's breaking apart," Cloud's End yelled. "The realm is crumbling!"

"Get those Garou out of the water!" Albrecht yelled, running into the water himself.

"The shore's falling apart," Evan said, watching as the sand began to run out into the churning waves, as if sucked in by an unseen vacuum cleaner.

The pack scrambled onto the eroding shore, helped there by the remaining Garou warriors. Only thirty-three warriors remained from a party of forty-seven.

"Out!" Albrecht yelled. "Head for the exit!" He urged the warriors onward, taking up the rear himself, falling behind.

"Albrecht!" Evan cried. "You can't stay! You'll die!"

"Somebody's got to make sure Jo'cllath doesn't survive this!" He waved Evan on.

"God damn it, no!" Evan screamed, breaking away from the others and rushing back to his packmate.

Albrecht waved his klaive at him. "Get out of here, kid! Go!"

Mari appeared, having slipped past the Garou trying to usher her out. "Hell no, Albrecht. You're king. I'll stay. I need to see this thing through more than you."

"Will you both stop it?" Evan cried. "This is no time for one-upmanship in suicide!"

John broke away from his pack and ran to Evan's side. "Albrecht, no one has to stay! The Animal Elders will see that the dragon is ended! You have to trust the spirits!"

Albrecht looked back at the island, which was gone. Only a giant whirlpool remained, sucking all the water into a giant maw. Ghostly animals hovered in the air above, making a cacophony of sounds. He turned back to Evan and John. "How can you be sure?"

"Because we're Wendigo," John said. "We know to trust the spirits. They are our relations."

Evan nodded, his eyes pleading at Albrecht.

Albrecht smiled and ran at them. "All right, all right! I'm right behind you!"

John and Evan broke for the tunnel they had entered from; its sides already sagged, as if its underground foundations crumbled. Mari waited for Albrecht to catch up and jogged beside him.

"You can be such an ass!" she said.

"Me?" he said. "You were lining up for a grisly fate, too!"

As they rushed down the tunnel after the war party, Evan stopped to look at the wall painting. "Albrecht! Look!"

Albrecht stared in open-mouthed shock. The white-glowing Silver Fang leader was no longer just a primitive stick figure; it was fully rendered, like a Romanticist painting. Arkady stood before a troop of Silver Fang ancestors, leading them against the dragon. Beside him, leading another troop, was Albrecht. Both of their heads glowed white, and the vague shape of a falcon wheeled in the sky above.

Mari dragged him and Evan away from the wall, which was already beginning to crack. Dust fell from the ceiling. "Move!" she yelled. They moved.

They were nearly blinded by the brilliant lights within the treasure room. Lore spirits whizzed about the cavern, infusing the treasure, returning it to its original luster from long ago, when its story was new. Loba paused to hold her satchel open, crying a voiceless summons. Some of the spirits broke away and shot into the bag. She sealed it and ran for the cave entrance.

The Garou flooded out of the cave onto the rocky plain below. Aurak Moondancer raised his hands high, calling the wind spirits that still waited there for them. One by one, they raised the Garou into the air and sent them spiraling off into the Umbra.

John, Evan, Mari and Albrecht were the last out of the cave. As he turned to see the entrance collapse behind them, John saw his spear, twirling in the air, as if caught in an eddy. He reached out to grab it and tugged it from the whirlwind. As he did, a single lore spirit trailed behind it, dripping with ichor. It had been trapped in Jo'cllath'mattric's very heart, and was now free. It swept past John, sending him reeling.

The rocky plain disappeared and he was back in the primeval forest when Jo'cllath'mattric was young and uncorrupted. He stood still, listening to a pounding sound, as of a hammer on an anvil. He turned to look behind and saw the wretched dragon beating his head against a rock, his eyes growing dim as his brain bled within his skull.

Then, floating down to light upon a nearby tree branch, a beautiful, red-plumed bird spoke: "Macheriel, I pity your plight, but you have done this to yourself. I pity more, however, those who shall live in the final days of the world, which your death will deliver to the earth once you have finally devoured yourself."

The dragon ceased his beating and turned to look at the bird. "Oh, Phoenix, lord of prophecy, tell me that this day will come soon."

"No. Your misery will be long and unremitting, until Gaia's Chosen free you from the cell of your own making."

The dragon cried in anguish and began to beat his head once more, shattering his own skull and sending rivers of blood down his face, blinding his eyes.

The Phoenix took to the air and disappeared into the immensity of the sky.

John felt a cold wind biting on his fur and realized that the sky was now dark. He was buffeted by wind spirits, flung along the Umbral night, far above faint moon paths. He saw his packmates nearby, tumbling up and down, over and under, dizzy with the speed of their travel. Seeing the landscape shift so violently made him dizzy. He closed his eyes and felt better.

When next he opened them, he stood on solid ground. Other Garou from the war party stood nearby, trying to balance on unsteady legs. Albrecht looked around and saw that everyone who had left the cave was here. He threw back his head and howled for their victory. They all joined in, their group howl echoing across the Penumbral landscape in which they stood, within the bawn of King Albrecht's caern.

Epilogue

John sat by the edge of the woods, watching the breeze ruffle the bare branches. A twig snapped behind him and he turned to see his packmates weaving under branches and around trees to meet him. He stood and tried to smile for them.

"There he is," Julia said. "The man of the hour, hiding out in the woods."

"Yeah," Carlita said. She had burns up and down her body, most of which had been healed by mystical spirit gifts, but some marks would remain. "What's going on? Everybody wants to meet you, man. You're someone they're going to tell their cubs they met years from now."

"It doesn't matter," John said, sitting down again. "We won. For now. But the Wyrm is still out there, corrupting everything. It will win, in the end."

"Whoa," Cries Havoc said. He leaned on a cane but was healing well and wouldn't need its support for long. "Where'd this come from? You stabbed Jo'cllath'mattric in the heart and he actually fell over! That is a major feat! It would have killed Mari and then all the Garou, not to mention us. What's really going on here?"

John sat quietly for a moment, arguing with himself whether or not to tell them about the final tale he had witnessed, from the lore spirit within Jo'cllath'mattric's heart. The tale the dragon had feared the most and had hidden deepest within himself.

Are you ill? Storm-Eye said. Her fur was still badly singed. Like Carlita, she had been healed, but some of the scars would remain, proud signs of her triumph. *Did a Lore Bane eat part of you? The healers will fix you.*

"No, it's not that," John said. He smiled again. "It's just all catching up with me, I guess. A lot to deal with."

"Sure," Cries Havoc said. "And the best medicine is renown. Come on, they're still talking about you back at the victory moot. Stuart-Speaks-the-Truth is there, and so is Mephi Faster-than-Death. They both want to hear the story straight from your mouth, so they can spread it far and wide to other septs."

John stood up, putting his hand on Cries Havoc's shoulder. "That should be your privilege, packmate. You were there. You did as much as I to kill Jo'cllath'mattric."

"We all helped," Carlita said. "A pack, right? All for one and one for all?"

"Right," John said, his smile genuine for a moment. "Okay, let's go back and get pointed at for a while."

"A while?" Cries Havoc said. "We've been offered a world tour! The Jarlsdottir at the Anvil-Klaiven wants us to come tell the tale. Konietzko, too, at the Night Sky. And I really, really want to see the Dawntreader again. I can't wait to hear his howl!"

"And Tampa," Carlita said. "That's our first stop. My homies got to know how down I am."

"London again," Julia said. "My sept deserves a telling. They did host us."

"Okay, okay," John said, hands up in resignation. "I get it. We'll visit them all. This time in peace. Just give me a few more minutes here, okay? I'll follow behind."

Cries Havoc looked at him for a few moments before answering, seemingly judging whether the request was healthy. "All right. But if you're not down there in five, we're sending the warders to get you."

John laughed and waved them on, sitting back down. As soon as they were out of sight, his smile disappeared. He lowered his head into his hands. "Oh, Father, I don't know if you can hear me, but tell me the last tale was a lie. Tell me the Phoenix did not speak of our doom."

The wind blew lightly, but it delivered no answers to John's ears. After a while, he stood up, his face stoic and grim. He knew how to shoulder burdens of loss and to swallow bitterness. He knew how to numb himself to feelings and shut out the worst of truths. He understood how knowledge could drive a person mad, if he had no means to alter it. He knew the secret of the dragon, and he kept it to himself.

He followed his pack's trail back to the moot, to the cheer and festivity, his heart numb to the fate of all those below, to the doom that now shadowed them with the death of Jo'cllath'mattric, as promised by the words of the Phoenix.

About the Author

Bill Bridges was the original developer for White Wolf's **Werewolf: The Apocalypse** storytelling game line and is the current developer of the **Mage: The Ascension** line. He has numerous writing credits on most of White Wolf's World of Darkness line, including the Werewolf novel **The Silver Crown**, which first introduced the conflict between King Albrecht and Lord Arkady. He is also the developer and cocreator of *Fading Suns* for Holistic Design, Inc.

It sent shivers down my spine."
—Tim Dedopulos, author of
Hunter: Apocrypha

Victorian Age Vampire™ Trilogy

by Philippe Boulle

Book One
A Morbid Initiation

Regina Blake believes her mother to be the victim of murder and conspiracy. Forgoing caution and propriety, she tries to uncover the truth and bring the culprits to justice. With every step, however, she uncovers more and more evidence of a secret world of danger, sensuality and sin. With the beautiful Victoria Ash as her guide, she peels back layer after layer of this benighted world, until the true horror of it all stands exposed.

Will discovering the truth be worth damning her soul?

Book One: A Morbid Initiation
WW11190; ISBN 1-58846-828-3
On Sale Now.

Book Two: The Madness of Priests
WW11191; ISBN 1-58846-829-1
On Sale in January

Book Three: The Wounded King
WW11192; ISBN 1-58846-830-5
On Sale in March

WHITE WOLF PUBLISHING